The Possession of Amber

The Possession of Amber

Nicholas Jose

University of
Queensland Press

Published by University of Queensland Press, St Lucia,
Queensland, 1980

Typeset by Press Etching Pty Ltd, Brisbane
Printed and bound by Graphic Consultants International
Private Limited, Singapore

Distributed in the United Kingdom, Europe, the Middle
East, Africa, and the Caribbean by Prentice-Hall
International, International Book Distributors Ltd,
66 Wood Lane End, Hemel Hempstead, Herts. HP2 4RG,
England

Published with the assistance of the Literature Board of
the Australia Council

*National Library of Australia
Cataloguing-in-publication data*

Jose, Robert Nicholas, 1952-
    The possession of Amber

    (Paperback prose ISSN 0156-6628)
    ISBN 0 7022 1537 6
    ISBN 0 7022 1538 4 Paperback

    I. Title. (Series)

A832'.3

To Sarah Lauchlan
and Scott Thornbury,
with love

Contents

ix   Acknowledgments

1   A Clean Place in Cairo
30   Harold in Italy
59   The Grand Nay
67   Coogee Spring
78   Stone's Throw
83   Beer and Wine
89   Troubadours
133   Mohsen Ben Dris
141   Cafe Children
144   Tunisian Nights
182   The Possession of Amber
201   Dear R.
208   Outstretched Wings and Orient Light
249   In Chinese
266   The Mares
274   Within the Hedge

Acknowledgments

Sections of "Harold in Italy" were first published in *Envisage* (Oxford) and *Ambit* (London), "The Grand Nay" was first published in *Quadrant*, "Stone's Throw" (under the title "A Development") in *Helix* (Melbourne), "Mohsen Ben Dris" (under the title "Leander out the Back") in *Helix*, "Cafe Children" in *Envisage*, and "Dear R." in *Public Works* (Canberra). Acknowledgement is also made to Arnoldo Mondadori Company Ltd for permission to quote from "Tuo fratello morì giovane" by Eugenio Montale.

Ma è possibile,
lo sai, amare un'ombra, ombre noi stessi.
Eugenio Montale

A Clean Place in Cairo

I

The roosters hadn't woken her but the alarmclock was a sterner taskmaster and Anna stirred herself obediently. It could have been any time in the dark room. She reached for the aspirins, squeezed the foil and swallowed a crumbly pill with the last of her bedside water. With gusto then she sprang across the floor to open up the shutters and the dazzle of morning. On the construction site next door the workmen had already broken for tea, squatting beneath the giant tree with beakers in their hands. Already the white undergarments of Mrs Mamoulian the landlady billowed on the line. As her eyes adjusted Anna made out a camel, through a gap in the buildings, bearing a mountain of lemons into the traffic. The fresh needles of light pressed her skin and pricked accidentally a nook of memory: to her amusement a bit of a prayer came to mind. *The remembrance of them is grievous unto us, the burden of them is intolerable.* She shook her cropped head free of the matted wisps of sleep. One of the workmen gestured slily to his mates, seeing her naked in the balcony doorway, and she ducked back into the shadows. A Moslem zealot had spied an English girl recently in nothing but bikini pants and the girl had been deported. Her robe was under a chair, filthy and crumpled, a blue striped galabeyah from Khan-El-Khalili. She smoothed it fondly. What was there to wear? Dust got on everything and the heap of dirty washing was higher than the bed. Ten minutes to be at work. The pressure in the shower was down. Instead of shampooing her hair she had to make do with fluffing it up and choosing her loopiest silver earrings. She rushed, took a pinch of mince out of the plastic bag in the fridge and plopped it onto the cat's saucer. Splashing in some milk, she carried it without spilling to a corner of her balcony, beside yesterday's empty dish. Mrs Mamoulian said she was crazy to waste food on cats. No one fed cats in Egypt, except to feed off them. But Anna kissed the air: "Pss-pss-pss." Then her folder of notes, her ample bag, her monster sunglasses — she was ready. She clipped the shutters closed, otherwise urchins and others would scale the wall. And hesitated. No sign of Terry, the fellow teacher who shared the flat, not a murmur from his room. No telling what he had been up to last night.

But perhaps he was better left. Anna lifted her head and settled her sunglasses so as to block out the front living area. With relief she was outside, descending the main steps. Behold the palm trees lightly sweep the spick-and-span sky. A great gang of high eager voices had filled the flat last night, when she had been tired. They all talked about the revolution, Terry grandstanding, shouting that they were all in Cairo in hope of a revolution. The shrubs round the entrance to the apartment building had a tiny charge of new greenness now. It was spring. Then and there, before she scuttled to the bus, Anna vowed to start a new life.

Terry woke shortly after: his night was still going, voices in the other room, other bodies in the bed — . The night *had* ended however and he was surprised to be alone, and dozed off again. It was easier than piecing things together. The bedroom was hot and airless, pleasurably parching in a way. The evening had had its excesses. Terry groped for his watch on the floor, nearly skittling a half-full beer bottle and lighting on a cigarette packet. He tapped the packet awkwardly against his chest and the one cigarette, slipping out, rolled down into the bedclothes. He retrieved it and fumbled to light it. The necessary smoke scoured his mouth. He felt like one of those salted fish on trays in the market. Shit, oh well, he looked at his watch. Half an hour's skipping off couldn't matter. He was the life and soul of Living Tongues Incorporated anyway. *Craving* liquid now. Great freedom to walk naked through the flat. He did so habitually but guessed Anna disapproved. Terry teased her about the sight of his unspeakable pendulous well-worn parts. It was good to have nothing on and to be bare like a sagging old horse.

The kettle took an age to boil. In the flat, capacious, primitive and cheap, none of the conveniences functioned as desired. He squeezed a couple of oranges while he waited and, a glass of sweet juice in hand, paraded idly from room to room. The flat was lovely. In the dark dusty nest of Anna's room sticks of sun poked through the slats. He circled her bed — she was reading *A Passage to India* . He observed her little black

3

diary, the clutter of creams, perfumes, eye-stuff, clips, odd chains. The sandalwood box in which she kept photos and letters. The key he knew was hung on a length of velvet ribbon around her bedhead, camou-flaged among scarves and pendants, and he smiled with respect. In the knowingness of their lives, where nothing was hidden, there was also a convention of privacy.

In the bathroom his socks had been soaking for a week and the water was squid-ink brown. He draped a towel round his waist and went onto the balcony to whistle for Gamil, the corner baker's small son. The kid normally played somewhere round the construction site. Terry called in his bastard Arabic that he wanted the *Egyptian Gazette* . He wanted to see if Libya had retaliated. The kid set off from his play nodding wearily, his lip stuck out like his father's when Terry had no small change. One ten pound note was worth four thousand loaves of bread: Gamil's father scarcely took that much in a long working day and it pained him to recognize in Mr Terry a shabby young Aus-tralian brand of Onassis. But his little son Gamil was allured more by the wonders of foreign life than by Te-rry's bountiful tips. The doorbell rang within mo-ments, ebulliently. Gamil had the English language newspaper plus a dozen loaves of bread "special for Mr Terry". He insisted on depositing the bread in the kitchen — a few piastres more. But when he saw the front room he stopped and gaped.

"Shoo now," said Terry, hitching up his towel and receiving the loaves into his outstretched arms, "Shoo." The kid slipped round the front door, giggling help-lessly behind his hand, and hopped downstairs. Terry's towel dropped. He saw now himself what a brilliant mess it was.

The front room was normally elegant, framed at either end by a curved arch, giving onto the balcony. From the ceiling an enormous brass onion hung, its surface pricked by rings of minute geometric holes which made a light effect at night. The furniture, ungainly King Farouk, was plush and filled the space. Usually in the corners there were potted palms, moderately healthy, but two of these had been coupled last night and draped with Anna's precious Indian wall-hanging to improvise a tent. In the tent, Terry more or less remembered, tarot readings had been given by Roma, the massive occult *professoressa* from New York.

He opened the shutters to let in some fresh air. Beer bottles were everywhere, dozens, and they shone with the advent of light. Blessed *Stella* the national beer was rumoured to be liquor of potato peel and onion skins — such was the morning-after smell. Some local wine bottles too, shamelessly labelled *Cleopatra* and *Omar Khayyam* , not quite emptied by people who knew what those wines could do. Glasses; the tea things; teapot, milkjug, honey jar and spoons, half-drunk mugs and those shallow blue glasses that hold a nipful. What numbers had passed through? He checked behind the couch for remains. On the low table an un-wrapped parcel proffered the last of the take-away *felafel* and *kebab* . The Scrabble board was alongside. Though the letters were strewn wide, at the board's very centre still intact on the red star, like a syllable for meditation, was the word which had provoked schism and finally violence among the English-teaching authorities. *OZ.* Was it a word, a valid word? The

5

interrupted score sheet awaited a decision. And then, wherever else Terry looked, the ashtrays. Ashtrays heaped with nutshells, orange peel, grape pips, pyramids of ash, and the butts of unreckonable hashish joints.

He surveyed the room proudly. The two plushest chairs had been piled in a corner to make room for a dance and, most puzzling of all, American Roma's gold-threaded caftan had been flung and now dangled by its neck from the lamp. Anna, seeing it, must have been furious. But Terry was content. Pleasure and freedom had blazed and he was tickled at the vestiges. But before he forgot he scribbled a note for Anna. SORRY ABOUT THE MESS. HAD TO RUSH. DON'T YOU TOUCH IT. LOVE T.

When he was dressed he perched on his bed for a minute to gulp the undrawn tea and feel satisfied at the energy he had spent last night. He had earned his quick burst of fulfilment with the clear equity of a fable.

At the quiet commencement of the evening Steve and Sue had called as usual to see what was happening. They were the other Australian teachers at the school and had been together successfully for years. Terry and Anna sat drinking with them lazily, talking over things at work . . . and plans.

Edgy Terry scorned a fellow teacher who'd re-painted her flat.

"She thinks she's living in fucking suburbia. Doesn't she realize the whole edifice of our lives here could come crashing down tomorrow?"

"If it does come down we'll be out of a job, mate," Steve commented. It annoyed him that Terry got annoyed at people who made an effort to settle happily. Steve slapped his knees. "Well, in the meantime, what are we going to do?"

Anna pleaded tiredness and a peaceful night. Sue smiled. She too was happy to sit. Sue was quite beautiful.

"What!" mocked Steve, "No one for a bit of excitement?"

Sue said she was content to dream about excitement. But Anna, when Terry stared at her accusingly, flicked her eyes from side to side and announced with prim confidence, "Yes, I could do with a spot of excitement."

Terry hugged himself and wheezed merrily.

But no one could think of anything on the spur of the moment so Steve rolled some joints and Anna boiled some rice and vegetables. There wasn't much music to choose from. Terry put on a cassette of Santana for narcotic contemplation and they waited until at last chance gallantly obliged with a diversion. Pounding at the door was Matthew Phaery the journalist.

"Let me in, you sods! Open up, sesame!"

Anna went to the door and he bumped straight into her. He swaggered exuberantly agog from fact-finding in Beirut, a litre of duty-free Glenfiddich squeezed into his armpit.

"My darling Anna." He hugged her and gave her a long slobbering kiss, as if to vacuum her mouth. Before the others could see he pulled something from his pocket and held it up to her. "My girl, for you." It was a capsule of cocaine.

"Oh ho!" she cooed. "Later." So it was her turn to be singled out by Matthew Phaery.

Matthew splashed the whisky around. He was full of stories about his trip, corruption on high and enticements below, embellished with his fulsome accent and pre-war interjections — "Gosh! What a prat!" — and he never stopped talking. He had read History at Oxford and was a raffish sportive man of the people, proud of his new suit from Lebanon. He had them all laughing. His mouth was huge and red. The generous greed of his conversation was his trademark. His eyes never left anyone alone. For a tall man he was pudgy, pretty and boyish, and when he finished an excessive spurt he rolled back cheerfully into his chair, unbuttoning his silk shirt at the belly. More of his flesh swelled out, pink and covered with fluff. "What do you say to that?" he asked Anna, and slipped her hand beneath his shirt. But he was hypertense too and shook convulsively when he tried to shell a nut. The whisky bottle was three-quarters gone when he revealed that he'd invited some other people to the flat and told them to bring friends. "We need a party — beauties — luxury!" A French couple and a male model who had been on the plane, getting out of Beirut; a quartet of American girls and Sudanese traders, merchandise unspecified; and a young man who had some connection with the President's sister-in-law: all these, apparently, would materialize. It was improbable enough.

Anna stood up and peaceably said goodnight. But Matthew came after her and caged her between his arms against the hall wall. He told her he had come tonight solely for her. His big mouth was gaping in front of her. His tongue wanted to slurp her up. You rosy mug, she thought. He had the cocaine bomb in his fist. "Not for the lady?" he queried. When Anna simply shook her head and pulled away, he tugged after her. "Goodnight," she said again and closed her door spinsterishly on all obsessive wants.

He pouted when he returned to the others. "She's got fastidious all of a sudden, hasn't she?"

Steve gave a grinning sympathetic snort. The journalist's carefree self-serving brought out the simple coarseness of adolescence in all the males. Matthew slumped disconsolately in the chair.

"I was looking forward to it. Getting to know Anna the cat lady! She wants to watch those tendencies."

The males laughed and the last trickle of whisky went round.

"Or some tea, Matthew?" asked Terry considerately. He was pleased to see Matthew Phaery thwarted. He was vaguely piqued that neither he nor his salon was Matthew's prime motive for visiting — but equally any emotional turmoil gratified him.

"Anna's been withdrawn lately," Terry reported. "She's going through something."

"What might that be?" inquired the journalist. "Easily remedied?"

"She gets fed up," Sue said defensively, sharing Anna's lack of taste for the males' lounge-to-bedroom swashbuckling.

The doorbell announced the French couple, who were ushered in. They were preciously, timidly polite, as if late for the play, and took up unobtrusive seats at the back. "English tea!" they sighed for whatever reason when Terry offered it and, when invited to relate the unhappy sacking of their Beirut apartment block, they really brightened up. They had managed a boutique. In the early days of the war the dummies in their window display had been picked out for target practice. The woman pursed her lips shrewishly as she recalled the violation. Then she began to complain that since she'd been in Cairo her pearls had been stolen. "Bof! First my dummies, then my country, and now my pearls!" Her grievances kept on. It might have been the rattling of a tape cassette, switched off abruptly when a hearty gang of the teachers from Living Tongues arrived with baskets of beer, prepared to play Scrabble but not to converse about desolation and loss.

Then the magnificent Roma appeared with her alternative daughter. Her gold-fibred robe was an allusion to Isis. She pronounced the night auspicious and, after a bubble on the hookah, was ready to scry. She had her cards — the spangled pastels of the Waite pack — wrapped in silk in her shoulder-bag. Flicking through she accidentally dropped the Ace of Wands, face up. "Oh goodness gracious me," she exclaimed, looking for eyes to catch. The card was a branch swollen with nodules and prolific with sprouting leaf: the power of the Phallus.

Matthew Phaery was fidgetty. Roma depressed him. He'd been to too many of her afternoon teas and slide shows. He gestured Terry away from his keenly entrepreneurial mastery of the ceremonies. "Look Terry, I hope you don't think I was planning to move in on you and Anna, and leave you stranded."

"There's nothing between me and Anna that would prevent her or you doing whatever you liked."

"Come with me, my old mate. At the Gouha discoteque at the stroke of midnight there will be someone worth meeting, an opportunity you'd be sorry to pass up, a divine oil daughter of sweet sixteen who loves ravaged old rakes. Let's go and get her. In my car Through the gloomy by-ways of old Cairo."

In the doorway Matthew and Terry jostled with the

two incoming Sudanese. Terry, always the host, guffawed to them, "There's a Scrabble game going you're welcome to join in."

"Now behave, you colonial prat!" reprimanded Matthew. "Those bewildered faces are my bread-and-butter." And Terry, reeling slightly, fancy-footed down the steps with Matthew's large shepherding hand to steady him.

The girl was called Amy. She was with her girlfriends at a table in the discoteque. The whole table was delighted to see Terry and Matthew, assuming that two men would be enough for all of them. But Matthew was wary of the others who were lumpy and frumpy, and convinced Amy in her ear that for tonight the single soul had better prospects than a bevy. Amy told her friends that something awful had happened and allowed herself to be marched officiously away between Terry and Matthew. Outside she threw back her long black hair and gasped, "It's a magical night. I'm so glad you got me out of that place." And to Terry with breathless hilarity, "Hey, what was your name?" Her tight white jeans were luminescent.

On the return journey Matthew stopped the car on the high battlemented terrace beneath the Citadel Wall (A.D. 1172). It afforded a view of the low ancient quarter once known as Babylon where the Copts lived. It was used for refuse dumping now. The vacant areas where the potters had their kilns were full of ragpickers waiting. At night the rubbish was burned off. Matthew, Terry and the girl sat in the car and passed the capsule of white powder from one to another. They could see black mounds of rubble down below, the glow of small furnaces, and the enormous orange jelly of garbage on fire. Matthew had chosen a safe spot.

They were shielded from the mad twining of traffic on the main road by the muddy wall of the city's highest aspiring sanctum. Amy, squeezed between the men, hissed a giggle and Terry paid her compulsive attention. Matthew was driving again now, pushing from lane to lane as if, like everyone else, to make the city circulate faster. When he jolted the back of a Fiat taxi, dislodging its number plate, he reversed on reflex and quickly drove — "Out of the way, cock!"

The front room of the flat was full and Amy was inducted straight to Terry's bedroom. Matthew was on his way through but encountered Salah, the living model the French couple had evacuated from their stable. Lofty with a swept back crest of waving hair, Salah stood like a wooden statue conveniently in a corner niche. He was receiving doctrine about sex roles in the Arab world from the fortune-teller's impassioned daughter. When Matthew led him off, he was glad to follow. Matthew knew, as he knew everything, that Salah was a superior masseur with more stamina than any in Beirut, and Salah owed Matthew a favour. He took Salah to Terry's bedroom and locked the door against all comers. Salah was invited to treat Amy first. Matthew and Terry sat cross-legged over the end of the bed while they waited, chatting idly about *Seven Pillars of Wisdom* . In the dim smoke of his bedroom Terry could picture the hard weak face of T.E. Lawrence and with Matthew sceptically conferring a second dimension of vision, the image of the turbaned Englishman was as vivid as if on a screen. Civilization seemed more pervasive than ever to Matthew. He sipped, smoked his cigar, gave literature his consideration, while over his shoulder the girl who would shortly get the best of him was being tuned up by the most primitive of arts.

"Haven't you got any decent music in this philistine den?"

Terry slotted side one of *The Magic Flute* into the cassette recorder. Only Mozart could find the divine harmony anywhere. He stretched out to listen. In the front room Mrs Mamoulian's fat son was yelling at the Sudanese. Was he really calling them hairy black lavatory brushes, with the unthinkable panache of Arabic insult? On the tape the Queen of the Night was beside herself. Matthew gave Terry a rough shove — his turn for the massage.

"No," Terry muttered. He was content to let it go at this stage. Salah, however, lingered sulkily, wanting to be included; but Matthew got rid of him sharply. Then Matthew and the girl were together and Terry's eyes closed, his body curled small along the side of the bed. The music continued high and loud. There was nothing anyone could feel that wasn't orchestrated by it. The pack of dogs that tetchily guarded the main entrance to the flats heard the music and came yelping and whining outside Terry's window. They yapped at the Queen of the Night's shrill anguish and howled at Sarastro's monumental rectitude, helplessly, tunelessly bewitched. Terry lay quietly, as one who listened to hear his heart's music. He kept sleep at bay, wrapping himself round with the wildness of the evening. When Matthew and Amy tried to pull him into their lovemaking he resisted. He thought instead of the letters he could write. This was himself at the fine prime old age of twenty-five. This was his life. God bless them all. Next door the voices had grown turbulent and the crash of furniture suggested — dancing? His com-

13

panions on the bed were moaning hungrily. What a
stone weight the music laid on him; how lightly his
drowsy body took it. The voices marched through the
air —

O Isis und Osiris schenket
Der Weisheit Geist dem neuen Paar!

The cars outside, the stars, the holy men for the dawn
turned by the same lunacy. Terry dreaming himself
now in the lowest-rental room of heaven's mansion —
The dogs baying at Mozart with his pony tail and
blessed wand — But Anna's door, closed to it all —

II

When Anna came home from school in the early afternoon she stripped her bed, bundled the dirty washing
into a couple of pillowcases and took it straight to the
laundry. Terry's apologetic note was attached to the
general chaos. Instantly and unshakeably she decided
that she would — quite simply — no longer consider
all those other rooms in the flat her domain. She
opened up her balcony and shook the stained rug over
the edge, sprinkling little Gamil who was below. Then
whimsically she threw it down on top of him and told
him to get rid of it. Briskly she swept the muck off the
floor and went at the boards with detergent and ammonia, mopping with thorough rhythmic thrusts.
There was dust everywhere, like fur round her fingers
when she touched anything. But every speck must go
and her zeal was greatest as she used her fingernail to
run a tissue along the inside of cracks and ornate carv-
ing on the furniture. She scrubbed at the rings left by

mugs and glasses. She pulled down her pictures and hangings and put them in a box. Only the walls remained, pale, dull, unobjectionable. Anna washed her body last. She spent a time under the shower scrubbing the dust out of her pores. When she was satisfied she put on her long dress of Indian cotton, made herself a cup of milkless, sugarless, lemonless tea, as weak as possible, and seated herself on the balcony, upright on a wooden chair. The air was tart with ammonia. The bedroom door was bolted. She had pinned a note to it. "SLEEPING".

Presently Mrs Mamoulian came out of the ground-floor flat to collect her clothing from the line. When she saw Anna she began to scold, shaking her finger humorously and half-enviously at the incessant noise of the night before.

Anna smiled gravely and serenely. "Yes, I'm sorry. It's gone too far, hasn't it? I feel so *tired* of it all."

"Why do you always make the party at home?" chortled the landlady. "Why don't you go out to the nightclub with Mr Terry? Like *we* always did."

Anna smiled again.

When the tinsel dusk set in she withdrew and closed the shutters. She just didn't want to see anyone — or be where she was. With a handkerchief she polished the little silver incense burner she had bought in India in transit. She often thought of floating on aimlessly and easily as she had moved already from country to country, situation to situation. It was brave not to seek shelter in a world which was benign and endlessly diverting to those it chose to love. The incense holder was starting to mirror and India was in her mind. Terry always spoke of it as the next port of call, when he was in that sort of mood. On Easter Sunday morning, a feast unacknowledged by the locals, they had been sitting in a cafe by the Nile, biting on pickled lemons, tingling with the smell of budding pink trees overhead. The first of spring had made them talk . . . of plans. After Egypt India was the only possibility, though it could never outdo Egypt. Living Tongues, evidently, was opening a school there. Anna had high hopes of India — Hindu men did not devour women as the Moslems did — and for his part Terry wanted to immerse in the Ganges' sacred filth of millions. And, as the man said, Everest was there. He'd always wanted to be a mountain-climber too. Passing, that moment, the imperturbable motion of a high-sailed felucca had given rise to a new fantasy. They could go by boat from Port Said via the Red Sea to Bombay, the two of them, regally on a barge.

Anna pulled herself up, rubbing hard at the silver trinket. Terry's plans only included her out of a spirit of poetic licence. The connexion between them was a purely contingent one. They'd established that from the start when they found themselves side by side on the incoming Cairo plane. They had been part of Living Tongues' annual shipment of new teaching blood. As they flew over the Alps they established mutual acquaintances, an arc thrown from Melbourne to London. Anna had come to the plane from a coastal retirement town where she'd been instructing French computer operators. Terry had dragged himself to the plane without sleep, he said, from some sort of small-scale North London orgy. Their perspectives on each other had been more or less fixed from that moment. When they landed Terry made cracks about gyppo air traffic control and intimated with his slack grin that in a spirit of Antipodean supportiveness they might share a flat.

Anna had complied with good will. Terry was companionable, he would tend her through the migraines and nausea this place would no doubt inflict, and his stylish scorn would match her own. "Johnny!" he had called to the solid huddle of taxi drivers at the airport that day — he got it from some book — then the meter hadn't worked; when they arrived at the school he braved the driver's curses and declared roundly, on the authority of his tourist guide, "Three pounds, my man! There you are!"

Anna stopped herself again. Those who shared a predicament could not look to each other for rescue.

She'd supposed many times that she would just drift on. Blocks of wood bumping in the stream was her idea of human contact. But now a different impulse was nudging her to reconstruct and make reparations. Her mother, a stubborn country evangelical, wrote to Anna routinely and told her every little thing that happened, on the assumption that Anna would shortly resume life in the family circle, Bairnsdale, Victoria. Anna might have been no further off than Lake's Entrance where they went for holidays. And accordingly when her mother's letters arrived Cairo became dull and a cheat. Its glamour wasn't enough to redirect her after all. Her mother spoke familiarly of Anna's homecoming as an article of faith. Prodigal Anna would return. Her sins would diminish in the distance and be forgotten. She would recover herself, clear, young and strong. Anna didn't really know what the chances were but it seemed under the circumstances a chance she might have to take. Fly to London, fly to Melbourne, be met at the airport, end of a chapter, moralizing her life as the strictest author would have wished. Comforting wings closing over her like a book's end papers.

Terry was back in the house, she heard.

He blundered across the floor until he saw Anna's note and became clumsily silent. He started busily putting the front room to rights. He carted the dishes off to the kitchen for a rinse, set the rubbish outside the door and smeared things over with the rag. It needed another party straightaway when he'd done. He was lonely, moving about restlessly with Anna cooped up in her room. Suddenly with his jacket and keys he dashed out into the street. Round his feet in the dust pins of quartz twinkled at the low sun.

He found people a-plenty downtown. The Riche eating house was a thin oblong of a place where the tables sat in sawdust under a hessian canopy. A body of men was gathered there round a distinguished old poet, railing fiercely agains the President's kingly pretensions. Bread prices would rise in order to fly the President's niece's wedding banquet in from Maxim's, Paris. Terry skewered his macaroni with passion, excited by the noise of committed life overheard. Two of the American girls round town lighted on him then, complaining about the bread prices too. There was a birthday party in Heliopolis and they invited Terry to share their taxi, and at the party he got involved, collapsing eventually, so it was another day before he was home at the flat. Anna was "SLEEPING" again. Was the note a decoy? Was she there at all? There was no answer when he knocked. When he tried the door it was locked.

Anna sat pat on the wooden chair, light because of her fast and indifferent to the extreme cleanliness of her surroundings. She'd swept the room again, done the mending, packed away her jewellery and make-up and was now engaged in a long letter to her mother. It wasn't a testamentary letter — simply an attempt to give clear and believable form to her desire to be good, to live a quiet life. Having returned to the country town perhaps she would become a nurse. All that she had fingered in the grim depths of life would then come in handy. She could be a healer. Through the shutters on the balcony the cats prowled and yawned. The dusk, trumpetted by the raw and lustful braying of donkeys in the construction site, was carnal.

"She needs a suitor. She needs to be opened up," Terry told Matthew Phaery after work, in a small unsavoury bar.

"I offered her myself," he replied, drawing sharply on his cigarette, "Myself at my most vivacious and most elegant, I might add, and she chose not to jump." He fluttered his long eyelashes to enliven his tired eyes.

"She takes time," said Terry. "She's not just another one."

The bar was Matthew's drinking choice, badly nautically decorated, with seashells, netting, a barometer and a carpet of aquamarine nylon. If it was intended for sailors it was stranded so far from the coast. Matthew was there hoping to rub up against a particular government official. It was rumoured that the President had briefed the army about emergency law and order measures. So Matthew kept his ears pricked.

It was, Terry reckoned, a mark of Anna's better taste that she didn't let Phaery crack onto her. Matthew was the first suitor Terry would have suggested to anyone, but a suitor bearing gifts and gab who would be turned down by any woman of distinction.

Matthew for his part assumed that once open to one Anna would be open to all. "Don't you think we could set something up," he wondered. Terry presented a sceptically romantic look. "I gather," Matthew continued, "that Anna wants an affair free of all the bed-hopping Cairene sordidness. We must be able to fix her up with someone who doesn't show his scars. Someone from another walk of life."

Terry couldn't help. Anna's temperament was too high and subtle to be tampered with easily. Where were the young men to match her? "She needs a suitor, something to toy with, not an accomplished fact."

Matthew's cheeks had a habit of reddening when he didn't understand something. "Getting down to practicalities, what about Salah? He's pretty flash."

"You certainly got what was to be got out of him."

"Now now, mate. Or what about a soldier boy?"

Terry raked his dirty black hair and finished his drink. He had to be anguished before he could reveal what Anna had once tentatively confessed. "She fancies that guy who plays acoustic guitar at the Gouha."

"Jimmy? Surely not?"

"She said he was cute."

"Jimmy Mandrax? That's what they call him. He's only held together with string, dreaming of smack and America all day. He wants to be the first Egyptian country rock star. What hope has he got?"

"Soul. He's an exile."

"Of course. I go to parties where there are Mediterranean exiles ten to the dozen, polylingual, polysexual, polyeverything. They can't stick in one language to the end of a sentence. But Jimmy Mandrax is so wiped he can't get to the end of a sentence in any language ever."

"It's worth a try," Terry decided.

Jimmy was the passive type, ready to accept a pleasure if it fell into his lap. He had simply to be told that Anna would be at the discoteque hoping to know him

20

better. But it would be hard to persuade Anna to come out of the house for the evening.

Terry found her examining documents on her bed, the door ajar. The twilight was unpleasantly muggy and it required an effort to be other than quiet, but Terry strode in with a jolly swag, clapping his hands. "How are you feeling?"

She looked up. Without make-up or earrings her face was unusually poised and determined.

"Listen, Terry. I've decided to leave Cairo. I'm going to London when the term ends next week. Sorry to be so precipitous — precipitate — whatever the word is. I hope it won't leave you in the lurch."

"Why?"

She laughed at him. "It's the right thing. I'm going back to Australia."

The passport folder flapped affirmatively in her hand. She was declaring allegiance to that kangaroo and emu embossed in gold on navy blue plastic.

"I thought you were waiting till the end of the year," he said.

It was no longer a matter for talking over and she didn't encourage him. He stalked to his own room, filled with bizarre and sumptuous bric-a-brac, and out of habit threw open the shutters, though the air was like lukewarm soup. He kicked his shoes off angrily and padded barefoot through to the kitchen to get a beer. Then back again to Anna.

"Okay," he said. "I hope it's the right thing. You'll make it right."

She wanted neither to look at him squarely nor to avoid him. "I hope so."

He had a draught of beer. It trickled down his chin. When he'd wiped himself he passed her the bottle.

"Cheers." While she took a token sip he asked, "Will you come out for a meal? To celebrate your decision? On me?"

"Why not? I've hardly eaten all week. I feel terrific. My body is cleaned right out."

She laid her passport on the dressing table and went to select one of her clean shirts with the creases still showing. Terry changed too and they caught a taxi to the restaurant they were fond of, Terry talking soberly of possible arrangements as if he believed Anna really would leave. She became sentimental during the meal and chose the most exotic dishes, raisin lamb, saffron rice, aubergine puree.

She ventured, "When you're sick of it too, Terry, you'll end up back in Australia."

"Egypt is the most important thing in my life." He called for the bill and suggested ingenuously over coffee that they should round off the evening at the disco. Her eyes flashed their old knowing nervousness.

"Yes," she said, under obligation.

Matthew Phaery was at the Gouha (but Jimmy wasn't) and ordered them expensive whiskies. "It's nice to see you out of confinement, my darling."

The music was loud, in a dead fashion. When Anna asked casually where the acoustic guitarist was her companions expressed keen indifference. Then Jimmy appeared and drank rounds of Terry's and Matthew's whiskies before his bracket was up. On stage he growled through the microphone that the first song was "For Anna".

"If you'll excuse me," Matthew said, "an appointment — one can't afford to miss a chance." He winked at Anna reprovingly, as if she had missed *her* chance, bowed and departed. Jimmy finished and came back to sit beside Anna, and Terry's discomfort was obvious. Soon he kissed her and said he had to go — — off into the young night — and kissed her again, and was gone.

"Terry?" she called.

But he was pushing through the tables, his head spinning, making for the toilet. In a split second he was alone and in the same moment he was aghast at the enormous task ahead, the procuring of rich and uproarious pleasure in the streets of Cairo. Till dawn. So he groomed himself and delayed. When at last he tripped down the front stairs of the club he saw a little scene fifty yards down the road. Anna was there. She was shouting. Half in darkness Anna stood impressively upright between a taxi driver and Jimmy Mandrax, speaking loud and firm. She was commanding the driver to take her away and she jumped into his car and slammed the door. "Come on," she shouted and the driver hurried to obey, clattering his car into motion. It vanished, as Terry watched, beneath the ribs of palms into the dark. Jimmy Mandrax was left shambling peacefully. His head nodded like a puppy's. When he saw Terry he shrugged loosely and gave a leer that couldn't be interpreted. *"Lissa, lissa,"* he shook his hand, his fingers formed in a bud. Then he was gone inside the sham music place, beloved of those who yearned for the West. Only now in the western sky there was nothing but a round humidified hieroglyph of a moon.

Terry stayed out all night again. In a break after the first lesson next day Anna came into his classroom, pale and shaky, her skin blotched like a pear's. But when she spoke to him she wasn't weak. The severity of her contempt was unequivocal and undisguised.

"Very funny."

Like a dog he didn't give himself away. "What?"

"The state of my room. I get the point."

"What are you talking about?"

"My room was ransacked while I was at the Gouha last night and I presume you know about it."

Terry stared.

His bewildered look didn't satisfy Anna. "My room was turned quite upside down. Only my room, not the rest of the flat. Sheets ripped off the bed. Clothes thrown out of the wardrobe. The contents of my sandalwood box sprayed across the floor. And my passport is missing. I hope for the sake of that you *were* responsible."

"Don't be insane, Anna." Terry took her and lowered her into a chair. "Have a smoke. Is this true?"

She let it pass. "All right, I can't leave the country till I get my passport back."

"I haven't got your fucking passport. What would I want with it? You stupid bitch."

Anna curled over, resting her forehead on her knees. "*You* left me with Jimmy Mandrax. What made him think he was coming home with me? Christ!"

Terry walked to the end of the room where the visual displays were. The school was in the forest of highrise blocks that ringed the city. Beyond, through the window, were fields and hovels, hybrid settlements, half-urbanized villages poor and stinking with comfortless extending families. It should not be.

Terry guessed that Jimmy Mandrax had thought it worth scouring Anna's room while the household awaited him elsewhere. Or someone who needed to do over a woman's room.

"Were you okay last night? It must have been spooky?"

Anna swung round. "*And* the taxi driver was one of those," she added brightly. "Showed me his merchandise because I was all alone."

Terry couldn't help sniggering; Anna sniffed too. "It's the third exposure you've had," he remarked. Then more earnestly, "Take the day off, Anna. Go home and rest."

It was as if the wind had blown a bucket of dust against freshly laundered linen and the rare rains had come, turning the dust to Nile mud, dying the sheets excremental brown. She shivered. "My room's such a mess. I can't bear to go back there. Someone's been through everything." Then briskly, "I'll see you later. I have to get a new passport so I can flee this place."

She lumped herself home through the desert suburban streets, eyed suspiciously from the doorsteps by sluggish sandy dogs — rabid, she supposed — and disregarded entirely by the housewives in black, lugging their goods like camels.

She lay fitfully awake for ten hours in the room until it reached eight o'clock, the busiest hour. But the whole place was so uncannily quiet that she might have thought her hearing had failed her too.

Terry, back, approached her re-ordered and re-chastened room apologetically. He knocked and went in to deliver the news. The government had brought down its threatened curfew. The first of the bread riots had occurred in the Liberation Square. Hundreds, thousands had gathered in the square, swarming, chanting together with a just passion. The army had crushed a row of them against the spiked fence of the museum. Now, that night, no one but the police was to be on the streets.

Anna heard quietly. Terry cautiously had something

else to add. Matthew Phaery wanted to spend the curfew period in their flat. He wanted to be within walking distance, across the Zamalek bridge, of any action.

And Anna shrieked. "The last *straw* ! GET OUT! Matthew Phaery will not come here and be bailed up with me and plague me for days! Isn't there anywhere in this city I can get a bit of peace? There must be somewhere out of it all — "

She heard her shrill self as if someone else were talking and in a laughably lucid second at once saw what she had said. Terry stared at her helplessly. In that same second, as she grabbed her bag, their eyes met and a spark jumped between them. But she had dashed into the street where a heaven-sent taxi was opening its door to her.

There was an hour to go and she urged the driver as fast as possible along the southern road, through the shanty zone of nightclubs and bungalows to the city's outskirts. There the taxi's tire burst, a soft noise like a fart. She heaved anxiously. The driver was so afraid of being caught after the curfew that he wouldn't see to the tire. He simply burbled. But Anna refused to linger. She was in the middle of the road waving her bag furiously, and because she was foreign and female a car stopped without delay. She was speeding on, bouncing uncomfortably in the prickly backseat of a VW. At the furthermost fringe of the Cairo oasis came a belt of canals and green fields, but it was dark. Beyond, as if life and sap were neatly severed, the abrupt desert. The road narrowed and sloped upwards. The driver was blathering at Anna in loud Arabic about her mad request. He wouldn't be able to wait, he said, he had to be home before the curfew. The Sphinx passed, scaffolded and gauntly lit for an unattended *son et lumiere* show. There were no guards about. Another quarter mile brought the pyramid of Cheops, its grandeur only a notion of dimensionlessness to the matchbox car which stopped at the foot. The place was quite empty. It was usually patrolled to check the lunatic exploits of tourists. But the guards had gone. A barbed wire fence was neglected like a demarcation line after the war. Anna's countrymen had travelled to die in this sand. She paid the car and waved it off, compelled to remain now until the next day's business began. The city from such a distance was a low luminous vaporous presence. The eye turned from it to the unending clarity of sand, and the blocks of the pyramid. The single block at the lowest corner was itself a monument, head high, pitted with holes as big as Anna's fists. She saw no geometry when she looked up, simply a swelling of stone from farthest left to farthest right.

She clambered, up the edge where it was easiest. At the meeting of two planes the pocks provided footholds and her hands could — as it were — hug the angle of stone. It took a very long time. Each of the one hundred and fifteen steps was a labour. But she pushed upwards to the most uncrowded spot around. Every ten steps a rest. The moon was bright enough for the sand to shed whiteness like bedsheet. From on high the city looked like a back-scratching loofah, dark and spongey. Once she slipped. The higher the more exilarated the more fiercely impelled to climb faster.

At one point she stopped to observe silence. A girl she knew had fallen from this pyramid, plucked by the wind, hurled upwards by the sail of her bright butterfly-patterned cloak, then down. Those who were there said she had been ejected out of time. Anna remembered the girl, but she wasn't frightened. There was no discriminating between the slightness of the strings that bound her to the girl or either of them to life. When her own skirt caught on a spur of rock she pushed on defiantly and strained till the cloth tore.

The summit. You didn't believe till you were there, one last step then perched atop — nothing. The far ground was silvery dark everywhere. There would only have been the sky to gaze at if the effort of the climb didn't make you sink on a ledge and, after all that, close your eyes.

"Anna. Hallo."

She would have fallen if he hadn't held her shoulder, anticipating the shock.

Terry didn't know how to smile. He didn't know if it was funny or not. "I was worried about you."

"What are you doing here? Did you fly here?"

"You told me you were coming. Telepathy. In your room you said, 'Somewhere out of it all — '. The penny dropped for both of us at the same moment. My taxi must have been faster. I thought you'd be up here already. You should have been." His lips curled. He looked at her with taunting, loving eyes. "I climbed the face behind. Stormed up like a digger."

"It's ridiculous."

"Lucky I didn't climb the wrong pyramid. That would have been a joke." He took out his cigarettes. A bit of wind made it impossible to keep the match alight. "I hope I haven't stolen your one clear place."

"I can't complain. With all this space," she replied. It thrilled her.

"I brought my camera," said Terry. "Shall I take a photo?"

"No, don't." She had a general air of contentment,

sitting together with Terry as on a parkbench. She didn't need a souvenir.

They sat, leaning against each other, and as the hours advanced the cold made them feel their bones. Anna wrapped herself closer. Next time she spoke she said she couldn't leave Cairo after this. "You being here, it's the last straw," she said. "The camel's back is broken."

A curious plant was growing two or three steps down in a crack. The weed, some sort of spindly thing, was flowering healthily, though there wasn't much accumulated soil on the top of the pyramid. Terry lowered himself and picked one of its little flowers. "Consider this the item in question, the straw which broke the animal's back."

She accepted with grace. It had a pert pungent nip.

The sun came up after a prelude of sombre colouration. It moved slowly and its shifts of shape and brightness could almost have been measured. It could have been a childbirth although unblinkingly remote from human things. Only at the last was the sun round and familiar, judged Terry and Anna from their viewing platform.

"That must rate three stars," she said.

A white egret flew past on its way, high up there.

"The sun going one way, the bird going another way, the pyramid not moving at all except with the earth, and you and me," Terry listed conclusively. "You're sure it's not worth a photo?"

"And I'm back to point zero," she asked him, "am I not?"

The first taxi was beetling along the road like a scarab with a spiral tail of dust. Its duty was to fetch them back. In the city the next teeming day somersaulted forward. Wide across Egypt the good folk kept up their agitation, squirming at the price of daily bread.

29

Harold in Italy

Italy, the paradise of the earth and the epicure's heaven, how doth it form our young master . . .? From thence he brings the art of atheism, the art of epicurising, the art of whoring, the art of poisoning, the art of sodomitry. The only probable good thing they have to keep us from utterly condemning it is that it maketh a man an excellent courtier, a curious carpet knight; which is, by interpretation, a fine close lecher, a glorious hypocrite. It is now a privy note amongst the better sort of men, when they would set a singular mark or brand on a notorious villain, to say he hath been in Italy.

Thomas Nashe, *The Unfortunate Traveller* (1594)

THE FIRST PART

On his first day the Contessa took him about the garden.

"Really we're waiting for spring," she said, "it seems so late this year."

On the lawns a few primulas had opened. The rhododendrons were still tight. The Contessa bent over to feel the health of a laurel leaf, then drew her shawl close about her. A compact woman, balding, she had a reserve of contentment in her voice.

"When the wind blows there are no clouds between us and Monte Rosa." She pointed across the lakes. "Ideal weather for gliding. Now — Harold. Come down to the greenhouse with me."

The Contessa managed the steep, stony garden paths much better than Harold. Down below the gardener showed them through the rows of jungle plants, orchids and herb trees.

"When it is winter for us, they have their summer," she told him, "so we always have something in bloom to take up to the house."

"How convenient," Harold replied.

While Harold was still walking among the shrubbery, the Contessa's children returned from Milan. He heard the shush of the car gliding up the gravel, and their laughter as they came seeking him, Paola's hand outstretched.

" *Ciao* Harold, welcome."

Gianfranco was more formal and led Harold inside by the shoulder, to give him a drink. He answered Harold tersely.

"Yes, we go to Milan to study and return here each evening."

But his sister was chatty. "There are always people here — my parents, my uncle, their friends, the butler, the cook. Have you seen her? Giuseppina — she's unbelievable! She's absolutely crazy!"

Then Paola went to make telephone calls and Harold asked Gianfranco about the demands of the family estate. Harold was free in Italy. He had come without ties and such obligations as he undertook were up to him. Gianfranco intensified his large eyes and explained the situation to Harold.

"They say that these days one family cannot survive more than three generations. I am the third generation. I must keep us in prosperity."

On the high ceiling of the "children's room" cupids hung among acanthus leaves. It was dark. Gianfranco systematically closed the doors and shutters to the garden. His father came into the room then, a big man, the Conte, who rubbed his neck. He told the two boys that the old grandmother would be there for dinner and they should dress accordingly.

Gianfranco was furious. "She only eats with us out of duty! Bof! *Nonna!* Do you know what ga-ga is, Harold?"

The assembled family had to receive the grandmother in the hall. Her driver helped the old woman as far as the door, where Paola had to take over and carry her through to an armchair. She gurgled as she went.

Harold was introduced but not registered. With impossible delicacy the Contessa was able to rectify the old lady's off-centre wig, and Paola declared compliments at her fine mesh dress. *Bello bello!*

Dinner was silent except for the grandmother's noises. She was too deaf to hear much, but her sharp eyesight made conversation impossible. A huge mauve orchid rose between them all on the table. The Conte announced his prohibition of his children's weekend in Tuscany. Travelling around was no longer safe. Gianfranco kicked his chair leg in protest and Paola accepted the paternal law calmly. Grandmother chewed and the Contessa seemed miles away. Harold's digestion was troubled by the unease at the table. Then the Conte asked about his plans and he had to feign linguistic incompetence. At last the dessert came, *marrons glacés*.

The plate was offered to grandmother first. She took her *marron* and bit it squeamishly. *"Aaagh! Aagh!"* she groaned and hurled it to the floor with fierce petulance. "Old! *Old like me!*"

Harold began to sweat. The cook was called in.

"Giuseppina," said the Conte, "my mother says the *marrons glacés* are stale."

Giuseppina shook to say that they were not. Her red hair and taut, redder lips made her look like a disinherited clown, hiding in a white uniform. But she would comply and, flapping her hands, vowed mutely to fetch a fresh box.

The grandmother wished to observe the actual unwrapping of the new box and Giuseppina obliged with a grinning, servile charade. When the old woman was satisfied, Giuseppina stood back, scratched her left mole and winked at Harold. Then she hurried back to the kitchen, from where her own account of the incident was heard to erupt.

Gianfranco cursed her.

Afterwards in the sitting-room the grandmother acknowledged Harold. She asked him to pour her a brandy. As he reached for the decanter, the Contessa deftly passed him a different one from usual. The old lady saw and moaned in a tremble, "No, no." Gianfranco whispered to Harold that she was always given watered down cognac. Then, over drinks, she signed documents, and eventually the driver removed her.

Harold removed himself too. His bedroom was high in a far wing of the house and he settled to sleep. That first night of residence in the ancestral home he dreamed of death. He had acquiesced too easily. On a blazing green mountainside the funeral of a young man wended its way. The body was covered with crimson flowers and followed by the Contessa under a veil. Harold's schoolday friends were in attendance, in jeans and bright shirts, straggling after the coffin until thin hot rain fell and the colours threatened to fade.

Harold woke up and heard an odd scraping sound on the gravel below. The old clock said three. The noise continued and voices were added. Very quietly Harold went to the window and put his head out. He saw Giuseppina the cook hanging out over her little balcony. In the courtyard a dark youth was grappling to fold a ladder. He was wearing overalls and not more than seventeen years old. When the ladder was compact enough, he hid it behind some pot-plants. Then he came back underneath the balcony and made a vast embrace to the air and to Guiseppina. She shooed him off reluctantly and at last he was gone into the garden. The watchdogs wagged lazily, used to such things. Giuseppina sighed, and sang to the dark in a low, strange voice: *Tonight, tonight, my heart is burning.*

Harold alone heard.

THE SECOND PART
(con sprezzatura)

The attractive Avvocato Pinelli slipped across the snow and into the chill morning-room where the Contessa waited with Harold. Opening his thick coat and rubbing his ungloved hands, he breathed cheerily —

"Burning cold!"

— And illuminated his remark with a smile dazzling as ice.

Harold had requested an evening at the "detestable" opera, so the Contessa had called in the family lawyer, whom the boy had met on various ceremonial occasions. Pinelli had arrived punctually and now took Harold, along with some brown-paper envelopes, out of the Contessa's hands.

On the autostrada the lawyer took no advantage of his right to aggression, though it was conferred by virtue of owning a midnight-blue Lamborghini. Instead he hummed benignly and smoked a cigarillo with Harold. Once Harold remarked on the litter all over the roadside.

Massimo Pinelli retorted: "We have a saying. To the pure all things are pure. So maybe there is some rubbish. It can be swept away. It is harmless. Because at the heart of our country there is health and vitality. Where things matter they are clean. You must open your eyes a little wider. That's what I have learnt. That's why I'm happy with my work. Happy with my Cinzia. Happy with life."

He smiled as he pushed a lock of hair behind his ear and hummed again.

The lawyer's apartment in Corso Buenos Aires was ultra-modern yet full of antiques. Cinzia the wife seized Harold's hand eagerly and persuaded him to a warming cup of English tea, while Massimo went off to his office. It took her some time to find the tea-pot, then they settled. Cinzia in her bottle-green top and bottom looked much more comfortable than any of the furniture.

"Your husband is a very happy man," Harold ventured, seeing it was common knowledge.

"When he moved to Milano, he chose for his new friends only those who recognized him as a saint. He found a good number of devotees. He's been lucky."

È stato felice. The desk brandished a colour photo of Pinelli smiling on the ski slopes, like a movie star, between the Conte and Contessa. A cat appeared from the kitchen and climbed onto the back of the sofa, from where he threatened to jump into Cinzia's lap as she sipped.

"Meet Harold," she told the cat, running her finger through luxuriant fur. "That's my Benedictine."

The telephone rang to announce that Massimo would be bringing Signorina Gadda to the opera as well. She was his accountant's secretary and the daughter of a business associate.

"Just out of hospital. Abortion," whispered a pitying Cinzia, hand over mouthpiece.

Cinzia and Harold rendezvous'd with Pinelli at a bar near La Scala. With him was the girl who, if she was for Harold, was in her mid-thirties and terrifyingly sensitive. She recalled how one summer on the drive to Portofino the lawyer had revealed to her Mozart's profound piety. They were to see *Don Giovanni* .

"An antidote against the cold," said Pinelli as he escorted his little flock across the square to the theatre.

The heavy-falling snow gave a special flutter to the

excitement inside the foyer, to the birds delighted with their aviary, birds of paradise, semi-precious and precious ones, vultures and starlings. Pinelli sent his party ahead to their seats and only just came back in time. In the first half the opera mainly failed to ignite, although once it did make Signorina Gadda emit a tiny cry and nearly slump against the lawyer.

In the interval Cinzia took Harold on a tour of the theatre. Thus it was by accident that he encountered Pinelli in the upstairs cloakroom being shaken and harangued by a man in a pale blue suit. The lawyer greeted Harold without surprise but with his crystal smile, which he then passed on to his assailant before disengaging himself. *Va bene, caro Massimo, beato te* , added the man in blue as Pinelli departed with Harold.

Oh, how the second half took off! Cinzia could justly fancy, on the way home in the car, that she'd been scorched, and Signorina Gadda had become reverentially silent. All it required now was one of Cinzia's culinary triumphs.

But dinner, despite the *ottimo risotto* , was a strain, for the Signorina discussed her hospitalization, in veiled terms.

"Only Massimo's advice got me through. He told me there is good at the centre of everything. What a vision your husband has!"

If it had been his own blood the lawyer could not have poured their wine more preciously.

When it was over, Cinzia retreated to the kitchen and Harold asked where his bedroom was to be. It was only because he could not find a light switch that he could stand in the shadows, an hour later, and observe.

The lawyer stood before the mantelpiece drinking and picking his teeth. Signorina Gadda timidly, yet intimately, approached him and slipped her hand inside his jacket.

"Only through the thought of you was I able to endure it. You're a saint, my darling one," she said.

Then Cinzia called and the secretary, quickly alarmed, went through to the kitchen.

Pinelli turned to the acre of gilt-edged mirror above the mantelpiece. He tossed his head back with pleasure and offered himself his most glittering, blinding smile. Then a sudden inexplicable convulsion overcame him. The cat Benedictine, startled, leapt on the instant from the sofa to the mantel and knocked the mirror askew. In his fright Pinelli dropped his liqueur glass. It splintered into crystal light.

When his wife and the secretary came running the lawyer was still shivering.

"Glass is meant to smash," said Cinzia to console.

THE THIRD PART

Before long Harold had become addicted to observation. He was able to imitate the particular dumb stare that accommodates all Italian curiosity, no matter how brazen. The more craven his desire to *see* became, the more he chafed against the Contessa's faded pleasantries, and at last when Paola and Gianfranco were sent to Portofino for a regatta, Harold had a chance to contact a different kind of name from his address-book. He had decided he must see Piero della Francesca's *Flagellation* . That would offer just the right stinging intensity. And who better to accompany him than his old art-history master, now resident in Umbria?

He wrote to Mr Thrush who cabled back a detailed, rather puzzling arrangement, and Harold decided to comply. There was a sequence of trains to catch and an uneventful night to pass in Florence, in order to arrive by midday in the village of San Sepolcro. One last shaky train carried Harold up from the workaday plain to the mountains, where green bushes and orange walls kept threatening to dissolve in painterly light. He hadn't seen the art master for five years or so, but could well re-capture those rousing post-vacation apostrophes to Italy. "Birdie" Thrush had been a sympathetic teacher, scrupulous and at times, when in charge of cross-country running, even hearty. He had at length completed a doctorate on "The Iconology of Martyrdom", published later as *Quattrocento Pains* , and had then abruptly left the school. Only the vaguest rumours of "research abroad" had remained behind him and Harold had had great difficulty procuring a current address from the ex-chaplain. A feeling lingered that Birdie had sold his soul, but no one knew if he had made a bargain.

At the small station an inconspicuous man came forward, in a mustard suit. "Harold?"

"Oh, Mr Thrush?"

The man paused long enough for Harold to admire the prosperous moustache on his otherwise exactly shaven face, and then opened: "Please call me Benjamin. I hope you don't mind not coming to me at home, but I thought it would be easier if we had at least a chance to see Piero's birthplace before going on to the *Flagellation* . I don't have a car and trains are at best erratic, so I've booked us in for a night here. With your permission."

Harold assented with his new deep stare. ·

"But perhaps first the *Polyptych of the Misericordia* ", said Mr Thrush. "Did you know it was here? And afterwards lunch."

It seemed easier to concentrate on the paintings first. Then an hour later in a restaurant on the outskirts of the village Harold turned his attention to the master. Benjamin had filled out, was at once perfectly groomed, gracious and informative, while also being, in his choice of yellowish suit, quite unconstrained. Interspersing his utterly precise conversation his syruppy laugh admitted of a dozen interpretations. "I suggest we begin with the *carciofi alla romana,*" he said jovially.

They were on a terrace, half in leafy shadow and half in the early summer sun. Only a few sheep, bleating as they stepped from grass to grass, disturbed the still green below. But their old waiter heaved, mopping his brow and squeezing his breasts, as he took their order. Across the terrace a party of businessmen was enjoying a traditional eating feast. The idea is to eat all the best dishes available, taking the whole afternoon if necessary. Those indulging lie slumped in their chairs, chatting wearily, until a vision of some gastronomic joy occurs to someone. Then he will raise his finger to summon the puffing old waiter:

"Listen, friend, do you have an exquisite piece of veal? — translucent, good and pale? — a nip of best marsala? — a breath of basil, fresh, you understand? — fried by your wife — That's what I want!"

"*Sì, sì, tenerissimo,*" promises the restauranteur, committed to produce whatever the feasters dream up. Another individual will then raise a finger to describe how he wants his tripe: "*Rustico! Rustico!*"

So Harold and Benjamin were left drinking red wine as they squinted over hills of the golden age.

Benjamin asked Harold what the world had shown him in five years.

"Has it far surpassed your schoolboy dreams? Have you surprised yourself?"

"There's not much I didn't expect."

"What about in yourself? Ah, our next course. The *lingue all'amatriciana.* We must have them."

"Tongues?"

"In bacon and hot sauce. Invented just the other side of the Apennines. An obscure kind of pasta, you see, and something you didn't know about. Italy surely must have accorded you many such revelations. If you have not been frightened."

Another of the businessmen suddenly called for deep fried kidneys stuffed with spinach and sheep's cheese. And more wine!

Benjamin ordered more wine too. Harold was staring his hardest to impress upon his former teacher that he had in fact seen and known.

"*Pollo in porchetta,*" was ordered.

A man crooned: "*Gorgonzola ben dolce!*"

"Whatever you please, my friend," called the crimson waiter.

Smiling, Harold closed his languorous eyes on the dizzy vine-leaves overhanging. He heard Benjamin request "Ice-cream for the boy"; and when he looked up again Benjamin was shaking his elbow reassuringly. "Even at school, Harold, I knew you would rise to the

challenge of the southern lands. The ability to sur-
render to one's pristine longings."

Harold giggled at a well-being he should have considered unimaginable, and the feasting party broke into
a raucous football song. *"Viva la Lazio!"* Their team's
national triumph had inspired their celebrations.

Mr Thrush paid the bill carefully and led Harold up
the hill to the Hotel Sole. Shops were reopening as
Harold struggled not to wake from his siesta dreams.
Mr Thrush locked the bedroom door behind them and
Harold collapsed on the bed. When Harold opened his
eyes, he found Mr Thrush advancing upon him with a
grin and his moustache flourishing. Why should I
move, thought Harold, and Birdie thrilled to the boy's
indolence, grinding his teeth as the centurion arose
within him. So Harold became the victim of a carnal
feast, a mass of body more spiced and thorough-going
than he'd ever before conceived possible. Past the twilight hour the two of them pressed, right into the dark
and afterwards a sleep of sheer stupefaction.

In the morning Harold told Birdie Thrush that he
would prefer to continue the journey alone. As he was
passing out through reception, Harold was called over.
The callow manager's son gave a side-long glance to
the bleeding heart on the wall and apologized sancti-
moniously that a chance double booking required both
English gentlemen to leave at once. But Harold left the
whole business to Thrush.

Our young man reached Urbino that afternoon, took
a room, and proceeded stubbornly to the Palazzo
Ducale. He would see the Pieros. He was in considerable pain after the night and had trouble walking.
Besides, the sunlight dazzled. At the ticket office he
found one guard, half-asleep.

"The *Flagellation* ?" asked Harold.

The guard yawned and muttered through his teeth. "Flagellation? You should have come yesterday, friend. It's been stolen. Too bad!"

A *carabiniere* appeared and eyed Harold suspiciously, hopelessly.

"Not the type," added the guard.

Harold walked back into the square and the light. He had to sit down. Across from him was S. Domenichino, stucco as white as the sepulchre. He took a seat inside in the cool and had a cry. There was a poster announcing a recorder concert that evening, and he decided to wait. Towards six the church began to fill. He shifted uncomfortably on his hard seat. A group of youths laughed, with stubbled greasy chins. Harold couldn't quite see clearly. The *Flagellation* gone from Urbino? Everytime he wriggled he felt the whips. Meanwhile the music of angels had commenced, fluttering upwards in an acoustic blur.

THE FOURTH PART

Whenever the old men playing cards started to talk about politics, the barman would wring his hands in his apron and swear: *"Comunisti — Fascisti — Vaffan-culo!"*; as indifferent to ideology as he was to the presence of ladies.

But the scene made little Pia Rossi stiffen in her corner of the cafe. Her boyfriend Augusto had taught her that such things did matter if the country were not to be ruined utterly.

She drank her coffee nervously. She had permission to leave the boutique early for this meeting. At half-past four she had gone to the cubicle and changed the boutique's outfit for her own clothes, and she had taken off most of her make-up with a tissue.

When he brought her coffee, the barman had gestured at the foreigner in the other corner. *"Sempre da solo, sempre da solo, quel giovanotto inglese,"* he had said, as if Pia should be interested.

And at last Augusto had arrived, breathless, babbling about his office from the first moment. As always he allowed Pia to smooth his thinning hair and pick lint off his dark office suit. Apparently the new season's units had come in.

"Why didn't you come last night?" Pia asked abruptly.

"I told you why on the telephone."

"You've never had work to do in the evening before."

"I wanted to finish my project quickly. I wanted to make an impression. You know that the world moves fast."

"Faster than your life?" she queried.

"I have to be up with the moment, Pia. I have to be on the crest of the wave."

She did not blink her eyes, the colour of the dusk and stone in the hills she came from. She felt sluggish and retarded. She cupped her hands.

"Will we get married, Augusto?"

"I think we should stop seeing each other. From to-day."

"From next week," she said. "One more time. Exactly one week from today, we can see how things are. Please? At least that?"

The young man resented her hint of circularity, but agreed. "At the bus-stop in Piazza Barberini, then." And left.

The barman brought Pia a glass of mineral water.

"Comunisti — Fascisti — Vaffanculo!" he said again.

She drank the water and waited for a long time.

Harold, from his corner, had listened to Augusto and Pia's conversation. A morbid, novelistic curiosity was the worst of his several habits of solitariness. But Pia's bulky, up-to-date cardigan could not disguise from him her touching simplicity and confusion. Even Harold, with his new passion for centreless Mannerist painting and his pursuit of the various national crises, was more at home in Rome than Pia seemed.

Harold knew that, a week later, he would not be able to resist going to observe the lovers' meeting at that bus-stop in the Piazza Barberini. He found such sentiment pleasing.

During the week a fascist bomb exploded in Brescia and killed nine left-wing students. A general strike was called. The people wanted the black-shirt party abolished, fearful that history might repeat.

At five minutes before five on the appointed day Harold was in sight of the bus-stop and Augusto was already there, waiting in his dark suit, unobserved.

Just at that moment a truck appeared, blasting music from loudspeakers on its roof. And a broad front of people followed straight after, marching, singing, spill-

45

ing from the Via del Tritone into the square. Banners and placards waved against the mild autumn sky and a swarm of kids ran down the sides of the procession spraying out leaflets. More and more marchers appeared, overwhelming the bus-stop and all the pavements, old men with mourning armbands, students chanting and giving fists to the air, working men twenty abreast striding out, and couples with their children on their shoulders. Huge sashes of red cloth bellied forward proclaiming the cry *"Avanti Popolo! Avanti Popolo!"*; and the square swelled and filled till the crowd became impassable. A man addressed them all, inaudibly, and was cheered, and still the mass of people increased. Exuberant shouts for "Liberty!" went up, and the host of faces shone with an enthusiasm greater than themselves. Then at last another song began and another music-bearing truck pushed from the rear, aided by a formation of motorcycles, and the body of protesting marchers rippled as one, thinned itself into a spear and advanced up the hill.

It was half-past five by the time the march had past. At first Harold had kept sight of Augusto who was pushed and buffetted for not joining in with the dominant movement. But in the end Augusto had sneaked away downhill against the throng, and had vanished.

Once the square started to empty a young girl opposite came out from the doorway where she had shielded herself from the march. She hurried for a few steps in the direction of the bus-stop, then stopped and looked ahead. Then she clutched her cardigan and handbag close about her and started to move again, this time heavily. Harold could hear her feet strike hard on the bitumen. As she got near the bus-stop she seemed pale and she walked now as if she wanted to resist what pulled her. Nonetheless she kept on, steadily, until she reached the gutter and could stop with finality.

Harold watched her. She turned half-heartedly in case there was someone behind her. She reddened and fumbled in her bag for a tissue.

After blowing her nose she threw the tissue contemptuously down the storm-drain.

But still she lingered, unable to stop gazing round hopefully. Her cardigan she let fall open. Leaflets lay everywhere, trodden underfoot.

Harold wanted to tell Pia that her boyfriend had actually been there. He wondered if he could do it. For a second she stared straight at him, without recognition, as if he might hold the solution.

But she didn't expect to have half of Rome pushing against her in the square —

Harold, to avoid her face, ducked to the ground and pretended to re-tie his shoelaces. When he rose again to his full height the girl had gone. She wasn't even walking slowly into the distance. She had gone into nowhere in the empty square "of the Dolphins".

THE FIFTH PART

Sabina had bovine features and chewed the cud incessantly. She began talking before she had even eased herself off the train and didn't let up till she and Harold got into their separate rooms at the hotel. But Harold was delighted to fulfil an old promise by showing her around eastern Sicily. After all, he reminded himself, only through deep-rooted friendships do the subtlest mysteries emerge. It had been a shock to discover how obsessive Sabina's ceaseless conversation had become, yet he hugged her warmly and rejoiced in the familiar rapturous light of her eyes. For all her awkwardness Sabina was uniquely pure-minded and had a radiance of spirit that matched the Catanian sky. She always wore long brown skirts, which swept the paths of light clean as she traversed them, and looked in the end like a Byzantine nun. By profession she researched the Patristic Fathers.

Sabina talked as if to convert Harold to her own eagerness; babbling now in a cafe about Tertullian, now in the park about Necessary Grace, now wrapping her tongue around odd slips of the local dialect. She barely stopped to savour the anchovies at lunch, the best in the world.

At last, in the bank, Harold had a chance to remark that Sabina was more energetic than he ever remembered.

"Yes I am," she replied as they herded round to change money. "I am different. I feel at last as though things have come together. My life is beginning to *flow* — do you know what I mean? — it's moving forward like a river at one with the spirit of things. I've learnt to channel myself, Harold, force myself in the proper direction for my studies and my history, and for this season of mankind. Can you understand that exhilaration? Heavens, how I've worked for it. But there has been the reward that at last I can feel the imminence. *Imminence.* The realization of what is ahead, the harvest, is just palpable. I see it, in glimmers only yet, but they are glimmers that trace back to the source of light. Oh I know I sound mad but words, words, what are they? Piled up to give some poor approximation. No, Harold, I *am* changed. For the first time in my life I feel as I am — a garden tilled and ready for sowing."

There was silence amid confusion as the teller reached out his hands for Sabina's documents. Not until outside in the bustling square could Harold convey to Sabina how much he envied her steadfast faith, and by then she was talking benignly about the exchange rate.

In their hotel a peculiar fellow always hung about. At first Harold thought him a porter, asked him to carry the luggage and got an insolent rebuke. Short, dark and greasy, but not old, the creature went about whistling through his cracked front teeth and bouncing in a hunched, ape-like way. He laughed like a watchdog every time Harold and Sabina passed through the foyer.

On the second afternoon they caught him dancing in front of the reception desk and wildly singing some sort of hymn. *"Benedetto, Benedetto,"* he called to them.

The manageress explained cheerfully that it was the day of his namesake, San Benedetto. He was the local half-wit and a child of the nearby Church of San Benedetto, where he still lived in a small room out the back. Officially he was the caretaker and guide, but since no tourists ever came to the church he spent his days lounging at the hotel. "He's a darling boy," said the manageress, at which Benedetto blushed rosily.

Sabina went forward to offer greetings for the fellow's saint's day and he responded with a look of perfect docility and a winningly sweet smile: *"Benedetta anche Lei."*

Meanwhile Harold had discovered in his guide-book that the Church of San Benedetto had a two-star rating as an instance of Sicilian baroque renowned for its fantasy of decoration. At once Sabina insisted that they visit it, straightaway, with Benedetto as guide. *"Andiamo,"* she said briskly.

They walked along the street and Benedetto yapped to and fro beside them repeating weird facts about the church. Harold gathered that the original tongue of poor San Benedetto the martyr was preserved there, curled up like a leaf in a jar, so as soon as they got inside the dark, dank church, they lit candles to the saint's glory.

Sabina was prattling about the power of relics and denounced any scepticism on Harold's part.

"I just don't want to see a dried tongue," he said. "I'd rather look at the scroll-work in the side altars. At least they're in the Michelin."

In any case Benedetto the guide made it known that the relic was kept in a niche high up in the wall in the Nuns' Choir, where only women were allowed. Sabina smiled contentedly hearing this, swept her skirt round and headed off with Benedetto.

The Nuns' Choir was a beautiful structure of gilded metal-work suspended from the ceiling at the back of the church. It was originally a cage for the holy sisters to sit in while they looked down on the Mass in safe sanctity.

Harold waited in the nave, irritated by Sabina's constant voice as she climbed the staircase with the guide. Then he heard Benedetto's keys jangle. A dim electric light came on, two baby bats dislodged themselves and Sabina emerged barely visible behind the golden grill. She was talking earnestly at Benedetto, to convey that she needed something to stand on so she could see the saint's tongue properly.

Harold walked timidly and reverentially towards the altar. The dirty, ill-lit vault made him conscious of his own failings.

Suddenly his reverie was pierced by a startled moan which modulated upwards into the shrillest ecstatic shriek. High in the back of the church he could discern Sabina shaking and her arms were flailing above her head.

Harold rushed down the aisle and stumbled up the spiralling stairs to the Nuns' Choir, where the iron door was locked. There was only a small barred window. Sabina was still screaming. He saw through the bars that she was quivering on tip-toes on a stool as Benedetto knelt before her.

"Can I help?" called Harold.

But Benedetto's back sloped forward, his head disappeared under Sabina's skirt and his prayerful mutter was heard — *"Tu sei la Madonna, la Madonna, la Madonna"* — while the woman screamed at her defilement.

Then Sabina was quite simply struck dumb. Catching sight of the relic before her eyes she gave her gaping mouth and soul to the shrivelled saint's tongue and became bravely, defiantly mute. Far below the muffled ejaculation of *"Madonna"* continued apace and Benedetto's feet wriggled fast as he pushed his head further up beneath the billowing skirt. But Sabina clasped her hands in an tight attitude of devotion.

And outside Harold thrust in vain at the iron door, which was built long ago to protect nuns and would never budge.

THE LAST PART

On the rocky bus ride from Siracusa to Agrigento Harold had felt his sins bump around inside him like the suitcases in the luggage compartment.

Now he sat in the spacious turn-of-the-century railway station and waited for the train that would carry him to the extremity of the island. A violent plashing rain outside seemed to have stopped most things and Harold read the local newspaper impatiently. "I KILLED BECAUSE I LOVED" was the headline. Harold's failings beat on his mind with the noise of the raindrops.

A tiny old nun came and joined Harold on the bench. Her black habit enclosed a general shadow out of which her eyes and her immensely bushy eyebrows semi-materialized.

"Are you leaving?" she said suddenly and Harold frowned. "Are you going home?"

"Home?" he repeated. "Yes," he lied.

"Then St Lucy has smiled upon you," said the nun, plopping her hands in her lap now, with satisfaction.

"What?"

"You cannot leave the island, sir, unless St Lucy has smiled upon you."

Harold demurred uneasily and, gathering his belongings, went to enquire again when on earth this train was leaving.

"Arrivederci," called the nun after him.

The train consisted of a single carriage which took both passengers and goods. Harold was the only passenger. The journey left the coast and travelled inland through a series of valleys which were obscurely grey-green in the rain. The slopes on either side rose into clumped stone outcrops and then lost themselves in the squalling clouds, while the black sky pressed down against the earth in the direction the train was headed. The sheep by the tracks sidled against the stone walls of their folds and no shepherd was to be seen. Harold could not even tell when the train came down from the mountains to resume the coastline. He sat slumped against the dusty cretonne curtains of the carriage, with his legs firmly crossed. He had done Italy effectively and was filled with an insinuating depression. He had seen Don Giovannis and petty tragedies and been unmoved. He had been unable to requite the Contessa's restraint and the art historian's way of excess. He had surrendered friendships to the quick jab of a scurrilous joke. And he had felt the blaze of sensation in his mind burn through to the ashen grey of a faded, neglected fresco. The evidence of his failure to — to what? — it all mounted against him and the burden was intolerable.

When the train arrived at Selinunte there was no abatement of foul weather. Harold left his suitcase at the station, to whatever thieves might want his well-read books and his clothes for every occasion. He had decided to travel on that evening . . .

He had his black umbrella and set out at once for the ruins, though the rain emerged in unpredictable gusts from the olive groves and would not leave him dry.

A baby Fiat beetled past, squeezed full of men who jeered at Harold. He had come to detest the coarseness of Italians.

The ruins of the Greek settlement were on a hill-top and not much intact. Harold traced the lines of the ground plan dutifully, reconstructing in his mind the ideals of that world. But the thick rain denied him all vistas. "Call no man happy till he is dead," he recollected.

He was lost in misery when a fierce gust of wind assaulted his umbrella and turned it inside out. It looked like it had spread wings, and indeed it yanked itself out of Harold's hand and flew like some huge tattered raven over the ruins. Its flight was only arrested by the one Acropolis column still perfectly preserved. The umbrella's handle caught on a corner of entablature and there it stayed flapping. Harold watched in horror and then with a cross manic calmness resigned himself to the inevitable drenching.

So he followed the curving road back, fed up by the water pouring down his neck and the biting, inescapable smell of wet eucalyptus.

He reached a bar before the village proper and had to go inside, although he was at once the object of excessive attention, back-slapping, head-rubbing and scoffing. He warmed himself with alcohol and, as soon as he could, stood on his dignity, reacting with chill ingratitude to the people in the bar. He preferred to suffer, for he knew he deserved this ordeal. He watched two youths shoving at a pinball machine and despised them for the combs they had in their tight rear jean-pockets. He felt a cold kind of pity for the hard, over-made-up woman perched on a barstool drinking a *digestivo* . And the man with one eye playing dominoes. Water was seeping in under the door and Harold's depression increased by the minute. The worst thing was that there was nowhere else for him in the world but this buffoon's imitation of hell. Such was Harold's obsolescence. He thought of that other Italian exile, queer Edward Lear. "He weeps by the side of the ocean, He weeps on the top of the hill, — that crazy old Englishman, oh!" And heaved.

Harold sat by the clouded window looking at the rain. With his finger he doodled on the glass and made a clear patch. He half-saw a motorcycle speed past, and its arch of spray. There had been a girl clinging to the cyclist's back and she wore a flimsy, bright blue blouse. For the split second of passing she too had stared, hadn't she, through the window at Harold, and her white child's face had had a supernatural clarity. It had been expressionless and her loose hair streamed out behind in ropes. But Harold was loosing his grip.

It was as if all the falling water had heaped itself up and broken in a single wave over his head. A total nausea overwhelmed him, a sickness to the death at his own damp, fetid impotence. He knew at that moment, that he did not care for anything and may as well not be. If only his inertia would drag him to the very bottom.

He walked in the steady rain back to the station where he was informed that all trains to and from Selinunte had been cancelled until further notice. For want of better he walked around the village then. It was early evening and he was alone in the flooded streets. In all the houses he could see the good Sicilian peasantry spooning down their hot filling *pasta* . But he refused to return to the bar.

He walked along the shore where twisted, formless waves spent themselves on the sand and the wind beat with a deep bass sound against the black hulls of fishermen's boats, pulled hastily up the beach. Across in that wildness out to sea was Africa and somewhere the angry, unappeasable throne of Neptune.

In the end, because he was exhausted, Harold

searched for somewhere to rest. He could not have been wetter. He found a brush-roof shelter near a boat landing ramp and went inside. In a dry corner he took his boots off, pulled his leather coat over him and curled up. He still could not ignore the rain noise and by the end his whole body was limp before he surrendered and slept.

Dawn was early. Inside the shelter there was at last silence and an incipient light as pallid as the white shingle Harold had slept on. He woke and tried to stretch his numbed limbs. His bare arms and his legs, laid across the ground, had become imprinted with sharp marks from the shells and pebbles and Harold felt as though his bones had become equally hard and white. He realized then that his coat was missing, and the boots from beside him. Whoever had bothered was welcome to them. But no wonder he was blueish and shivering.

The cold and the stillness left him helplessly calm. He stood up, tried his stiff joints and walked outside in his socks. There the light, so pale and early, had an extraordinary modest intensity and Harold squinted. His eyes watered at these signs of the pre-natal sun, sending ahead the palest pink and grey wash and causing a sky to form from the thinnest thought of blue. A limpid quiet milk spread across to Africa.

He walked unembarrassed along the sand. The yellow house-fronts had their windows open and the bakery already had stacks of oven-trays cooling. The place looked utterly transformed. Behind the village the squat *campanile* and then the bristling hills and the unfolding olives, here and there an odd worn intrusion of antique remains. The day was born imperceptibly

56

and there were slow changes in the very medium in which the world was sunk.

Harold climbed up onto the pier, a ricketty structure of blackened oak and pungent from slime about its base. He walked to the end and sat with his feet, still soaked, dangling over the edge. The warmth increased, the sun yellowed and voices from afar got going. The first vehicles set off for work.

Presently a girl with a sprightly walk came down the pier. She was a schoolgirl and had a wooden tray beneath her arm, her father's fish which she was to wash in the sea from the end of the pier. She took no notice of Harold as she climbed down the slippery steps to the water's surface. Round the bottom, and round her bare ankles, the water lapped in quiet, indifferent curlicues. She lowered the tray into the water and the fish stirred as if alive. Then she tossed the fish a little, making them flop silvery, and some she took in handfuls and dunked thoroughly, so water streamed through their gills.

Harold coughed and she turned, looked up. He recognized her as the girl he had seen flash past the window in the rain last night, clinging to the motorcycle and the rider's back. She was still wearing the same cotton blouse. When Harold stared at her she didn't look away or make her placid face tense.

"Bon di," she called. And she smiled.

When Harold looked at her still white face and her hair brushed for school, and the tiny oval mouth that had spoken its blessing, when he caught the glint of her silver-bellied fishes and the sure way she crouched on the edge of the milky sea, he grasped that he was witness to the miraculous. He was hit with helpless glee, a feeling that he would burst his skin, and he wished that he was worthy.

But the girl made no further acknowledgment of Harold. She simply finished her task as quick as she could, settled the tray on her hip and was off. Watching her climb the steps Harold remembered the nun's prophecy at Agrigento and he blinked in wonderment.

"*Addio,*" he called to the girl, but she had started to sing and did not hear him as she walked away. She was slim, with hair to her waist, and in her very motion withdrawn from him. He had seen her smile and stared after her until she grew small and lost herself forever among the yellow village houses.

Full morning had come and Harold was filled with a consuming gratitude. The new-born day had intervened to throw off the burdens this dark land had imposed and better now, Harold was free to go.

Fishermen were putting out.

He took off his socks, and rolled them up and dropped them into the sea. Then to his great astonishment he declaimed in full voice across the waters, as if on the opera stage:

"Addio, island that smiles."

The Grand Nay

Bethany was due in about an hour. Warren settled to wait with great unexpressed excitement. In the classic manner he chose a corner table, from which he would measure, through salt-smeared glass, the conversion of the harbour's gun-metal to copper. He pressed one foot against his suitcase, as always, just to be safe.

The Nubian waiter delivered Warren's coffee.

"Mafeesh," he said, as Warren gazed round rapturously. "Finish — Alexandria — all finish."

"Oh no, I can't agree," exclaimed Warren. "It's beautiful — magic."

The waiter shuddered sceptically and hid his hands in his robe before slapping back to the front bar.

Warren couldn't stop himself grinning. He tingled with Alexandria and the prospect of Bethany. To be itinerant still, at thirty, was his monstrous fait accompli and it pleased him enormously to be once again an arrival in a new town. He'd managed so far to avoid all upsets, which was as he wanted it. The first class train from Cairo had slipped luxuriously along the Delta and the city had surpassed his dreamy expectations: the marketplace of *homo sapiens* itself. How strange that the clattering sea-front square with its seventeen palm trees would witness the transaction of his life. Without making a display of himself Warren positively bounced as he waited for Bethany.

The Grand Trianon cafe might have been a ballroom. Columns encrusted with tarnished knobs supported a fantastic ceiling, and a chandelier hung, disappearing slowly in the dusk. On the walls a line of huge red Sheherazades, dirtied over by the years, danced with Arabian sheiks and on the floor, moving among the tables in their costumes, the old waiters kept up a similarly mad, choreographic decorum, learnt no doubt long ago when they were bright hot youths at everyone's beck and call.

Warren glanced at himself in the mirror. His fair hair was long enough to let a boyish wave show still. He checked his watch. She was due any minute.

It wasn't characteristic of him to make a rendezvous in a cafe but for her sake he was willing. In her connexion he was a penultimate romantic, not sufficiently an ironist to have terminated all mysteries, though he had shorn away most of his ties. Only to find himself the more dependent on Bethany — Bethie — the girl who had accompanied him through his suburban teenagehood.

The waiter returned with the sticky delicacies Warren had ordered to wile away the time. His state of expectancy made him greedy for the sweetest things in Alexandria. He was on holiday after all, but it was no accident that he and Bethie should intersect in Egypt. Warren's firm was these days directing its attention more and more towards the Middle East. All the developing countries wanted installations and Warren's boss was eager to oblige, not just because of the oil money, but also, burdened with mercantile guilt, to seek a kind of philanthropic absolution in the countries round the Red Sea. The way the boss brooded over Arab interests, it was as if he were grooming some uncouth heir-apparent. When Warren mentioned going to Egypt for a holiday, the boss had seized upon him as an unofficial ambassador. If Warren could bear Cairo, there'd be a chance of an important posting there, in charge of a new agency. So this trip was a try-out.

Warren didn't pretend that he liked the job nor that he was good at it, but there was no doubt it provided opportunities. "I've landed on my feet," he told himself. Not only had he defiantly cut his ties, but he was in debt to no man. He had made it as he wanted it and could be doubly proud. His only obligation, which need hardly be considered, was to his father who had introduced him into a seedy import-export company once when he was at a loose end. He had discovered then that business need not be a commitment, but could be a means to keep him exploring and unattached. He had been posted all over the place and had seen that trade, if nothing else, unites mankind. He took the world slowly, crawling like a snail with his house on his back, not surrendering to any of the communities he encountered. Everything he needed was in the worn Samsonite case at his feet.

Certain memories lingered, despite being packed away inaccessible to everyday use. Among these Bethany was the brightest and Warren had kept track of her movements as far as he could. Odd acquaintances saw her at airports, or else he could procure her latest address from the family at home. Occasionally she responded to Warren's correspondence and her own trail had been linked to his by frail sinews here and there.

But it was the larger pattern of things sending her to

Alexandria. She'd been in Beirut, on an uneasy footing in the house of a young Australian diplomat — Warren hadn't precisely gathered their relationship — and when Lebanon blew up there had been all sorts of bureaucratic problems about her evacuation. She ended up being flown out to Cairo alone, standing most of the way in an overloaded aircraft.

Warren had this information from a sleek journalist he came across in Cairo. The journalist could also confirm that Bethie had an appointment in Alexandria. But he was vague and incoherent about it, so that Warren assumed Bethie had been evading the man's nosy importunities. The Australian embassy in Cairo had also seen Bethie, though the diplomat she'd been living with was still sitting it out in Beirut. Things being what they were, there were good prudent reasons why the liaison plans were not less flimsy.

The news that Bethie was to be in Egypt was proof that she, of all women, could make anything happen. As a matter of course he'd written to Beirut to inform her of his Easter holiday, and he'd casually reminded her of their old fancy one day to stroll together along an exotic corniche. The reply had come: inside an envelope, as a registered letter, a postcard of the Sphinx. "Warren dear — let's meet for drinks on Coptic Good Friday at le Grand Trianon, Alex — B." He'd written back and agreed, and had gone further. With no small amount of self-love he'd outlined the streamlining of his life, his paring away of involvements. He confessed without shame that she was virtually the only person he wrote to, that for the record he'd meaninglessly had several women, that wherever he'd gone he was reputed to be unloving and in the end unloved; and all this, he intimated, was tribute to Bethie's power.

Now it was pitch dark and she hadn't come. Warren ordered *arak* and stared at the frenzied dancing on the murals. He endeavoured not to think about what was happening. It was proper to sit out the time in deference to her romantic arrangement. Every person in the cafe was replete with a Byzantine mystery that struck Warren as gaudy. Perhaps Cairo was to be preferred to this vulgar coastal town. He despised suddenly a cheap conjuror who was doing his rounds with babboon and barrel-organ. Cairo had been impressive. One could live there, despite the desiccation. On three of the mornings the dust had come in, had dried him out and completely finished off the English teachers he was staying with. They'd become rather attractive old heaps. "Dead dust. It drives you barmy," they said. The museum had been a veritable hall of dead and dust. He'd wandered among the gold and black Egyptological glitter. There was a tray of dried-up rose petals. Intact but entirely dust, once they had scattered the innermost canopy of a king's tomb.

It was near closing time. He admitted that Bethie wasn't coming. She'd never be coming. He paid his bill and left a big tip, making the waiter perform again.

"All finish — Alexandria — *mafeesh* !"

Although it was late the famed Hotel Cecil was glad to see him and provide a room. No go-ahead businessman likes to be thwarted and Warren wasn't an exception, so he took a few drinks in the hotel bar before going up to bed. There wasn't a soul to talk to, let alone anyone to relieve himself on, and he knew he wouldn't sleep.

Instead he'd pass the night in a chair on the balcony, half-dozing, bitching at himself, groping in chill sea air.

Bethany had of course been "around", with her raven hair and her forehead of unquestionable integrity, had even at times seemed sluttish. Even if circumstances were responsible he blamed her savage independence. Still, it was his own fault for clinging. He'd clung without penetrating. It was a mistake never to have slept together. Such quaint adolescent hesitation had only prepared the way for obscurity and easy forgetting. Now his last bearing on her was gone and she might be anywhere, anything.

He was free to rise like a balloon. He chewed over the imitation continental breakfast which had arrived with the sunlight. The harbour, waltzing in the blue morning, appeared to challenge him. The sea, virginal blue, had the texture of mother's milk. But it was as if the madonna had leered and mocked. He could hardly think for the spun, inescapable beauty of the bay. Effortful futility, Alexandrian languor, perfect freedom, almighty effort. He had to realize the achievement of his masterlessness, and gave up. The woman's absence wouldn't leave him alone and he couldn't get away from his sense of romantic propriety.

He shaved and cut his neck deliberately to provide an excuse for pampering. He took morning tea on the balcony and ventured down only to re-confirm his room for the next night. The Greco-Roman museum was closed for restoration.

"I'll just sit here in the air," he said, and some time later, "hellish boring."

At one stage he threw down all his small change to the boys in the street.

He wanted to see if at the end of the time he could

re-imagine the woman and his love. At last he admitted he'd been duped. He knew nothing of the woman. She had lived all along out of cachets of otherness. Just how many lives she may have had and how wide he may have skimmed by in the blue, as if water-skiing, were things closetted behind her impenetrable pluralism. The postcard which had launched his ship was one among a thousand faces, without mercy for the rare, tawdry scene it had called up.

He took a good thorough shower before leaving the hotel, and groomed himself well enough to impress anyone. As he paid his bill he smiled and told the clerk he'd be back.

"Alexandria is beautiful for visit," said the clerk.

"Also for business," added Warren. "You have the open-door policy, which means you lie back and take everything."

"Yes, sir. Thank you."

To see a different aspect of the country Warren decided to travel back to Cairo by the bus which took the desert road. He caught it beneath the tatty palm trees in the square. Presently he and his case found themselves careering through the desert, and hot. The indiscriminate space on either side of the road was extraordinary. A few huts and the odd installation were the only novelties in otherwise interminable waste. In a place like any other a soldier got off the bus and set off for the horizon. Then nearer Cairo the dust blew up and Warren remembered that he was returning to the city of the dead. The windows and the roof of the bus were open to the hot dusty wind and Warren felt it come round him from every side. If he was free, he was a creature of the desert too. The coastal city had not been kind and had bereft him of his last familiar, the last rooted thing in his waste of sand. But he would not be taken in by Alexandrian delusions again. He would report favourably to his boss about Egypt and would start up an agency in Cairo with a vengeance. He would be "in" installations completely, amongst the street life that appalled him. He could reside in Cairo after all and make that his necropolis. He would accept that he had been promoted to a dead freedom and when he heard later that Bethie was far-off and content, he would relish his entombment with full Pharaonic pizzazz. He'd been blown and blown with the dust but he too could settle out over the teeming inland city.

The bus arrived in the Liberation Square, in the corner between the Egyptological Museum and the Nile Hilton. Warren wiped himself down and got a taxi. He set off to find the journalist to tie up the loose ends, before he joined the collapsed English teachers for an evening's drinking. For evermore he would hide the cruel miniature of his trip to the coast, his acumen sharp as can be.

Coogee Spring

I

A boy called Steve Baio had a spring birthday and didn't know what to want. Last year he got a skateboard and spent the summer afternoons edging and veering down Beach Road until the wheels were black with tar and the nose abraded flat. But last year he was fourteen, and this year he couldn't ask for a surfboard because you couldn't surf at Coogee Bay unless you'd been out with the frog boys in their wetsuits qualifying all winter long.

He came home from the bus-stop after the first day of third term, up the zigzag of concrete steps to his pale blue house, 147 Titania Street, a moored fibro galleon with a pediment of weatherboard and a hooked terracotta prow, afloat on a drooping bank of pigface and buffalo. He walked past his mother, taking sunny tea in the kitchen, and got to his place, formerly the verandah, high above Titania Street. There he wriggled his shoulders and considered the season to come. He could see to the west the city, glinting like cellophane, and seawards down the street the old and the new flats. From the window of an upper unit a chintz curtain blew, with a palm behind and a slack powerline aslant. From his house, his ship, the vista was familiar, right to the ocean blue beyond.

He prickled his way out of his uniform and dumped it in a heap. Once in his ordinary clothes the afternoon felt good around him. Impatiently, then, he spread his homework out on the table. They had a new English teacher, a Lithuanian whose name was spelled Babitis. Miss Engels, the old teacher, had gone to Asia. This new one had red hair and his skin was flush pink, from shaving too severely, they decided, or from suntan and skin lotion: "Baby-itis". Steve stretched his arms out to their full length and bowed forward over his book. As he did so his finger reached for the radio and its released words mocked: "Are You Old Enough, Oo-Oo, Are You Old Enough?" He really didn't know.

He finished while it was still light enough to go out and he told his mother so. There would be possibilities in the shops. But once he was outside things were different altogether. Titania Street felt peculiar and urgent, and the boy hurried. Opposite, the block of Carthage Court flats loomed like Kong. He strode, past the closing corner shop and, crunching, across the shattered windscreen diamonds at the intersection. His thongs clapped against the ground and an Alsatian pup yapped at him. He stopped only for a moment to flick a stone at it, then headed uphill towards the horizon feeling good at last in the warm sweet air.

At Coogee Bay people were in the bus shelter, people were on the beach. The shops had closed already, surf, music and pawn, a net of alternatives he was glad to escape. He shouldered his way across the zebra, in the crowd, and drifted down to the beach. The chill sand spilled round his toes and before him the waves pursued their curvacious variations. Nothing was required, for his birthday, because nothing seemed possible to Steve Baio, a boy like any other, shoulder-length hair cut straight across the bottom, knowledgable and confused. He kicked at the sand to unbend his leg, like an unpretty flamingo in the dulling grey. Then hands in pockets he turned his back on the sea, hungry, if resentful at the walk home. As he crossed the concourse a sportscar hooted to make him step lively. He was only young. He was worried still by the straggly shadows round the lantana and banksia bushes on the esplanade and arrived eagerly into the light of the corner pizzeria.

But there had been a woman on the bench near the edge of the grass, near a rubbish bin. She watched him slip past timid like a faun. A handkerchief was crumpled in her hand and a package of fish and chips sat beside her. Steve Baio felt her impressive weight on the bench, and the darkness of her, dressed all in black. Yet he couldn't look at her in passing. She had a trail of silver running down from her eyes. And afterwards he could only glance back fleetingly, to see her smile.

Black-clad in wool, as Greeks wear, the woman had stepped off the bus uneasily at the Coogee Bay terminus. At first she'd walked forward as if on the way home, then stopped to look about her. The driver and conductor, yarning against the shelter, thought she was looking to them. But she saw nothing around her, in a quiet way that drew little attention. She stood about as if waiting for the bus to return her to the city, but she declined to get back on board when it left, wandering instead further up the footpath, and the bus-men could let her slip.

Ileana had come to appreciate that the proportions of her life were classical: the word was preferable to "remorseless". Only there was a new force currently building. She hadn't left the bus at her home stop. She'd gone, whether to follow or flee the new pressure, the full way to the open greyness of the seaside evening, and sat herself on an empty bench there, in a grassed area, to inhale the damp air in comfortable rhythmic heaves. Anyway she didn't want to go to her little flat in Carthage Court, Coogee. She never managed to tidy away her piled-up losses there. And at work she was always jolly. They called her Lily because Ileana was too much in the mouth. It was enough, now, to have resorted to a patch by the sea.

Eventually she crossed to the fish-shop. Her order was prepared in the mournful roughness of the Cretan tongue, and she felt the vestiges of her old oppression upon her as she took the portion of food, bundled up in newspaper layers. Then she returned to the bench, waiting. Something in this adopted life must touch her. If it didn't she would die.

II

The new English teacher was an odd one. Steve had resented Miss Engels who was a depressive and dithered about communal self-expression when Steve had known his self to be too green and sharp to blend in a stew with the expressed selves of his classmates. But this Mr Baby-itis, with his blood-shot eyes and scarred, dimpled chin, was different. He talked about the symbols of everyday life and claimed there were correspondences between all things, for the beholder. Hidden threads that tied up reality, he said. They were doing selections from the classics and had to respond freely to one who wrote about Paradise. Mr Baby-itis chanted at them like a race commentator:

> The birds their quire apply; airs, vernal airs,
> Breathing the smell of field and grove, attune
> The trembling leaves, while universal Pan,
> Knit with the Graces and the Hours in dance,
> Led on the eternal Spring . . .

Steve's freest reaction was to let it waft over his head as he hunched over the desk and doodled. Bronwen Krapan had sent him a note. She was going into the city after school. She had an almond face and honey hair. Steve thought about her happily but didn't want to sit with her and friends all the way there and back in the bus. He supposed he'd go home to Titania Street, as if there was anything for him there.

Over Coogee spring had conferred an exuberance of lawn-mowing and after-work exercising, and Mrs Baio was weeding. The boy went into the house and lay on his bed. All of a sudden things were unendingly slow. Annoyed now at his time to spare he turned his head sideways into the pillow and wondered what he was feeling. Was he as thin and insipid as the lilac paint on his bedroom wall? He traced the shapes of stucco boronias and ferns on the ceiling, almost able to insinuate, under his shirt, his fingers between his ribs.

"Steve, are you doing anything?" she called.

"Yeah."

Leisure was his only prospect. The boys who'd left school had to spend whole days hanging round the beach. Leisure was his estate. So he rose and slipped on his nylon swimmers. The water would be almost warm; a paradise lagoon bath run for him.

Across the road Ileana came out the main entrance of Carthage Court. She'd added sunglasses to her black dress. Her day had been spent inside, off from work, and only now was she out on an errand at the bay shops. She hadn't always clung to the coast. When the ship first delivered her she had gone inland. She'd acquired immediately with the new land a new husband and his small business. It had been far off, and hard, and horrible. But she learnt soon that a woman could exist singly in this country. There were places for her in the city and so she hadn't retreated to the life she'd let go of. It was better to be an exile in a country of them. Her thoughts ran on routinely. In this new country her old tragedy had become a dead broken tooth. You lived with it without pain, until now.

The kid came leaping down the steps opposite and without wishing it she gave an odd twitchy greeting. Steve Baio passed by briskly on the other side, whipping his towel. Woman of tears! In a concrete front garden two cats, a white and a blue, sprawled while a lady cut dead-heads from her tubbed magnolia. From under a car stuck out a man's pale naked belly. Steve was on the look-out for symbols. A rosemary shrub flowered strongly. The beach-front palms sprouted erect. Outside the Oceanic some musicians and their girls were unloading equipment for a night of sweat and celebration. He could read the signs.

The waves were lazily solid. When he dived the water pressed round him, cold and chaste, and didn't relieve him. Over the head of the bay the Babylonish heaps of flats and houses, and the brick spire of St Bridget's, were fired opulently red by the last sun. Afterwards he jogged along the beach to dry off. Couples were airing, one lanky and one squat old lady, and two men in tight shorts passing demurely the wall which read "SHAME ON YA BOURGEOSIE". One of the men, who was fluffing his red hair with a strap of towel, gave Steve a showy wave. It was Baby-itis. But the boy felt himself solitary and awkwardly half-ducked his head, shying from the connection. He meandered, wandering by himself around the rocks until the only choice was to head back.

The woman was there again on the bench. She was sitting upright, her eyes wide and, it seemed, unfocussed. In her lap she clutched a paper bag from Lethe the chemist. She grinned in a kind of shock when she saw Steve.

"Why are you laughing?" he asked.

That made her truly laugh. She'd been crying hitherto. "What's the matter?" he went on.

"Do you live near Carthage Court flats?"

"Yeah."

Shivering in his towel shawl he looked as womanly as she did.

"You must be about fifteen."

"Nearly," he said, shifting away. "See ya later," he said.

"See you — tomorrow."

Before getting into bed that night he stood in the window and contemplated the block of Carthage Court. It was mostly dark or else curtains were drawn opaquely over ghosty television lights. The woman of tears was somewhere there, he knew terribly. She'd be crying out through the fly-wire to the sharp night air. His body shivered for its own thin singularity.

But she was still on the bench, where she would sit out her time. It was an anniversary, the day she had left Greece behind. She'd had a baby there and seen it die.

She'd had love and, accursed, had been brought to hate her love. Her tragic vision hadn't much more flesh than that. Only its lines remained now, quite clear tonight, sharp as wire, fifteen years ago.

III

Next day Mr Baby-itis explained to the class that "vernal" meant "pertaining to spring". He said his aftershave of the day gave off "airs, vernal airs" and surrounded him in seasonal bliss. Steve Baio didn't understand. What sort of a guy was this he whispered to Ted Brook slouched beside him. He was meeting Bronwen Krapan at the Coogee Bay Pizzeria after school. They'd have tea together and do something afterwards. There was only one day left till his birthday. What should he want?

Bronwen brought two girlfriends to the meeting, and her brother, and Ted Brook. They sat on high red stools in a circle round the pizzeria table and ate, exchanging triangular slabs of the distinguishable tastes. They spooned froth off their cappuccinos. Bronwen's brother, who'd left school, wanted them to go back to his flat. Bronwen tossed her hair with pride that her brother promised so much. But Ted Brook was keen to join in the pinball tournament next door and once there, like a fiend, he never stopped getting free games. The silver ball kept rolling down the chute and ages passed before they could re-assume their own track down the night. It was proposed to walk out round the cliffs, where members of the public were warned, to Bronwen's brother's. She tossed her head and twiddled with Steve Baio's t-shirt.

"Coming?"

"Nah. Gotta be going home."

They dismissed him from their employment. He loitered about the shops until they were gone, then came back to the front. The mysterious dark was up again, deadening the sand. From a parked car Steve heard "I dare you to run into the sea with your clothes on. If you love me." And the man did, plunging like a cat over the high beach wall.

Ileana was on the bench. If she'd been crying she was no longer. She'd composed herself.

"Hallo," said Steve.

She indicated that he should sit down. When he asked if she was waiting for a bus she replied that she just liked sitting on mild evenings, that she couldn't sleep if she'd been cooped up all day. Although smiling, she looked so sad.

"I'm a sea person," she said.

They talked. She'd only been at Coogee a while.

"I'm glad you're here," she told him. "It's a hard day. I can't tell you about it. It's too long ago. You're nearly fifteen?"

"Yeah." He didn't really follow, and yawned. "Mum'll be wondering."

"I've seen her in the garden. I can see your house from my flat." The woman had a soft firm voice, like her body. "Put your head against me if you're tired."

He snickered and felt a frightening pull.

"If you want to," she said and took hold of his hand.

He let his head sink down quietly on her. He didn't mind, as she pressed her head against his and stroked his hair, for many entirely peaceful moments.

Not seeing his particular face, but feeling him there, she could imagine other existences for him.

Then he sat up nervously. "I've got to be getting home."

Her face opened into a fully gracious smile. "Good-bye now," she said and released his hand from the bud of hers. "Thank you."

Steve half ran to Titania Street. He didn't know if he was gladder to have been there than now to be away. Yet his head was wondrously clear and the hills of Coogee were higher and purer than anything in the world.

His mother and father were watching television in the living-room. He stood behind their armchairs. For the first time ever he wasn't sure how he'd appear to them.

"Where have you been all this time?" his father muttered.

"I'll be fifteen tomorrow."

"Not till then."

"Come over here," called his mother, wanting to look at him. She plucked a long black hair off his t-shirt and frowned onto it. The hair grew grey at the root and she sighed, too tired this time to speculate.

Steve said meekly that he was going to bed. But still later he wasn't asleep. His lilac bedroom was too full of discovery. At midnight by the hall chimes he took up a position in the window. He'd only be visible as a dark shape. Down opposite in Carthage Court was a square of light uncurtained and clear. Within the room a dark woman stood before a dressing table mirror. She seemed to pick hairs from her jumper and hold them up, like inexplicable gossamer, to rapt scrutiny in the lamplight. Her reflected face, absorbed in its task though night looked on, was content. Long blonde hairs, knew the boy, his own vernal hairs. The ex-change was wound round his finger like a tendril.

The birthday morning was luminous and fresh. His parents gave him a watch, with jokes about his lateness, and a penknife. While he waited for the bus he carved in a paling of the shelter. Then as the bus which had collected him rocked forward he saw the Greek woman emerge from the flats, ready for work in a bright green dress. She walked quickly towards the bus-stop — but traffic cut off his view. He hoped she'd see his mark. He hoped she'd read in the wood what could never be taken away, that he existed, that here and now was his: STEVE BAIO 29-9-78.

Stone's Throw

I

He was out in a flurry in the morning. From the back
garden he could see the sea where the suburbs ended
run off into lighter blue to become the sky and stretch
round, reaching the hills, the house, the fat lordly sun.
In the chookyard he found two eggs, stuck with straw.

From outside through the screen door the house was
cavernous. The boy went in, laid the eggs on the table
and drank a glass of milk, panting. He stood on tiptoe
before the open door of his parents' bedroom and saw
them curled up still, under a sheet. His mother's face
was without expression, quiet as flesh can be. His
father's arm was laid across her back. It was brown and
unbendable. The clothes fallen on the chairs were
heavy round the figures on the bed. The boy realized
he was alone, and free, and although he wanted to tell
about the morning, now it wouldn't be told.

Down the hill was the dam he wasn't allowed to
swim in. For weeks he'd been fiddling with a net made
of chicken wire, with red meat for bait that became
pink and stringy in the water, trying to catch the
cranky old yabby who lived in the dam. Today he'd go
himself and dig that yabby out with his feet.

The water was the same brown as the boy's skin and his legs disappeared in it. The wet clay was like cream. Each step deeper he twitched expecting the yabby's nip. But it never came. The old man yabby had been frightened by a bunyip coming to drink at the dam and jumped out of his shell, and the spectral serpent in the gumtree overhead thought he looked so funny he turned him into a cicada that flew far away in search of wild orchids and star-flowers. When the boy remembered this he dived right into the dam and weaved round underwater. He lay back and kicked and the sun in his eyes made him squint. Best of all he lay on the sloping bank of the dam in shallows and lolled in the creamy clay till he was all over white and silky, squelching behind his knees and on his belly like a fish. When he was skinned completely he rose from the water trying not to bend and stood still and upright till the sun baked him dry. Soon he was a clay-white statue. His body had contracted. He was made of earth and his two white feet were trunks that grew out of the dam side. He stood as a clay-man for ages getting hotter and hotter. Then it was enough and in a huge leap he threw himself into the water, swam and splashed till his skin was all off in the murk. More preening was needed when he got out. He picked off the scales of clay one by one and his downy hair shone through again. One last dive to make himself glisten in the dapple of light in the glittering water where his arms and legs darted.

Then it was really enough and he followed the path back to the house, paddling his feet in the dust. Mum and Dad were in the kitchen having breakfast.

"Hi."

"You haven't been swimming in the dam, darling!

Your hair's as white as flour. You look like an old man. Doesn't he, dear?"

His mother had boiled the eggs and there were toast-fingers and tea. When he put his hand on his stomach he felt it slosh together.

II

His mother taught him "swam not swimmed". He hammered with his father who wanted him to watch the generator get fixed. You found things that were sweet or smooth to put in your mouth and had twigs scratch against you as you pushed through bush and grass inhabiting for a moment the chambers of shade and stillness formed beneath the lowest boughs.

His mother worried that he didn't play with other children, that he would break off in the middle of sentences. His father reminded her that school would come soon when it started in earnest. But she looked forward to the subdivision of the hills' face which would bring others whose children could be shared.

The boy's favourite path was the one behind the hedge to the rose-garden. At dusk it was complicated with shadows and all the smells of roses; some the colour of blood when they prick you, lip roses and tongue roses that bat against the wind like moths. His own paths in the garden criss-crossed aimlessly, as he thought of what had been that day — a dam, an egg, and sweet minty saliva. He thought of journeys to the sun and to the rose. There was a white one he cupped in his hands and wanted to snuff up or eat. But he let the rose-head bend back out of reach. His mother could never have followed his paths through the farm, sheep-tracks, creek-beds, roads.

She hugged him as she put him into bed and fretted at the contours of his face, for which there was no map. She wanted to find islands! oases! emerald moments! to believe that her son would be licked and loved, and would discover, for a week, in particular towns, that all was joy. But his eyes wouldn't reflect. She kissed him with feathery lips, sniffed, tucked him and left him.

III

On Monday morning he ran out and found his particular rose full-blown and browning. There were questions to be asked. He marched down the hill to the old creek overhung with gums and willows. He followed the dry bed to the narrowest point where he'd built his own dam once. The pile of rocks and sticks was a huge effort that didn't work to stop the spreading water when rain fell for days. He'd used a round white pebble as a foundation stone. It was somewhere here in the dirt. He searched for it on his knees and found it a few feet off, half-buried. Quietly he enclosed the pebble in his hand. He blew on it, rubbed it on his trousers and licked it to make it shine. Between his thumb and forefinger the silvery quartz veins tangled and glistened.

Now he turned to face up the hill, over the roof of the house, to the sky. He pulled himself upright to oppose the sun. He couldn't help squinting. It was all very well hardening, but withering and shrivelling, why? He held the pebble at the sun and it fired magnificently. It was immense in his eye. He would avenge the rose and wrap the wind in a paperbag. Taking off on tiptoes the boy charged screaming at the sun and at last catapulted his stone into the air. It curved for ages towards the height and gave off fatal sparks. He was delighted and quiet. He had threatened fiercely, and would continue, though the winds rebelled and men came over the hill.

Beer and Wine

They were given to experiment in those days. If anything was learnt it was forgotten soon enough.

Jon picked Brett up from his parents' place by the
beach. A new crowded Burger King stand defaced the
poetic sea.

"Nuh. Stobie poles and hamburger joints are as
beautiful as everything else," said Jon. "As ugly too."

Their chat was embarrassed as they drove towards
the hills. In the few months since school they'd
developed in rather separate directions. Jon disagreed
with Brett's scathing remarks about the music on the
radio. He steered the car exultantly along the hills
highway, leaning hard against the door.

"Can we stop at a pub?" said Brett. "Get some
beer?"

"Yeah, but wine?"

"You get wine. I want beer."

"We can't afford both."

But they wouldn't compromise. They stopped at the
Crafers pub and Jon gave Brett his note reluctantly.
While Brett was inside trying to act the legal age, Jon
heard a song on the radio which made him glad, *It
Don't Matter To Me* , not because of the lyrics particu-

larly, though he agreed that nothing could matter enough to worry about; but just because. Brett returned with six cans in a carton under one arm and a flagon of red under the other.

The cottage they were to sleep in was a little place down a hill. Brett had the use of it for a few days. Inside there were all sorts of posters and artworks. Brett chose the armchair by the empty fireplace and set himself up with his beers and his tape-recorder around him.

"We can hear something really good now. Bessie Smith."

"Superb," said Jon.

Brett said you could trace the development through from her to Joplin.

"Yeah, she's really great." Jon had the flagon open between his legs. He sloshed the claret into a peanut butter glass. Red wine made him feel sensual even if he wasn't.

They had discussed, in fearfully detached terms, the heated curiosities of their schoolyears together, and did so out of habit tonight. The room was dim. Jon's flagon was emptying and Brett was getting drunk too. You could see him watching Jon, making sure his friend had more than he did. Brett started to talk about his admirers. "You know, a lot of people say I look like Mick Jagger."

Christ, thought Jon, admitting that a resemblance was conceivable. Brett had an aggressive, desirable way of holding himself. He was working, temporarily, as a brickie. But although the conversation had taken its customary sexual course, Jon wanted to tell Brett about his philosophy.

"It's a gas. Life is a gas. Really. That's what I think.

Good and bad, ugly and beautiful, black and white. They really don't matter if you look from high enough.

Brett sneered at his friend's silliness. "You miss a lot if you think like that," he ventured. "What about love?"

"Love makes you happy. That's how you decide."

"Bullshit."

"It's up to you."

Brett began again with precision, first settling his hair back behind his ears to achieve his finest logicality. "If you're *sincere* in seeking to fulfil your emotions, then you *can* direct your morality that way."

Jon had broken a cork in half and was juggling the bits. "I think moral judgments are crap," he pronounced and emptied his glass.

Brett drank up too. "I quite agree. Conventional morality."

Jon was chewing half the cork. "Can we have something to eat?" he mumbled.

"What?"

"Toast. Vegemite."

"Okay." They went out to the kitchen, which showed the familiar signs, and sawed up a stale loaf haphazardly. While it was under the griller they both stood silent, respecting a sudden communion in the heart of the house.

Brett rushed the browned toast from the oven to the plate, cradling it in his hands, and Jon spread on butter and vegemite. They bit and smiled. A line of butter dribbled down Jon's chin.

Afterwards Jon went into the garden. Under the pines it was misty and shadowy. He walked through the damp grass into a grove of hydrangeas and pissed there. It was a gentle place.

Back inside they took up their seats again, opposite each other, and raised their drinks while the last of Bessie Smith played.

"Have you done anything with anyone?" asked Jon. He was curious about Brett's body.

"I nearly made it with Jane. You know the girl from the bus. She's only fifteen. Incredible for that age. She's coming back this weekend." He threw his hair back.

"Hope it goes well."

"I've also got hold of a book by Genet. *Our Lady of the Flowers*. It's banned. It's stunningly beautiful. Our Lady is a teenage boy and everyone wants to make love to him. Shall I read you a bit?"

Brett would have read all night, adoring his imaginings, but they were tired and, paradoxically, restless, wide awake. Jon was kept from relaxing by a pulse of energy testing his blood. He lay back in his chair with his legs apart and looked at Brett reading. Each was anticipating a move.

"Do you think sex is mind or body?" asked Jon.

"I don't understand."

"I think true love, even with sex, is spiritual. For want of a better word. But sex can exist on its own. Pure physical delight."

It was a persuasion to fit the drunken mood. Brett ran his hand over his chest.

Jon said noncommittally, "I feel lustful."

"So do I. But if we did anything we'd be using each other."

"Can't you see it all doesn't matter? If you want to or not, I don't care." Jon spoke against the undercurrent he felt, hobbling across the ambiguities and hesitance of desire. He stood up suddenly, grabbing the flagon, and said, "I'm going to bed. See you tomorrow."

Brett packed up the tape-recorder disconsolately and stripped for bed. He was drunker than he'd realized but his drunkenness hadn't achieved anything. He stumbled through to the kitchen for a glass of water. The door of the room where Jon was sleeping was shut. He couldn't bear to make the decision so, half-oblivious, he fell against the door and pushed it open, slumping himself against the doorpost, framed against the light.

Jon was awake and looked at Brett's thin shoulders and hips, and the undeveloped muscles beneath the skin. He got up slowly and walked across. Brett stayed still obediently while Jon put a shepherding hand on him and brought him over to the bed. They lay on their backs, watching the ceiling, smoothing each other's bodies. Here was wonder. Then Brett pulled up the sheet to cover them and, rolling onto Jon, tried to relax and enjoy. At last they were romping happily in the different textures of their bodies.

It was when a climax was imminent that Brett exclaimed, "No! Christ! I'm sorry, but Jesus, we might as well masturbate. I've gotta go."

"It doesn't matter . . . does it?"

"But you understand?"

"Go by all means."

"You think I'm a bastard."

"Go if you're going. I really don't care. We might as well get some sleep."

Brett left Jon gazing out the window. The fields were pale blue, as if enchanted. He thought of Peter Pan never growing up.

In his own room Brett was pulling himself hard, the

image of his ideal love before him. He came and filled his navel hair with the spunk he'd worked up on Jon.

When Jon woke he didn't realize where he was. Brett called "Good morning" from the kitchen where he was cooking sausages and brought Jon a towel. The bathroom was concrete and reminded him of his grandparents' farm. Brett called out to him under the shower, "Do you want tea or coffee?"

"Tea. What are you having?"

"Coffee. I'll make you a tea-bag."

Jon was gazing out the window again as he dried himself. The grass was bright with dew and the morning was wonderful. God's in his heaven, he thought.

At breakfast Brett said, "I really apologise about last night."

"Don't worry."

They were tired and had to leave by eight. Jon put his overnight bag and the near-empty flagon in the back of the car. Brett locked the cottage. The sun already had the full warmth that comes at the beginning of a scorcher.

Jon drove Brett to his worksite and thanked him for having him. Brett said it had been good to see him and hoped he didn't mind . . .

But Jon had slammed the cardoor, turned the radio up and pushed down on the accelerator. He began to sing vigorously, until he noticed a fruity smell. The flagon had tipped over and the wine was running everywhere. But Jon didn't much care. The smell was faintly intoxicating and he kept on singing.

Troubadours

I

There was no deep water, only a series of troughs and sandbars. We waded in timidly, one step up to our thighs, the next up to our ankles, horizon-wards. It was a question, as always, of when to take the plunge, when to dive to avoid the agony of the chill sea creeping inch by cruel inch up your crotch. Both of us misjudged. Leo dived too soon, in a shallow place, and was floundering in six inches of water. I left it too late, tempting Leo for so long with my dryness that he leapt from behind and pushed me under. There we were, wet in the sea for the first time that summer and at a loss.

At half past three the school kids came down, rare perfect girls and others with puppy fat and a hotdog in hand. There were boys with thick floppy hair, skidding on their bikes to spray sand at older girls. There were housewives and their mothers and dear distended old people wading hand in hand through the water. A girl flounced past with her transistor blaring. *We-ee may never pass this way-ay again . . . .* That month the hit-parades were starred with songs of farewell, shipwrecks and the like.

Towards evening the sand became greyer so we put on our shirts and sat with arms round knees, gazing out. We had just finished our terms as students and it was natural for us to think of our own futures in terms of the futurelessness of the world.

Leo said to me, "You've never been creative, actually, have you?"

He turned the knife, grinned and lay back. It was one of his routines.

Even then one of Leo's fans might have been saying, "Leo's got the whole world. He's really going places. He's bright, good-looking, just enough genius and such a warm heart underneath it all. He's got the lot. It'll be interesting to see how he ends up."

We moved eventually to the beer garden of a pub.

"Listen, Si. Wouldn't you like to try? Just once?" Leo was off. "I want to assault them, physically attack the public and drag them into our game. Even if I have to make the stage around them I'll have them up on it."

"Give it a go."

"You help me, Si. You and I can go along the beaches performing. Why not? We can work up a few routines.

He planned to set off in my old Jaguar and perform interludes on the southern beaches, ending at Victor Harbour, eye of resorts, for New Year's Eve. He would create an event that utilized all summer things, natural and synthetic, and he would devise techniques to force involvement on the audience. We would be troubadours for the public and lay our caps down for pennies. We flew high on beer and ideas.

◆ ◆ ◆

I sat below in the theatre bar because I couldn't bear to see the show one more time. Leo's student revue was set in a fantasy world *(Once in a Blue Moon)* which precisely resembled Adelaide. All the comfortable awfulnesses of life were there. But perhaps I shouldn't call them awfulnesses. I too have turned to the blue fizz when the release of sleep escaped me. Our own continent was a blue moon where anything might have been possible; where now in the end the same old things flourished. The last night of the revue was in any case not one of the best. So I gathered from Effie, a gem of the cast, Leo's girlfriend of two years, when she came down in the interval.

People accused Leo of favouritism in having her in his revue. She had no stage skills, but being herself was so extraordinary that she could reduce a full house to hysterics. She was unusually pale and diminutive. Some of us called her the White Mouse, which was unfair because her plaintive face made her look more like Alice in Wonderland. She was accomplished, could sing, draw, dance and play the violin, all quaintly. She perceived other people's behaviour solely in terms of passions aimed at her: rivalry, jealousy, possession and lust. Her little ambition had been to enter a beauty quest until Leo derided it. No one knew what kept them together. We all assumed that privately they must reach *heights* of rapture.

I submitted to another drink and Effie left to prepare for the final *coup de theatre* . Afterwards everyone was off to a cast party in the hills, but I waited behind for Leo, who stayed dutifully until the set was struck.

"How do you feel about it?" I asked.

"Bloody glad it's over."

He'd lost interest in the revue when it stopped needing his inspiration.

"Effie was good tonight," I said.

"She has no idea what she's doing."

"Like hell."

The stage was empty but for the stage manager.

"Effie's a joke compared to Glinda, Si."

"Come on — Glinda can go through her paces,
that's all."

"No, she's got more than that."

The hall had immediately resumed its original form,
without a trace of the energy we'd expended. Leo
twinkled at me, taking my shoulder before I could scry
his true emotion. "Come on, Si. Let's get out of here."

"I'm not sure I want to go to this party," I said. "It's
over now."

"You have to come, Si."

"Why do I? Do you want a lift home afterwards?"
We always used my car and were considered insep-
arable.

"No, no. I'll go home under my own steam. But
Effie would love to see you there."

This was bitter. There was always hostility between
Effie and myself, kept inoffensive but moist beneath a
wrapper of pleasantry.

The party was high on a slope. The warm air had
been freshened by a sea breeze, the moon was up. Wine
and music rippled. Leo wandered into the kitchen at a
loss. He was accosted with complaints, compliments,
advice, and bent to each one with a blank spongey
expression until he devised an excuse for moving on.
He looked visibly bruised, his eyes lost in cavities of
crinkled blue skin, pasty despite our day in the sun,
the places he'd scratched for inspiration inflamed.

At one stage Effie rushed to put her arms round him and he pushed her away, scolding as if she were a child. "Go and talk to Simon, sugar. He's dying to see you."

I noticed Leo find Glinda subsequently and lead her outside. I had feared it. Now Glinda was on the pedestal. He told me about it the next morning.

I woke him towards midday. He still looked haggard, took his time showering and shaving so he could emerge truly refreshed. A few matches were scattered over the squalid kitchen floor and I put two cups of black tea together.

He began flamboyantly. "I'm in love."

"With Glinda?"

She was the current first lady of student theatre, popular in society. At a twenty-first birthday dinner dance she had been photographed with the host by the local paper. But this was all her mother's doing, Leo assured me. Her wide mouth had an immense capacity for beaming. I thought of her as terribly athletic because she was well-built, having swum as a child, always tanned, obtrusively healthy, and had once slaughtered me at tennis. She was bitchy and bored with everyone because they were inconsiderate and immature — except when she wanted something. Then she could communicate a special intimacy. She would teeter pertly on her soles.

"Is Glinda in love with you, Leo?"

"That's what I wanted to ask. Come on, Si, tell me. You know about these things."

"Me?"

She'd been furious with Leo at the party, apparently, and had called him childish, arrogant and pretentious. He had pleaded overwrought and confessed that he loved her. He was frightened they'd grow apart and he wouldn't have a chance with her. She'd smiled condescendingly and ignored it all. "How's Effie?" she'd replied.

"I'm serious, Glinda."

"It's hard to believe you. Why don't you go home and sleep on it?"

But he had worked on her for hours and hours in the moonlight, sitting at the bottom of the garden away from the rest of the party, talking of oddments until finally they were conversing softly about each other.

"We've been in such close contact for weeks," she said. "It's natural we should have affected each other. Let's face it, we're both powerful personalities. But that doesn't mean we're cut out for each other."

"How do you know?"

"For a start it's you. You're frivolous. I'm pragmatic. I'm what you'd call bourgeois."

"But you've got extraordinary talent — in the right hands."

It was dawn when she dropped him home and he took an audacious peck.

She was leaving for two weeks at the beach and Leo wanted to visit her in a few days to follow things up. It was too hot to think. When evening came it was still hot so we bought some more bottles of beer. We composed a letter for Glinda together, with all the tricks of sincerity. "I don't usually feel like this about people . . . ." She'd be moved. Leo did earnestly want to be a troubadour along the South Coast because it would bring him to Victor Harbour where Glinda would be. But the city still had a hold over me with the rest of the dusty Christmas crowd egged on by tinsel and canned angelic choirs.

Just then Effie appeared. She had suspicions about

Leo. With a swallowed sob she rushed to lay her head against his chest. She'd gone home from the party with the burly stage-manager and under duress had slept with him. But it meant nothing. She loved Leo. She put one arm round his neck and stared sadly.

Leo rang me the next day and cursed Effie. He couldn't stand it any more. His heart bled for Glinda. Would I leave immediately?

I wanted grace. In a few days he'd choose Effie again. It was another side-show trick. Under which egg-cup was the pea? But presently the city came to seem a circle of retribution and offence. The sins were dreams of abominable excitement and unnatural escape. The penalty was uniform imprisonment. "Grant Us Thy Peace" was the seasonal salve, but how much more accessible that would be on sand against blue. We arranged to leave.

II

We took small suitcases full of theatrical bits with us. Leo slumped in the passenger seat in a boater and mirror-glasses, like a weary entrepreneur, and I drove, mythically, towards the southern beaches. The Jaguar glided along the arterial road. Who has not struggled in vain to make a wise choice from the range of service stations which proffer themselves along the highway's edge? Who has not paused, self-hating and unwilling, at the hamburger joints there and taken from the black-and-yellow girls with marvellous hands a cheeseburger with egg, draped in a sodden tissue and coddled in an emblazoned bag; and then sat sucking it down to every last bit of hair-like lettuce? At last one enters the country proper.

"The best way to get them in is to promenade flamboyantly down the beach, then to stick a sign in the sand and both of us to squat under it curled into little balls, each wearing an outlandish hat. We'll stay there curled up for half an hour if necessary, until a crowd gathers."

I had my doubts. Christie's Beach was enough of a resort once to have to this day a smattering of mansions. The bay itself was almost horseshoe. Large waves tumbled onto the beach and red cliffs rose behind, eroded beautifully.

"These are the people we have to reach," said Leo.

We had a milkshake and a roll, yet failed to achieve any rapport with the locals. We decided to wait in the milkbar till midafternoon.

"Just keep confident, Si. You've done more embarrassing things than this before."

When we were ready I parked the Jag at the top of the wooden steps to the beach. Leo stepped out blinking like an airport starlet, flaunting the banner ("Mid-Coast Mimers"), descended. He was in a complete white suit with rose in lapel, boater, shades and glittering silver boots. I trailed behind with a wicker basket of props, wearing a jerkin, jeans and a brown corduroy cloak. On my head was a wide-brimmed felt hat with plume.

A kid looked up at us from her sunbathing and called out, "Eh, Looweeze, come 'ere!" Two boys who were lugging their bikes up as we came down muttered to each other, "Fuckin' pooftas!" That was more attention than the rest of the beachgoers gave us. There were lots of them, settled with their brollies and tents, stretched out drunk in the sun. No one called out to us, no one swore at us directly. An extraordinary number of people managed not to notice and those who did only gazed with wondering eyes, presuming, since they were looking into the sun, that we must be an illusion.

After two hundred yards we found a suitable patch of sand. Leo stuck our sign in and began to dig a square shallow pit with a beach-spade and then he raised a sand platform. Meanwhile I drew a large circle to describe the acting area and with a beach bucket began to fill the pit. When Leo had finished we broke into a brief softshoe routine.

Oh when I am there beside the seaside
I am beside myself with glee,
There are lots of girls besides
I should like to sit beside
Beside the seaside, beside the sea.

Soon enough people did begin to stare at us and some brave curious souls came closer. Immediately the song finished we crouched in our egg positions on the platform of sand and waited. A small audience gathered and when there were a dozen or so we began our seaside mime. Leo, ever seeking to befit time and place, had devised a twee tableau of marine science. He was the Sun. I was the Water. I had to lie in the muddy pit and when he rose be evaporated and when he went under fall as rain back into the pit, taking up Minerals from the Earth and from the Sea. Then he became a Human Being who, replete with deckchair, sat by the shore sunning. Meanwhile I became a Fisherman and using our other two props — a net and a rubber fish — mimed the getting of Food from the Sea. We accompanied this innocent mime with noises, bits of rhyme, contortions, and the children seemed to enjoy it. At any rate they stayed wide-eyed and smiling and, as Mummy would have warned them, a safe distance away.

One girl was quite forward and joined in my wave noises. Leo took her aside at once because we needed a child for the next part of the performance and I heard her memorizing, reciting in a cocky Midlands voice, "Uffta sooch kahndness thut wd be a dismal thing ta doo . . . ." Other bodies had gathered by now too: an aged couple, two Italian youths in dicky-bag trunks, a nubile trio who might have worked together in a bank, a long-haired lad and lass who looked earnestly sympathetic. One person asked if we were from the television. Part of our policy was not to talk to the audience out of character, but to draw them into the scene we wanted to create: now the beach at Brighton, England in the late nineteenth century. The next bit was underway: Leo strolled to and fro, doffing his boater and proclaiming gymnastically:

> The sun was shining on the sea,
> Shining with all his might,
> He did his very best to make,
> The billows clean and bright —

All at once a huge pink man pushed through the crowd and blurted to Leo, "Excuse me sonny, what do you think you're doing?"

Leo pattered on pertly. "And this was *odd* because it *was* The *middle* of the *night* ."

"Listen 'ere," said our gentleman. He was pear-shaped and wasn't set off to advantage by his olive green swimming outfit. He was one of those men who have on their bodies just a few very long wiry hairs. "Listen 'ere," he said, seeking support from the crowd,

"I'm only doing you people a favour, but I'm a member of the shire council" (his voice rose on the last syllable) "and I think you should know that there are laws against this sort of thing . . . ."

"What sort of thing?" said Leo with an imbecilic smirk.

"I mean — you need permission to perform in a public place and I'll have to get the police to move you on, if you don't stop, that is."

"We're not doing any harm. The kids like it, don't you?" But there was no spontaneous hurrah.

"You'll have to clear out. That's all," said our rosy pear and bowing his burnt head swaggered back to his family group with dog.

Leo and I conferred a moment. In reality we were greatly confused and furious, but to maintain dignity we announced that the next performance would be at Southport Beach in an hour's time.

"Would you like to come with us in the car and be in the play at Southport?" Leo asked the Midlands girl. She had wet salted pigtails and smiled very wide and keenly.

"Yeah, that'd be great!"

At this juncture, however, someone else had her sense of civic duty moved. A woman in a towelling robe wearing an orange bathing cap called out from the back where she'd been standing.

"I wouldn't go with them boys, little girl. Not with strangers. Anything could happen. You'd be asking for trouble. Remember about those little Beaumont kiddies disappearing from the beach — "

Her companion joined in. "And there were those lasses from Wanda Beach. In Melbourne. You read about one tragedy like that every summer. It's always in the papers over Christmas — "

"That's right, and there was Harold Holt drowning one year too. No, I wouldn't go off with them, dear."

Their insinuations made us flash with rage. We walked across with the girl and Leo addressed what portion of the face showed under the woman's tight cap. "Madam, I don't appreciate your way of thinking. My friend and I are both perfectly reliable ordinary people. We have brothers and sisters, some this girl's age. We've worked with children. We like children. We like making them happy. If this little girl wants to come with us, if she'd enjoy it, that's what concerns us, not whatever you may dredge out of your newspapers."

"What's your name?" I asked the kid.

"Sandy."

"Would you like to come with us to Southport, Sandy, and we'll bring you back after?"

"Yeah."

"Where's your mother?"

"She's back home."

The two women watched this and stayed watching us pack up, their grapey eyes almost bursting. They couldn't speak for their pursed lips, even to each other. As we walked away we heard the diminishing, worried rise and fall of their voices.

Sandy sat in the back while we wound round the coast to Southport. Leo told me basically to give my performance more oomph. At Southport you have to park the car miles from the water and traipse across a footbridge over the river, then round the sandhills to the front beach. We decided to make this walk our procession. Our outrage from Christie's lent us an air of confidence and glamour, and by the time we were in front of the clubhouse we had a gaggle of followers. Sandy was marvellous, never stopped smiling and danced quite unabashed along the way. And she cheeked a lifesaver.

As we squatted in the sand to attract our audience, there was an unaccountable buzzing overhead, so I hatched myself to look up. A shark plane was circling and all the kids had left the water. Dripping, huddling in their towels, they all came over to observe. During the ecological mime at the beginning, one of these beached surfers took off his wetsuit, making excruciating noises which were the ideal modernistic accompaniment to our evaporating and condensing carry-on.

By the time the Walrus and Carpenter Mime had begun enough young children had shoved through to the front to make it work. Leo strode back and forth blockbustering the crowd with his rendition of the introductory verses, while I shuffled after him, a dour-faced humourless Carpenter. He the Walrus came to the lines:

No birds were flying overhead —
    There were no birds to fly . . .

and pumped them full of the rending tone of the most desperate anti-pollution documentary. In fact there was one seagull arcing away. Then Leo took out his hanky, blew his nose and breaking into thumping sobs turned to me (with a wink) to take my hand. We spoke:

The Walrus and the Carpenter
    Were walking close at hand:
They wept like anything to see
    Such quantities of sand . . . .

In our pathetic well-practised dilettante voices.

If this were only cleared away,
   We say, it *would* be grand!

And continued exhorting each other —

If seven maids with seven mops
   Swept it for half a year,
Do you suppose (sob sob sob)
   That they would get it clear?
I doubt it (I said
   And shed a bitter tear.)

Then pacing round our acting circle and aided by Sandy we gradually took the hands of likely looking children and led them into the centre, Leo crooning enticingly —

O Oysters, come and walk with us!
A pleasant walk, a pleasant talk
   Along the briny beach:
We cannot do with more than four
   To give a hand to each.

Quite willingly little sand-covered kids gave us their hands and joined in our perambulation. At this Sandy, the eldest oyster, turned and gave very knowing leering winks at the older onlookers, who would turn to each other, whisper and snicker, but turn back for more. Now the narration passed to me while Leo mimed the brushing of their oyster coats, washing of faces and shining of shoes —

And thick and fast they came at last,
   And more, and more, and more . . . .

I muttered mournfully as really quite a few children joined the huddle round Leo. When all were gathered Leo the Walrus stopped, seated himself on a deck-chair from our props basket, spread a table cloth and orated —

The time has come . . .
    To talk of many things:
Of shoes — and ships — and sealing wax —
    Of cabbages — and kings —
And why the sea is boiling hot —
    And whether pigs have wings.

Into which Churchillian intonation Sandy broke in plump North Country —

But wait a bit . . .
    Before we have our chat;
Fore some of us are out of breath,
    And all of us are fat!

Then I, taking my position by the table cloth, mumbled, "No hurry!", to which Leo bowed and urged the others to thank me muchly. He patted his vested paunch and droned again, now the connoisseur,

A loaf of bread . . .
    Is what we chiefly need:
Pepper and vinegar besides
    Are very good indeed —
Now, if you're ready, Oysters dear,
    We can begin to feed.

He beamed at them and smacked his lips before dissolving into an expression of pontifical sweetness. Sandy piped up again, more or less getting the words straight.

"But not on us! After such kindness, that would be A dismal thing to do!" Walrus Leo, oblivious, replied stretching a complacent arm to the orange sun over the sea: "The night is fine . . . . Do you admire the view?" And gradually as he spoke further I who had spread our fishing net was taking one child after another, beginning with the most assured, and putting them inside the net.

It was so kind of you to come!
  And you are very nice . . . .

"Cut us another slice," I'd mumble as I put the next
child in under the net, "I wish you were not quite so
deaf — I've had to ask you twice!"
Leo was building his speech into something akin to
the rising cathartic moments at the end of a tragedy.
There were even clipped consonants in the Olivier
manner entering his voice. And how he postured!

It seems a shame . . .
  To play them such a trick.
After we've brought them out so far,
  And made them trot so quick . . . .

I pushed another squealing kid under the net which
was getting full, and growled in my best gravel, "The
butter's spread too thick."
The climax:

I weep for you . . .
  I deeply sympathize,
With sobs and tears I'm sorting out
  Those of the largest size,
Holding my pocket-handkerchief
  Before my streaming eyes.

At this point Walrus Leo was to promenade in slow
march round the circle while I suddenly tightened the
rope that drew the net closed and dragged the tumbling
mass of shrieking giggling children along the sand a few
feet, intoning the epilogue:

O Oysters,
  You've had a pleasant run!
Shall we be trotting home again!
  But answer comes there none —
And this is scarcely odd, because
  We've *EATEN* every one.

Now I released the children who scuttled off frightened from the wriggling heap of snakes and with Leo, who'd hastily thrown all props into the basket, was to scuttle off myself in a walk not so different from hunchback Richard III's, over the hills and faraway, both of us mumbling and wailing: "We've eaten every one . . . we've eaten every one . . . we've eaten every one . . . ."

The end was successful and Leo escaped. The play had progressed to its crest of terror and then, all the children-oysters gobbled up, we were gone!

But slouching my way towards the car I ran straight up against a hard body and nearly toppled over.

"What in Jesus' name do you think you're doing?" The brash unfinished voice registered at once. I looked down at her golden-haired legs. It was Shirley, ex-girlfriend, fanatical surfer, denizen of Southport where her brothers were lifesavers. "You're the end, Si. You really are."

It's unimaginable how imposing she was, arms akimbo and legs apart before me, brown muscular body and yellow hair, her pretty face stroboscopic with health and her huge eyes laughing at me from her position of confidence, beach-ownership and a day's obliterating sea-immersion. We talked and I explained what Leo and I were doing. I couldn't stop my awkwardness, and my new free feeling slipped back as I realized how fixed I was in the elements of my old life. I felt like one of those puffing blow-fish, stranded by the tide, prodded by a disinterested beachcomber. We said goodbye and she swaggered on down to hear how the others were judging her weird friends. I hurried to catch up with Leo for a re-charge and he talked non-stop as we crossed the bridge to the car.

"We had them exactly, Si. Do you realize that?"

He didn't let up. We took off to the nearest pub for celebratory gins, fearless. In the toilet after his second gin the lad pissing next to him glanced down at the silver boots and burst out:

"Aren't you the guy from that thing on the beach? Really incredible! Wow!" And splashed the silver toecaps a little.

I was blasted with play ideas for our new piece. It kept on expanding, a jigsaw puzzle mystery that worked from a moment of total annihilation to a perfect edifice, a formal equivalent of Void. My head fell back on the rough hessian that covered the hotel windows. The sundown light through the orange drapery made us both look rather demonic. I started to explain that my new idea was problematical and vaguely monstrous.

"I don't know that I can have it ready by tomorrow."

"Why not?"

"We need other people."

"Never," scowled Leo. "Can't you use the audience? Why not advertise ourselves in the next town as bearers of fame, dispensers of lustre, Father Christmases of glory?"

"Harbingers of paradise?"

"Why not? Ask people to bring their own acts along. *Children* , Si! Before they learn that it's not nice to perform, while they *want* to dance and scream and cry, 'Me! Me! Me!' Look at today. That little girl."

"Sandy," we gasped simultaneously. "My God. We forgot her."

"That's terrible. Come on, we'll have to go back. She'll be desperate."

The beach was almost empty. There was no sign of Sandy. We called, and roamed over the sand in front of the clubhouse gesturing with our arms at the sky. She was nowhere. We could only presume she had managed her own way home. She was a smart child. The tide had swallowed the beach area in the short time we'd been at the pub and the water running where our enchanted circle had been marked the beginning of the night that was to absorb the traces of the weekend's activity. Leo and I felt guilty about Sandy, though the feeling was atmospheric as much as anything.

We ended up in the cliff-foot carpark for the night. Leo chose the back seat and lay face-down, awake till morning. I was granted the front, with the roccoco pleasures of the gearstick. The dark was interrupted only once, by an inquisitive bloke with a torch.

III

We decided to drive all the way to Robe, an abandoned port with historic appeal further down the coast. The road went dead straight over the ranges.

"Tap the petrol gauge, will you please?"

Leo tickled the dial dandyishly and then gave it a vengeful thump, so the needle leapt from one side to the other before falling back where it had been — on zero. We stopped at a spanking new station at the bottom of a hill and Leo took advantage of the telephone to ring Glinda. I dithered about the front end of the car tapping and tsking, hoping that by fierce magic the car would cure its own enervation. The attendant regarded me, minimally, with disdain. I felt uncommunicative and inside it pained me to watch Leo procuring the telephone information with which to trace Glinda. The waitress seemed to begrudge me the hot water for the coffee powder. Leo was abusing the local operator who was possibly the waitress's supply-line for the darker mysteries of life. Leo was chattering like a canary to Glinda's mother, wheedling numbers out of her.

He turned to me. "Jesus, she's staying with Mark Harcourt at Victor. Fucking hell."

Finally he got through to Glinda herself. "Nice to speak to you at last." There were long pauses. I was glad for Leo. She must have been doing a lot of talking. He told her that we'd be in Victor for New Year's Eve and hung up. "No, we won't be extending," he added to the operator.

"Well?"

"On Thursday she went skiing with Mark. She kept falling off but Mark kept getting her back up. On Friday she had a counter-lunch with Mark. She had drinks with Mark. She's met some really nice kids."

I laughed.

"I'm going to stay with Mark too," Leo added. "He said it would be great to see me."

"He's a nice guy. A nice honest guy."

Leo put on his dark glasses. His sullen withdrawal was the *coitus interruptus* of the phone call. The door was hung with anti-fly dangles. He scattered them as he pushed out. I was left to offer the woman the money for our coffees.

"Forty cents, love." She gestured casually at Leo's poured cup sitting cold. "I s'pose he didn't want it after all."

Outside the attendant wrung his oilrag. The gears crunched and the car shuddered uneasily into motion.

In the dusty rear-vision I could see the attendant lift his eyes from the rust-pocked body of my '58 sedan, up to the clouding sky whence hosts of Hell's Angels might descend.

It started to rain and tiny spurts of summer dust were sent up. After so much heat the fine rain made the engine and the road steam. The wipers didn't work. Leo and I settled low in the seat for the hours ahead. He tried to sleep behind his hat brim and glasses while I twiddled the radio dials. A voice rustled across the rainy distance from the city that the Adelaide C.I.B. was investigating the disappearance of a girl; then all metropolitan sound ceased.

"It's impossible to sleep here," said Leo. "How can you bear this heap of a car? Look at the seat-stuffing? Can't you talk to me, Si. What's going on in your head? Something must be."

The road was grey and straight through the beginnings of the ninety-mile desert, wide land stretching out of sight on the left, low hills formed by windblow, furred with grasses and screwed-up scrub; Lake Alexandrina made chaotic by rain; reeds beating the sandbanks that had once stopped Captain Sturt's final breakthrough to the sea; all blurred by rain.

"Is there anything I can read, Si?"

There was only the first part of Proust which I had vainly embarked on. It was full of sand grains which trickled out into his lap. "I'd be happy to tell you what I'm thinking, Leo."

He began to flick through the book, then threw it down. "The continual wanking, the never ever coming?"

"You need to have absolutely no interest in what happens next," I instructed.

He huffed and sighed. We were passing now through a town. The main street was so wide it seemed to lay waste the proud buildings that lined it, the Stock and Station Agent, the Memorial Hall. It was a relief to see the final billboard — for private cabinettes on the lake.

"If only we had an author carrying us forward, Leo, towards his climax. That would be sublime —

"OH NO! FUCKING HELL!"

I'd gone flying on where all the luminous signs pointed, not perceiving the dull bent one that veered off to Robe. I stopped and reversed across the middle of the highway.

"WHAT? DEAR GOD!"

Astraddle the white line the car had conked out.

"It's seized utterly."

The trudge through the rain, the hitch, the garrulous mechanic, the towing, the rust particles in the petrol filter, the roadhouse kitchen where Leo returned his plate of fish and chips. We reached Robe after midnight after not speaking for two hours.

The next morning we drove out of the town so we could enter again triumphantly, trailing the streamers we'd picked up at the local newsagent. We were both in foul moods. Our sleep had only been a hiatus and we were scowling at each other before we were out of our sleeping bags. Robe is at the mouth of a working river. During the pastoral boom graziers had built a batch of sturdy holiday homes there, hidden now mostly by hedges and shrubs. There were some older bluestone houses and some ambitious new constructions. The town creamed enough for survival off the surfies who came like bees when the waves were good down south.

The grey raininess of the place was softening. I

followed the river inland for an hour's solitary ramble, among birds playing in the cool and sprays of insects darting and crisscrossing in the moisture.

We were supposed to parade on the beach with a sandwich board but the drizzle kept up and the whole thing didn't seem likely.

The only place we could perform indoors was the Mechanics' Institute, a sandstone chapel with white highlights. It was necessary to get permission and when finally we tracked down the Town Clerk he was not obliging. He had loosened his tie and laughed, rubbing an imaginary object between his large palms.

Finally in the evening word came of a party along the road, in a clearing under a group of old trees. People were swigging claret enthusiastically there when we arrived, a raucous merry crowd. We joined in. When I left, Leo was sprawled face-down across a ti-tree bush moaning with pleasure and nausea. He came back to the car very late and woke me up, unable to find the open end of his sleeping bag.

In the end he managed to slither only half way down into the bag. His face showed up all night. The tenacity of its whiteness in the dark car made it seem like an ideal marking which would be preserved on the wing when the caterpillar metamorphosed; maybe the next dawn, maybe the next day. When Leo crawled out of his cocoon in the morning he found inexplicable scratches round his nipples. He blinked and couldn't remember. He'd had a wild night.

We conferred. Things hadn't got off the ground in Robe, though the new day was brilliantly bright. I would return to the city for Christmas and Leo would push on to Victor Harbour in search of Glinda.

IV

The car was trembling more than ever before but
caught a glimpse of its former streamlined glory at
sweet ninety miles an hour. We had the windows
down and our hair flew out, desiccating in the air. A
family-sized cola and two chocolate bars passed between us, and we poured water from a gallon flask over
our heads to air-condition us. I put my foot to the
floor, out of mind, out of sight.

Then a small female hitch-hiker appeared on the
road side. Leo grinned instinctively. The girl waved
back, screamed and ran after us as we slowed.

"Can we pretend not to recognize her?" whispered
Leo and then: "Hi, Effie! For crying out loud — "

Effie was already in the front door and on Leo's lap.
We all screeched at the coincidence involved. Had
Effie known we were coming that way? She could
easily have contacted Robe to find out our time of
departure. Anything was possible to her wizardry. But
she was thoroughly vague.

Leo declared he must have a piss. We stopped and
winking directorially he sent Effie off to the shop
while he hustled me into the men's.

"How did she do it, Si?"

"It's just bad luck, isn't it?"

"It can't be. What in hell is she doing down this
way?"

He clasped his head at the chaos of things as if he'd
been clapped between cymbals.

"Anyway the fact is that I'm going to Victor Harbour and she *isn't* !"

"Don't she and Glinda get on?"

"You know perfectly well. No, Si, you'll have to

take Effie to Adelaide and I'll get off at Strathalbyn and hitch down. That's the solution."

"Fuck you. No way. Can you imagine me and Effie alone together? In any case we don't go through Strathalbyn."

"A slight detour. I'll smooth it over with Effie."

"It's impossible. You can't palm her off like this."

"Listen, Si. This is vital and mortal. You've got to do it."

I squirted the liquid soap onto my hands just as the swing door opened and Effie appeared.

"What are you boys up to?"

"Just coming, sweets."

We came out together into the glare and took our places in the vehicle. Effie was in the back now, for comfort, but leant forward to whisper in our ears. After five miles Leo had begun his diplomacy. He told Effie that he was going to Victor Harbour to stay with Mark Harcourt and that I was returning to the city for a family Christmas.

"It's been planned for days."

He had overdone it and she detected fraud.

"Why are you going this way if you're going to Victor?"

"I'm going to hitch from Strathalbyn."

"Strathalbyn? Yeah? Your route's a bit of a dog's leg then?"

"Si's coming down after Christmas. Why don't you come down with him?"

Effie took it up quickly. "I'm going back to Adelaide now, am I?"

"We're going to perform on New Year's Eve. Mrs Harcourt invited me but said we'd have to bach because she was terribly busy. We want you to perform with us. We've got this playlet. You can be the child star in it."

Keep talking Leo, I thought. I was in no mood for improvised bluffing, but he was sparked by possibilities again.

"Si and I will be the hairy old ringmasters. You'll be an innocent child in a sequined bikini, made to perform, exploited, corrupted, just to delight our depraved fancies. Sound good?"

Her eyes were made to glint for a moment at this apotheosis of herself. She settled her straggly hair behind her ears and gazed out the window. She began to sing, as piercingly high and pure as a silver wire. *If pretty little bluebirds fly beyond that rainbow why oh why can't Ieeeeeeeee?* Leo was giggling. We had arrived in Strathalbyn.

We put away three schooners each in the main pub. No one else was present. The dwarf barman was lost in a shadowy dream about the pool table nobody used. The sun through the venetians cast faded bars on the felt.

The scenario took over: Leo stood like a telegraph pole outside in the dust. Effie reached up on tiptoes to his face and they kissed formally. "I love you," she said. "Get your act together," he said. She took her place as if rightfully in the front passenger seat.

"Happy Chrissy," we called.

It was sunset, powdering Leo's Giacometti body with dust and distortion. Effie looked back as the limitations of human vision took her beloved. She sniffed a little. She and I might have been the lovers.

Soon we were within the metropolitan area and heard the News. A local woman wanted to connect the disappearance of the Christie's Beach schoolgirl with

114

the appearance of a UFO. Then once more heavy rock thudded out over the plains.

When I deposited Effie she made a precise arrangement for travelling back to Victor Harbour with me after the festivities. Such devotion could not go unrewarded.

The roads are perilous on Boxing Day because once Christmas has been survived people feel no further need to worry. Effie and I reached Victor at midday, and I stopped at a phone box to warn Leo. Mrs Harcourt answered. When I told her my name there was a dreadful pause until, pulling herself up from oblivion, she cried wondrously, "I know you!" Leo was on the beach with Mark and Glinda. When I told Effie she exclaimed in sparkling naivety, "Oh, Glinda's down here too?"; and shrugged her shoulder in its tiny velour jacket.

On the shore Mark and Glinda, laughing, were playing beach tennis and gaily skipping into the shallows. Glinda beamed like a cheese chunk whenever the sandy ball bounced into someone's picnic salad or across an oiled belly, and she'd apologize with such eagerness that no one could mind. In her deep crimson bikini, heart-shaped and frilly, her outsize sunglasses and a bluebird hairclip, she dashed. Mark was all bounce and torso, leaping and patting blithely at the little white ball. Leo was on his towel watching them vacuously behind glasses and thick sunburn cream. Effie stumbled across the sand to him in her flowing floral wrap-around, clutching the noble hat that was her only hope against burning and blistering. Leo hugged her like an invalid because of his sunburn, frightened she'd stick.

Confronted by the two couples I felt self-consciously on my own and plunged at the water energetically. I swam right out deep towards the wild blue. The white strip of beach looked cleaner and smoother from a distance. Behind came the bushes against which our cars were edged, a road, then the houses in blurred mosaic, the hills and heaven beyond.

Our accommodation presented a logistical problem. Glinda made murmurs about how flustered Mrs Harcourt was with all these visitors, but it transpired that the girls could take Mark's room with the extra bed, while Mark would have the spare bed (which had been Glinda's) and Leo would sleep in the car. I went up the road to the house of a gorgeous surfer, where health food was eaten and natural gods bowed down to. Stephen, the proprietor, had forsaken his career as model and barman in order to cruise the southern beaches seeking perfect rides and incredible surf shots. He was waxing his board and his tremulous drawl put me at ease immediately. I was able to doze there on the verandah, under his presence, until the stubborn dusk became night.

The Harcourts' esplanade house was called "Happy Days". We gathered in the bar area to find refuge from the sullen hot evening.

"Would you like a drink, Glinda?" asked Leo.

"Mm, yes. Gin?"

Mark got drinks for the rest of us.

Glinda sipped, in a shift that let most of her olive legs slide over the barstool she perched on. Mark and Leo were dolled up too, their brands of aftershave clashing in mid-air. Effie had only herself which she laid out along the foam sofa.

"This belonged to my grandmother in the twenties,"

she said rather sadly of a cross round her neck. "Leo, did your parents like the painting I gave them?"

"I haven't heard."

Mark said "Cheers" to his second gin and turned on the television. "Anything on?" he called across to Glinda who was near the programme guide.

"The News."

"What is the news anyway?"

"UFO sighting," I said.

"They still haven't found that girl," Effie said.

"Gone without a trace."

"A clairvoyant's being brought in."

"Why can't she be left alone?"

There was nothing on TV.

Leo picked up an old conversation with Glinda. "I'm interested in romantic roles while I'm young," she sighed.

"There are plenty of those going," muttered Leo then stuck his head into his drink like an ostrich.

"What was that?" asked Effie.

"Nothing."

"Leo!" She did the nagging wife so perfectly that Leo kissed her for it and flopped across her lap. Glinda in syncopation moved into Mark's arms and whispered something.

"Who wants a game of table tennis?"

No one. Mark went to the toilet, leaving Glinda in the doorway.

"You look superb in that pose," Leo said.

She made her silver eyes gape then changed face and smiled warmly at Effie. Effie had sunk into the sofa with the weight of an overtired child, one arm carelessly fondling Leo's knee. She reverted to primal innocence when she was too lazy to cope with the evils of day to day. Her eyelids closed over those last chinks of blue purity and in that moment all of us in the room lost something.

"Is Effie asleep?" I asked Leo. "Do you want to talk to me?"

He didn't. He was busy accusing Glinda of being bourgeois, *sotto voce* .

Later we played pingpong. Tk-tk tk-tk tk-tk. The tiny ball danced in its green squares, skimming the tattered net that made the point yours or your opponent's.

When the others went to bed Leo and I set off promenading along the foreshore. Our rubber thongs clapped against the ground and sprayed up dirt as we shuffled. Leo's monstrous feet rocked beneath his rippling trouser legs. We were sweating in the darkness and he wanted to tell me about Glinda.

"I know you don't like her, Si, but I refuse to be defensive."

We followed the train tracks. When they veered towards the station we headed off through a dusty park to the sea. Leo had picked up a palmfrond and was cracking it to bits. We reached a bench by a hibiscus and stopped to talk. He loved Glinda utterly, he said; in her he'd at last found warmth and humour and tenderness and no small amount of celestial fire.

"She's whole."

He had separated her from Mark on the first afternoon and they'd gone photographing on the island. There was a fine shot, apparently, of Glinda regarding the Bluff. That night the weather had become freakishly hot and they'd gone swimming, alone. He'd taken her hand in the water to allay any fears of nocturnal bogies. Once reassured she had let him go and dived forward in the pins of phosphorescence. He'd swum after her and they chased each other amongst their limbs until Leo pounced and hugged her. Before she'd shaken herself free of sea-weed and water he had kissed her. She'd let him because they were both immersed in sea anyway. Until she saw the doggish look in his eyes and flipped backwards, underwater to the shore.

Leo, drunkenly calm from kissing her, had back-stroked elegantly, observing the moon his confederate squelched by his watery vision.

"Kiss me, Glinda," he said, running up dripping.

"No Leo!"

"Come on."

She skipped ahead rubbing her hair briskly with a towel. Leo watched her fade into the sandhills that shielded the train tracks.

"You can't get away," he called. He caught her up and they walked side by side back through the park.

"You're sweet, Leo, but it's too complicated," she said flouncing. He swung round a palmtree to intercept her with his arms.

"No."

He watched deflated as she paraded down the avenue. Then he ran ahead by a different route, shinned up a tree and leapt down almost on top of her, bawling like an orangatan.

"Aar-aa-aar-aa-aar!"

Finally she took his arm. They stopped to drink from a brown fountain trickling noisily. When they rubbed together they felt salt. He pushed her up against the wire screen door of the closed kiosk. She stretched out an arm to allude, in pose, to melodrama, and threw her head back to the sky which was hot and crossed with clattering palmleaves.

After ages of kissing her he drew back to gauge her

madly gratified eyes. Their shadow was silver and gold.

"You *have* got something," he said. "There's something inside you. That's what I want."

"Don't be ridiculous." She was offended· that he didn't appreciate her *style* and ran her hand through her hair to give it body. Leo pressed against her breasts. He curved his arm round her and tried to move her. They were heading for the sandhills, but she had withdrawn her flesh again. They crossed the railway tracks and frightened a huddle of kids smoking. In a neat valley of sand he grabbed her by the shoulders and tumbled her down. While he giggled innocently, she struggled then subsided, the less wriggling, the less sand in the hair.

He didn't give up. "We love each other." His body was so long. He began hammering at her and heard in his ear her spontaneous gasp of pain. She was pulling away from him.

He didn't protest, except to fling a limp hand after her rising body and then to roll, wallowing in sand, to the bottom of their dune. He lay in the sand and watched her head off. She was more mysterious from behind and at a distance, edged with moon and willowing at him. He wanted to feel like a martyr, but she had stopped apologetically to wait for him.

"Come on, Leo. I'm sorry. I've got nothing against you personally."

That night was sleepless for Leo as he lamented that events had followed the snake not the ladder. He glossed over the mooniness of his desire and convinced himself that only the walls of the house kept Him and Her apart.

She was nice to Leo all the next day. They spent the afternoon at Boomer Beach with Mark, drenched in oil

120

on giant towels. When Mark was in the water they strolled off up the beach and weren't seen for two hours.

"You're wasting your potential, Glinda. You could do anything. Given a good director."

A fourteen-year-old girl way out in the waves yelled to her friends that the water was divine. "Come on in!" The deathly heat was making Leo dizzy and Glinda gave him her hand.

"I can't take you seriously, Leo. You don't understand."

"Where are my glasses? This light is blinding."

The waves broke endlessly into smithereens of blazing glass.

"Perhaps I should go to another town, Leo."

He knew she would be a success and wondered how big a fish one must be to feel blissfully secure in the ocean itself. Even then there would be the sky beyond, glimpsed in a mirrory distortion through the beady fish's eye.

"Have some oil! You two look frazzled," said Mark when they returned.

That night they went drinking and afterwards to the sideshows. It was a boiling Christmas Eve. Wily Glinda wanted more of Leo's bantering praise. Her arm in Leo's she circled the fairground, with Mark attending. They watched the bucking horses. Two teenage girls were riding them in a frenzy, spurring their painted bodies to the utmost defiance of gravity. The one in front, red-haired and ring-flashing, screamed: "I want to die-ee-ee!" Leo's eyes danced secretly for the crazy rider, until Glinda leant against him to keep the two of them aloof from all this lunacy. She had only to run her fingers over his chest to arouse Leo and bring him back

121

to her. He kept telling her how gorgeous she was, what potential she had, how alluring was the stone at her centre.

"Let yourself go! Here's the space for you. Let it all out, Glinda, I'm dying for it. Shall we ride the horses?"

"I'm too big for that, Leo."

"I thought you'd lost weight."

They decided instead to ride the sedate big wheel. It worked out to everyone's chagrin that Mark and Leo were in one carriage together while Glinda dangled above them alone. It was the operator's practical joke. Then, when the boys were ushered out, Glinda's compartment went sailing past, again and again. Round and round she went, suspended regally above the fair. Leo gazed upward through the slats at Glinda's legs. As she circled, passing through fairy lights, she became red and green and yellow. For Glinda the cars and people formed a complex filigree, but their noise was overcome by the shushing of the sea and the carols from the amplifiers on the palms. The sea was black and the country was black as far as the Bluff. Leo waved at her against the stars, then she was down the bottom, then up. After twenty minutes she came to a standstill, reeled off through a maze of fences and tottered into Leo's arms. Mark had looked a little shocked and hugged her possessively when his turn came.

"She's fantastic, Si. She's passionate and brilliant. She makes real demands. She's tough."

Leo had finished explaining it to me and folded his arms. It was a little unexpected and his fanciful nature showed in his eyes. His face looked like a mask in dough that could be turned from merriment to tristesse with just a pinch. I put an arm on his shoulder. I was simply close to him, happy in his happiness. We only had one summer, and he looked like a gollywog.

"Don't forget you're the star," I said.

.

V

Everyone was type-cast. Through connexions we had acquired the use of a private theatrette in a colonial mansion, a sprawl of local granite. The immense room had a high ceiling which made things cool and shadowy, and was draped with velvet the same thick green as the stage curtain with its old gold braid. The house sat in a sea of lawn kept bright by dozens of sprinklers working in intricate synchronization. We sat eating packed lunches on plush antique chairs and I unfolded our new opus, a who-dunnit tragedy called *The Mystery of Hindmarsh Heights*. Leo would play the benign old aristocrat with an eye for the ladies. Effie would play his precocious daughter Alice, a bad seed. There would be a teutonic governess called Fräulein von Kulp — Glinda — and I would play Rev. Breezy Transcendence the family chaplain.

Glinda fidgetted showily. "It sounds very involved and camp to me. Will people like it?"

Effie gave a few positive bounces and Leo chuckled at the awfulness of my ideas.

They were to improvise their lines, and there was no lust for rehearsing yet. We wandered out to the mansion's back porch where the Jaguar was waiting.

"We'll drop you off in town," said Leo to Effie, who wanted to go shopping. That would leave him alone with Glinda, and me.

Then, the moment she'd been left at the chemist's, Leo suggested that the rest of us drive out to the old whaling pub at Encounter Bay.

"Give us a kiss, Glinda."

"Fuck off."

We chose fiery spirits and watched the jukebox swaying the mermen and mermaids in the pub.

Leo touched a white scallop of skin revealed by Glinda's brief shift. "You'll have to wear a different costume in the sun," he warned her.

She stroked his cheek. "And you need a different make-up base, honey."

As he tickled her thigh, staring out the window, she collapsed against him in giggles.

At the jukebox a guy offered me some really amazing dope.

In my absence Leo and Glinda had interlocked, cooing and blowing. She laughed mockingly and he would push her back to arm's length, observing the miracle of the face.

We didn't find Effie back at the Harcourts'. Poor angel! She'd fallen asleep on the beach in front and her protective hat had blown off her face. Her veiny eyelids were unspeakably vulnerable, the colour of raw chicken. Beneath them her eyes flickered in a dream.

"Effie!" I shook her and she woke quickly, horrified.

"Si! How long have I been here?"

I put my palm across her blinking eyes, to shield them, and she felt her face desperately.

"I'm so hot. I'm red. I'm going to blister."

"Come on, we haven't been gone that long."

"With Glinda?"

I picked her up and she brushed herself free of sand.

"I can't peel. I can't lose it all."

"Come on, you couldn't have stayed white all summer."

We hopped across the burning road.

"Si — " she said, as if about to confide.

I looked at her appealingly.

But she had already checked herself.

We were too preoccupied with our senses and our souls to rehearse much. Yet Leo planned, to continue our troubadouring into the New Year.

"We can't go back now," he said.

"We can't go on forever," I replied aimlessly. "Will Glinda come?"

"Sure. We've been getting on like a house on fire."

"You'd be better off if I didn't come."

"No, Si. Your solitariness is just the spark we need."

Out of an unappreciated sense of obligation to friends and followers we were destined to mount some sort of performance for New Year's Eve. The evening, it turned out, was piquant, gaudily mauve and odoriferous. I saw Effie in the garden, moving round a flowerbed in half-hearted waltz, and she came up to me.

"Don't worry, Si. Leo's not serious about all this romance. I know him really."

"That's what I should be telling you. Is that true?"

She was on the verge of tears. Her pallor had resisted the sun's boldest threats. "He's a bore about it, that's all. He wants to be a sad pierrot. Isn't that silly for someone who's six foot three and obsessed with his prick."

"How well you know him."

"Better than you. You actually believe in Leo. But he'll always come back to me. Only it's more of a strain each time."

"Will he get away eventually?"

"You think he can fly. That's why you like him."

I had never talked to Effie before.

"I wish you could help me. But you're too airy-fairy about Leo. I was his first failure. His strongest vision. No one else can ever be that. So he'll always come back." She was partly gloating. "He knows all this. He's wiser than you are." Her face was transfigured with slack understanding.

"I don't believe in happiness for myself. But for some people."

She made a tipsy arabesque, a sort of kick against the way things did, inevitably, fall back.

Mark, acting as stage-manager, signalled us and wished us good luck. The lights went out. Glinda, on stage, yanked the thick curtains apart and gave the hellish scream which set the piece in motion. Our performances flowered into mad impromptu unleashings of bravura, and when it was interval the small audience was heard to snort approvingly.

We actors sat at the top of the garden taking the air. Leo poured huge gins for himself and Glinda, rolled a cigarette and beckoned her to stroll about with him. Effie and I looked queerly at each other. Leo was unusually determined and now led Glinda, by the hand, towards a dense grove of rose bushes.

"Do you remember we started off like this at that party after the revue? Remember?"

Leo was certainly projecting.

"Yes."

"Well, we did split up and now we're back together.

It was the inevitable thing. Now it's time to get down to the nitty-gritty."

She stepped ahead of him, crunching over the leaves. "Speak for yourself."

"Stop fighting me, Glinda. I want you to come touring with me and Si."

"I'm sorry, Leo. I can't."

"What are you talking about?" he screamed at her. "Fucking Christ."

"Calm down. Have you always had your way before? Is that why you set such a store on having me. Well, you can't."

"Bitch. Stop it. You've got something extraordinary about you."

"And I want to keep it."

We heard their voices on the air, but saw nothing.

"And Leo, I'm not interested in other people's fantasies. I want to preserve myself."

He was tugging at a rose bush. I nudged Effie to get up. She walked forward towards him ever so slowly and quietly.

Leo said, "I do love you." I don't know who to.

"It's all stage fright," Glinda finished roundly and came romping down the hill with a rose she'd souvenired. "We're running late," she said.

Effie was beside a rose bush. Leo passed her without commenting; she came along behind him meekly.

We stand on stage and bow once before the languid applause. Then Glinda steps forward for her special finale:

Plays, like everything, must come to end;
To cope — my help as Epilogue and Friend.
Our boys and girls pile dead on stage,
Today such nihilism's all the rage,

Which would show a metaphysical bent,
Like the *Atheist's Tragedy* or *The Malcontent.*
But what a balls-up here! Who t'invoke
When revengers are revenged and all such a joke?
Hamlet tho' messy at least had his words,
Here all is cliche, tricksy and absurd.
True, nothing new in the sun — so what?
Why go on saying this same old twat?
Okay, let's give these kids a chance,
But I prefer guts to a dandy's dance.
Simon is pretty and Leo is sweet,
If stagey, if cagey, if squashily effete.
Simon will posture and revel and bow
In the red satin cloak of holier-than-thou.
Leo will tumble and tap for his honey,
Retailing jokes he thinks are funny.
If an eye offends, they'll pluck it out,
If a leg — off! — sure cure for gout —
An arm is boring — where's that axe?
Or their heads — off! — they fuck up sex.
And groin goes and belly and heart,
But fiercely they cling to one last part,
For they love their souls, their own basic bit,
Which never palls, never becomes shit.
They flirt with the Void, murky and fun,
But spurn in fear that bottom-most rung,
And as long as they shirk that heroic line,
It's Happy New Years till the end of time.
For which I have one resolution to give,
Eat, Drink, Be Merry — tomorrow you LIVE!

After a quizzical pause they clap again. Glinda
seemed to have snatched victory once more, and shot
off swiftly in the last of the year's moonlight to some
circus celebration. And the audience was gone too, to
its parties. Chairs and the green curtain remained.

Leo shuffled shyly towards the front row where his bag was and where Effie sat.

"Come on," he said to her cursorily.

They kissed and took each other's hands; I joined them, grinning stupidly.

"Yeah yeah yeah. I know," said Leo to pre-empt any commentary.

"It's been fun, though."

Effie cuddled up to Leo in the back seat — dreaming perhaps of babies and houses — and we drove to a party.

"We'll have to spring clean your place when we get back to town, Leo."

We stayed awake long enough to see the New Year in. We managed it by dancing and dancing, round and round, in circles and circles. At midnight a fireworks of gay cries exploded, passion, beery foam and a girl arcing round with tearful eyes. There was a bonfire and people danced round its flames with their arms criss-crossed.

"Happy Days! Happy Days!"

Effie melted against me when we kissed, to say that she and Leo would return to Adelaide the next afternoon.

"That's fabulous."

We danced together, a ludicrous drunken gesturing dance, imagining ourselves to be archangelic visitations in the firelight. I disengaged myself from the circle finally and as I walked away looked back only once at Leo and Effie in the ring — long enough to realize that all his excursions were described about her centre. She had a grip on things. The lawn and the house were tattered with faint light. I was fumbling on the floor of my car for my keys. Could I prevent the annual melancholia? I drove riotously to the Bluff, the high cliff at the far end of the curve, solid granite and solidly black by night.

Even finding the track was difficult once you left the main road. I careered over gaping potholes and into stoney embankments disguised as grass. Coming across the shoulder of the hill that took me to the top I stunned a couple of rabbits with my spotlights. They sat blinking in stupefaction before recalling that they should flee such an invader. I parked at the very outermost point of the Bluff, as close to the steep drop as I dared to go. The car radio was on loud and I could listen to it as I staggered about. My eyes hadn't adjusted to the dark and I stumbled constantly. Below there was a neat sandy cove where sizeable breakers rolled in white bars. I was too frightened to clamber down in the dark because I'd been menaced by a wild dog in a similar night-time cove once in childhood. So I sat on top of my car roof to be even higher up and I felt through the car's body the radio's music and the string of New Year messages relayed by the disc jockeys from one listener to another. They announced that the missing girl from Christie's Beach had been found in a metropolitan caravan park and was selling her story to the *News* . Truthfully it was a relief to be apart from the adventures of the past weeks. They'd unravelled themselves pretty predictably. I knew as well as anyone that there was no choice for Leo but to return. I should've been doing the same. I endeavoured to clear my head on the Bluff so I could regard the twinkles of Victor Harbour without being drawn compulsively to metaphor making. The night was so compatible that you could simply forget the element you were immersed in. I had one hand on my head and one hand between my legs. We beat on and we beat off. Before I knew it the light was coming up all the way across the sea from the South Pole, sheening the leaden water and quite dissolving the corporeality of the sky. The shadowed rocks began to warm up and bake.

Clambering downward before the freaks of half-light had dispersed I fell and scratched myself, clutching at weeds. I wandered for hours round the rocks and pools and in the shallows, until the sun was properly high and I could strip. Searching the shore is the most unformed activity and summons you back to your earliest years. At the same time, being without intent, it is the simplest, most graceful picture of a future. I picked over crabs and shells and debris. I waded to my thighs. I went around the point and discovered another bay, not as nice and sadly under the way of development.

Coming back, much later, I noticed the fresh sand of the little cove was spattered with more feet than mine. I looked out to sea and discovered a boy on a surfboard paddling out. When he stood up on his first ride I realized that he was the health-food surfer, some time barman, that I had been staying with. I didn't wave. This must be the location he'd told me of secretly, for his wondrous surfing film. His teeth had tinked like piano keys against his charred skin and strangely blurred eyes. Yet the sign on the cliff-top read, "This Inviting Ocean Is Notorious For Drownings". I sat on a rock to admire this seeker of perfect rides.

He paddled out very far where most of the smaller swells were barely formed, out where the sharks cruised. The ride shorewards was of remarkable duration and he smiled blissfully at the end in gratitude. I fell rhapsodically into thought, the wide blue space before me. Although we've never conquered the inland I felt all at once that this new land of ours had been exhausted after all. I should forsake this island and sail across seas, so I could re-imagine our upside-down country as an infant's past paradise where things awful and lovely would be remembered in their first brightness and held in balance. And one could go on, forever, skipping and striding, limping and waltzing, making trails around things. Yet every time the beings of the green fields will turn out to have escaped. Perhaps it's the blue and the light only that's paradisal, leaving the reachable boy on his board quite out of it; only a flicker of a haze the thing you can't forget.

It would be unfair to canonize Leo, to cast him in bronze like the Gallipoli hero in each country town. That would be to fix the stained water running in circles and surges through his veins. And greenness needs, when all is said and done, that careless wanton spraying of his sprinkler heart.

I started into action. I'd left the car radio on and, accidentally, the car lights too. The battery would be low. Everything depended on the first try.

Mohsen Ben Dris

Mohsen Ben Dris was sent to Oxford because more education was available there than anywhere else, and he was allotted a room in the suburbs with Mr and Mrs Neape. Life in England was mysterious and free and Mohsen had looked forward to it passionately. Immediately on arrival he had bought jeans, a tight leather jacket and a blow-dryer for his hair, and he was not disappointed. The cars, the crowds, the women on bicycles, the shoppers in queues were if anything more fantastic than he'd heard. Only his language let him down. He could never speak in time and hadn't managed to meet anyone except a smooth Tunisian at the Polytechnic and a girl who offered him Christian comfort. Whenever he made a joke to a perky shopgirl she would freeze more snappily than a well brought up Moslem. After thrilling to the streets poor Mohsen would have to walk back lonely and unrequited to the Neapes.

Mr and Mrs Neape laughed a lot and lamented a lot, but were nicely unsuspicious. Mr Neape sat guarding the television mostly while his wife prepared her abundance of awful food. Mohsen's room was upstairs at the back and he liked to get away, even when obliged to spend hours in a quiet agony of metallurgical study.

Then sometimes his legs would disobey, would stretch and twist under the desk and cramps would seize his thighs. His body protested for want of use and to calm down Mohsen would have to pace the room, hand on crotch, swearing in Arabic. Luckily the room had a large window which opened onto the flat iron roof of the kitchen, Mohsen's "balcony", and on these occasions he could climb out to the cold air. Surveying the house-tops he felt better.

Worst of all were afternoons when he heard football noises from the field a block away. The shouting and raw cheers made him long for activity. But he observed the unaccustomed green of the grass and resigned himself, returning again to his book and its puzzles.

On Saturday afternoons he would wash his hair and blow it dry with the machine. Then he trimmed and shaped his moustache as his father had done, and afterwards he would dress in his tightest newest clothes, kept specially clean for Saturday, until at last filled with a pretense of well-being he could resume his desk and his day-dreams.

When evening came Mrs Neape would knock and ask if he'd be eating in and whether he wanted to watch the television with her and her husband. And their dog, an unclean beast Mohsen recoiled from touching. But on Saturdays he liked to eat a hamburger in town, go to the cinema, drink beer in the pub, and stagger back fuzzy, so he told Mrs Neape he was going out with a friend.

Only when spring came and less dark was he happier. After washing his hair he would climb out the window onto the balcony and sit in the polleny sunlight. He would buy a bunch of grapes to remind him of home, and although they were always sour and from

Spain, he would eat them and remember his Egyptian friends, lounging in the streets, day in and out.

That was when he first noticed the neighbours' garden. Their house was one of a row in the street round the corner and adjoined the Neapes' yard at the side. From his vantage point Mohsen could see the lines of baby lettuces, the rippling tendrils of marrow, and there, lumbering along the path, two tortoises. They were just waking out of their sluggishness, looking like camouflaged army helmets, waiting for an engagement. Mohsen grinned, threw down a grape and missed the target.

He was about to aim another when a man came out of the house and walked magisterially to the end of the path where the tortoises were. The man, short and big, did not see Mohsen, who was still grinning above. The man belched, then turned round and stomped back up the path. Mohsen could at last appreciate how weirdly futile to an outsider is the life of a neighbour. After a few minutes he threw another grape and hit the larger of the two tortoises. The protruded head swayed and rose. It extended itself further and then finally drew in. Mohsen continued to bombard it with grapes but the animal was entirely stone-like.

"They don't like grapes," called a shrill woman, emerging from a shed hidden from Mohsen's view by the fence. She looked up at him, beamed and put one leg forward. "They only like my nice lettuces." Then she tossed her blonde hair and careered up the path inside. Mohsen registered her as the unlikely wife.

◆◆◆

That week at the post office Dulcie Bond saw Mrs Neape, who was posting a letter to Egypt for Mohsen. When she'd gone, Dulcie said to the postmistress:

"The Neapes have got a new lodger."

"That's right. He's a foreign boy."

"He's a lovely looking boy too," said Dulcie, upon which the postmistress asked how her husband John was. "Same as ever, thanks."

"My son saw him at the pub the other night. They had a few together apparently.

"That'd be right." Dulcie tossed her head. She wasn't a woman to be drawn into other women's charities.

When the warm weather came in the next Saturday, Mohsen spent the afternoon on the balcony and then walked into town dressed up, wanting something. He lingered about the cafe and the ice cream shop trying to talk to the girls working there, but ended up in the pub swallowing many pints of beer. He had a corner from which he could stare at the young women with their low light summer armour and their strange done hair. One girl, when he was buying a drink, almost slid her body into his. When she turned and saw him she squealed and apologized giggling. But Mohsen didn't care if she'd mistaken him. He took hold of her arm. All at once she was shoved out of the way and her boy-friend was dragging Mohsen outside. He turned out to be an Arab too, which made the insult worse, and he treated Mohsen to a wash of rank fetid abuse in the mother-tongue. Then, laughing proudly to impress the girl, the boyfriend clapped Mohsen on the shoulder and left him, out in the street against a wall.

Mohsen didn't recover. He simply didn't bother to remind himself where he was and he stumbled home bewitched by the paring of a moon. When he got to his bedroom, he lay on the bed spinning almost unconscious with the jasmine his memory was inhaling. For hours.

In the end he only wanted to urinate. He opened the window but again seeing the crescent moon was drawn outside to the warm-cool air. From the balcony he directed his piss over the kitchen roof onto the blackberries that tangled the fence dividing the Neapes' yard from the Bonds'. A peaceful draining feeling overcame him. He could have been on a roof-top in his own country, under the moon, giving way to the fantasies of the blood that rise from horse manure, dust and perfume. When he had finished he let his cock lie in his hand and soon it hardened. With the unbound desire of an exiled warrior he started to fuck the sky. He manipulated himself slowly and royally until the trees too started to shudder at his pleasure. Then he heard a window-sash scrape and saw opposite through the curtains in the neighbours' upper room a vague pale shape and a movement, slow, blurred, in time with his own. And when finally he sprayed into the night, bent double by the power of it, he was aware that the globose shape too had shuddered in a sudden jerking series of spasms. Then, before shame and the here-and-now could claim him, he groped his way back through the window to sleep.

◆ ◆ ◆

The next night was Sunday. He had seen the woman's husband parading in the garden, in the morning moving tentatively and painfully as if hung over (like Mohsen) and in the dusk as if preparing for a proprietary evening ahead, of home-grown vegetables and conjugal rights. Mohsen waited until one in the morning and stepped out onto the balcony once more. There was no response from the neighbours' window and Mohsen felt too chilly and foolish to take on the sky.

The next night again nothing so he decided to wait.

As before he spent the following Saturday afternoon lolling on the balcony, drying his hair in the sun and watching for signs of response from across the fence. Then he went out and passed the evening quietly, having only a few drinks to prime him for his nocturnal mission. He was home well before midnight and stretched out on his bed in the dark, to welcome his dreams of love and to wait. At a late hour he climbed out through the window and stood naked facing towards the neighbours' house. He gave one low whistle and presently the curtains parted opposite, the window was raised, and blonde Dulcie Bond stood there lifting her nightdress. Across the fifty feet tract of vegetable garden they each started to act love, in rhythm, patiently and tenderly. Coming, coming, the moon itself bobbing. When finally it was over they blew kisses and spright-like tiptoed to sleep.

The third Saturday Mohsen prepared himself once again and after closing time, as he made his way home, he passed the male neighbour on the hill. The man staggered along, with one breath exhaling a song fragment, the next forcing sour vapours from his belly. At one stage he slumped around a lamp-post. Mohsen smiled to see his rival so thoroughly incapacitated.

After midnight Mohsen appeared on the balcony as usual, already erect in eager anticipation. Dulcie soon came to the window and instead of commencing their rite, she gestured that he should climb the fence and meet her in the garden — for the real thing, she made clear with her fingers.

Mohsen didn't hesitate. Stealthily he climbed down from the kitchen roof and with the utmost erotic delicacy began to negotiate the blackberries and the galvanized iron fence, so as not to damage his bare skin.

He landed with a plop in the lettuce-bed.

At precisely this point a click was heard in the back porch where Mohsen had expected Dulcie and a sheet of light was thrown out over him. He curled up to hide his naked body and blinked at the brightness. She was standing in the doorway in a posture of triumph, clutching her robe about her. She shouted:

"John! John! Help! Come quickly! There's someone in the garden."

And her cackles were half screams, half shrieking laughter.

Mohsen boggled at the traitress.

But no one stirred in Dulcie Bond's house. Her husband had been rendered inert by his evening's carousing.

Mohsen dashed forward in rage, grabbed Dulcie who had given up yelling, pushed her down onto the lettuce patch and opened her robe. It was his first touch of other flesh for months, his first touch ever of English flesh, and he was welcomed into her easily, despite herself. It was delicious. The woman was sweet, like the milk and rice pudding he loved at home, *mohalabeyah* , moist to the squeeze and warm as blood. In the full greed of desire he bolted through it and in a quick minute was finished, gone.

Poor Dulcie sprawled. She *had* put up resistance, her body stiff as a shield to protect the lettuces. But the earth beneath her shoulders and the hot air had couched her for him. In her own kitchen she would have wiped down the smelly smear on his skin, but his moustache was as brisk as a new scouring brush and his tongue was . . . marvellous. She smoothed her dirt-spangled hair. She feared that she'd been seen but worse was the fear that John would discover the wrecked lettuces: she would sneak out of bed before him in the morning and make a giant Sunday salad with all the bruised leaves.

And the one person who *did* see the affair trembled. Old Mrs Neape, sleepless, looked down from her window. Dim of eyesight, she had seen a strange monstrous beast, pale, many-limbed, convulsive, disporting itself in her neighbours' garden. She took it for a diabolic visitation and felt her way feverishly back to bed — to pray. Hell had opened between the Bonds' lettuce rows and worse might happen if East Oxford were not soon put to the purging.

Cafe Children

In passing, in Oxford. The cafe has six round tables with three chairs each, the chair-backs curved. The table-legs flower into ornamental fronds. The patterns might be prison bars. In the first window a birdy girl faces a man with a patch over an eye. His fork circles towards the Black Forest gateau and sounds out its sponginess before crushing it. I am on the first cup of coffee, waiting for the boy.

The man beside me has street clothes that look like a uniform. He's waiting too. His swarthy face, the hairs curling out of his collar, his convex belly match the easy placidity with which he waits, snapping at ten minute intervals for more coffee. His date is crucial. What is his chance? If I capture him in the mirror opposite I can make him seem to be eyeing me off. Otherwise he's looking to the four tumble-locked girls at the second window table. They're nestled in clothes and bags. Paper beige, a mustard and the pale green of celery are the colours of the year. They will be swirling together in decor displays throughout the fashionable West. I know, I've been there. That's why I want to read my neighbour's keys as some sort of codified cravenness. In fact they're lying quietly in his palm.

Each one is numbered and probably opens an ordinary door. Feeling a tiny bit desperate he goes to the jukebox now. *I tried to fight her but I tried to fight her but I can't resist her never knew how much I missed her.* The girls have begun a timely giggle. An Arab boy has taken up the wall table and cocked his head. *Sorrow.* He would give them all head. The whippy waitress moves in. She's humming.

I am on my second cup of coffee, waiting for my friend. He has been at the hospital for over an hour, one of the last hours before we finally wear the hole through things. He is going back to Los Angeles. I've been *there* in my time too and know all about *that* . The door opens and lets in a young man who could be anyone's lover. He has a great bunch of chrysanthemums which crowd his face until he reveals it suddenly, smiling, and gives the waitress the flowers. She's foreign.

"*Moi,*" he says as she squeezes the flowers.

"*Merci, merci monsieur,*" she says, "*pas mal, pas mal.*"

It emerges that the flowers are for the tables and the man is for the cigarette machine. He unlocks the front where stacks of packets sit in anticipation. They'll become chain smokes. With a rat-a-tat-tat the coins shoot into the money bag. The waitress figures I am to be pitied and brings to my table a vase with one yellow flower that grins. The Arab boy gets three big red ones which cause him to mutter. His noises mock the insipid giggling of the window girls who he is threading through his Phoenician curls. An elipse-shaped woman slides past outside, looking as if she's towed.

The patch-eyed man and his girl are leaving, and jostle my friend in the doorway. Here he is. Through at last.

"Sorry."

"I've been here so long I'm part of the place."

We get the third and fourth coffees.

"How was it?"

"I *have* got it. I can't drink or have sex."

"You chose for it to be that way."

But neither of us chose the jukebox music. Doo da doo dad dooda —

"How does it feel to be part of the world's great venereal chain?"

"It's kind of a rush. We're all part of a flower."

The aptness of the Guru's words seemes questionable. No matter where the camera might angle from we're in a cinematic frame. The dead arrangement of tables, the foot-tapping waitress. She's got to get that old da-do going.

"Just think, I'm leaving the country. I'll take this moment with me, honey. It'll be so good to be intercontinental again. I only hope I've got all my stuff."

"You left some of your blood at the hospital, didn't you?"

He nods. Some new clients upset the lassitude. The waitress has delicately slipped us the bill. We must calculate ten per cent and then split the reckoning. His face opposite me is losing its sharpness. I suspect he's using too much organic moisturizer.

"And they gave me this. Look, a special travelling venereal passport."

He had a blue date-stamped document.

"Lucky you. Love rules O.K.?"

Tunisian Nights

I

It was imperative not to dry out in the bleached North African summer. Ed, accordingly, after riding home from the embassy, had had a few drinks, had rubbed himself with sunmilk, had gone to a thorough work-out at the beach and now was showered, shaved and scrupulously dressed for the evening ahead. He took his orange Barracuda, the biggest of the Americans' cars in Tunisia, and drove indifferently to Marsha's. If he swung too wide round corners he didn't care. It would pay the locals back for laughing at him earlier. They were naive to think that pedalling along in the dust reduced him to their level. He'd had to yell at the gardener, who was dozing under the bougainvillea and hardly bothered to get up when Ed addressed him. The car had been filthy, but the old man shrugged vaguely to say it was pointless, washing a car on a hot dusty day; but for reasons of state he'd obey.

An invitation for seven had to be honoured. When Ed honked at Marsha's she hurried out. She kissed him and he jollied her waist. He found her difficult but who else was there? Yet their attachment couldn't have its

144

head. It was little more than routine for a newcomer to the diplomatic community to take up with the most likely old-hand. It made transition into the life easier and the transition had to be made, if never completely. Anyway, Marsha wouldn't have touched a local. A black career-woman nearing her prime, she hoped to look back on Tunisia as the last of her underprivileged postings. So that left Ed, who was glad of a steady companion.

The French ambassador's residence was of pink stone and he greeted them with a roseate glow to match, before they were ushered to the terrace for drinks. The lighting, cast subtly from behind creepers and statuary, gave a bloom to the company which made finer distinctions at first impossible. Yet if local wine was being served the party did not rank highly. Marsha reached for a glass of *rosé* and turned to notice the ambassador's daughter. Ed had meanwhile been convoyed by the American ambassador, as a specimen of health and vigour, to a group of Tunisian worthies. Ed chuckled naughtily with a relation of the President who asked if he found their country romantic, and he gave tips about the life to a pair of brothers going to study in Washington D.C. He was practised. No one could say anything interesting in English, their French was mere gloss, and by definition he didn't give a damn for whatever subtleties they might convey in Arabic.

"Vous aimez la Tunisie?" asked a woman hung massively with pink glitter, and in the same moment Marsha was addressed by a businessman, *"Vous aimez la Tunisie?"*

The Americans flashed wearily, *"Merveilleuse."*

When the conversation drifted to the truth about the Tunisian Left, Ed veered towards the drinks tray and a trio of French officials, led by his own well-evolved counterpart in the other embassy, surrounded him. Ed offered his hand but the man, handling a nut, evaded and instead introduced one of his companions. There was nothing to say, however, and shortly the Frenchman, put out by Ed's grinning silence, steamed away with his countryman. The third man was left and he was not, Ed realized, one of the French.

This man immediately gave voice to the conversation that had been suppressed between the two trade officials.

"The factory at Memsil-Temim is progressing satisfactorily?"

"Yeah, it's pretty impressive considering the way things get done in this country. You don't mind me speaking like that?"

"My loyalty's not to Tunisia."

The man's dark matt face seemed to combine the after-effects of too much continental high style with the sulky wounded quality Ed associated with the natives. His posture was finely and effectively statuesque. "Actually I am Italian," he went on, "but I was brought up in Tunisia. On the other hand my experiences have made me French. That is why I'm here with the ambassador."

Ed assumed at best he was only half-Italian and wanted further confirmation. "You're in the French embassy?"

"Oh yes." He reached into his admirable charcoal suit for a packet of French cigarettes.

"I didn't get your name," asked Ed.

"My name is Claudio, Mr Brady. But you must call me Claude. That's what I associate with *les americains* ."

146

Ed's mouth drew in distaste at these cosmopolitan intricacies and he bluntly ordered the man to call him Ed.

"Shall we have some more wine, Ed?"

Claudio turned and pushed behind the backs of other guests to the table of drinks. Ed assumed he was to wait while drinks were fetched. The man returned with full glasses and swept ahead down the steps into the garden, allowing Ed to follow.

"Such a beautiful evening!" said Claudio.

"You think so?" In the garden one was more than ever vulnerable to the local vegetation, gardenia, jasmine and green-black foliage.

"Are you busy with negotiations about the mouldings factory?" Claudio asked.

"Not busy exactly. No, not yet. Are you involved in it?"

"I know something about it because Memsil-Temim is my village." He beamed seraphically. "I love it very much."

Ed wondered where he was being taken.

Claudio added, as if it were in doubt, "The village is glad to be developed."

"Really. We're led to believe they don't like to change their old ways."

"You Americans have so much energy. So much power." Claudio could say it with shameless pleasure. "It frightens the old people; but it excites them also. Their imaginations are weak — easily overwhelmed."

"You talk very philosophically," snapped Ed. The chatter from the terrace descended in difficult harmonies. Fixing his eyes boyishly on the toes of his shoes, Ed speculated. "We have weak imaginations too. Beneath the sky. We are easily overwhelmed too, by

147

the magnitude of what we can get away with. We are frightened by what rebound may be working towards us."

Claudio arched his neck to stretch a muscle. "And excited?" he plausibly mocked.

From the terrace it looked to Marsha as if Ed were awkwardly engaged. The ambassador had left so there wasn't much point in staying. She came down with a slow bounce, sidling up to Ed finally and murmuring, "Do you object if I take you away from all this. I think we should be getting on."

Claudio bowed deferentially, managing with insolent slightness to imply a sense of affront which unsettled Marsha. *"Bon soir, monsieur, madame,"* he said and dashed ahead, leaving the American couple to mount the steps at their leisure. Marsha took Ed's arm and lent against him. These parties were such a disappointment.

"Who was that man?"

"Sorry — Claudio something — he's on the embassy staff, I guess."

"I thought he must be a journalist. I thought maybe he had something for you. Or vice versa."

As they crossed the pink terrace Ed and Marsha sensed the usual perfumed mystery yet again invest their evening.

"I've seen you enjoying yourselves," said their cocky host as he farewelled them, twinkling first to Marsha and then more eagerly to Ed. " *Vous aimez la Tunisie* , evidently."

They walked without speaking to the car. Ed was a disappointment too. Although she didn't need stability from him, Marsha at least wanted him to come close enough, forcefully enough to give her a good time.

After all Tunisia couldn't offer less than that.

They went downtown to a club she liked, where you could dance for hours. But Ed was lethargic and poked at his fish grilled on fennell without comment, typically suspicious of its hygiene.

"What are you thinking about tonight, Eddy? Hey? You may as well tell me. We've got all summer together."

"I'm fed up with this place. I'm sick of the murk of the place."

For a moment she tried to translate his words then gave up. "Shall we have another bottle, Ed? I know the disappointment feeling too."

He drove her home afterwards and they sat for a while in the car, talking in the air that was almost too laden to breathe.

"It smells like incense," Ed said. "I've always been allergic to incense." He lay back across the seat in a posture of piety, mocking the figurines he'd prayed before as a child.

"Getting ready for midnight mass?" joked Marsha and tickled him in the ribs.

"God knows when I went to my last confession," he said seriously.

"Only God." She leaned over and pressed his tense body against the seat.

He kissed her politely, sitting upright and avoiding her as he did so. "I really appreciate you, Marsha."

"Do you want to come in?"

"No, I better — "

As they sat ready to separate the local percussion group came prancing up the street, chanting and bash-ing. A straggling dancer struck his tambourine on the car bumper before passing into the dark. Marsha and

Ed felt parodied by the half-witted show of nocturnal fire and Ed switched on the ignition sharply.

"See you tomorrow honey," called Marsha, slamming the door.

"Night. Thanks."

His car moved strongly forward and a surge of bitter, archaic righteousness welled up in Ed. His rejection of Marsha was the shadow of a heroism which could lead to greatness. No street musician could ever appreciate his act of denial; no random tympany after midnight would ever get God on its side.

II

Ed locked his car and whistled into the huge house allotted him. On the rug was a telegram. The letters were muddled but the message was clear. "ARRIV JUL16 ROM GENOAA 19HRL OVE JUGLIAN". He stepped round the rug, blood-coloured, from his last post in Barbados, and poured himself a large nightcap at the bar. He adhered to a bedtime ritual with the utmost strictness, in fear of what might happen if he deviated. Then he climbed the stairs slowly, with the drink and the telegram, like an old monarch. He turned the light onto his double-bed, set the glass down and went into the bathroom, where his eyes peered into themselves straining bloodshot, as if that would dispel any of the flecks and spectres he was familiar with. The crumpled telegram was beside the basin. He might as well not sleep. If he slept he would only dream unrealistically of seeing Julian again. If he was awake he could at least contain his innocent pleasure.

150

Early in the morning Ed drove round to his little butcher in Sidi Bou Said. To get prime cuts it was necessary to be there before eight and he wanted to turn on a good meal for Julian.

"You're bright and early," said the secretary when he arrived at work. "You must feel as great as I do."

"Good for you."

"Aren't you going to ask me why? I've finally decided that this country is paradise."

"Sure. Is Marsha in yet?"

"No sign of her. Maybe she's feeling strung out," hinted the secretary, a fat girl called Darlene. "Hey, there was a call for you too, from a guy called Claudio. Didn't say why he was calling. Said he'd call back. Who is he? My girlfriend Gloria knows a guy called Claudio — "

"Sure, Darlene. Thanks."

From his office he telephoned Marsha to see if she was all right and to tell her about Julian's arrival. He couldn't help sounding enthusiastic. Marsha had seen Ed's slides of Barbados where Julian had stayed with him fresh from college in Australia. Ed had showed her the green photographs of their trip into the tropical heart and the bright blue photographs of their fishing expedition.

"That's great," quipped Marsha, "a nice new innocent for Carthage."

"Just what's needed," Ed blurted gleefully. There was an odd pause. "You'll have to come round and meet him, Marsha. Tomorrow," he clarified, "come tomorrow night."

"I'd like to. Right now I want to sleep. I'll come in later if I feel better. Okay, Eddy? Thanks for ringing."

"Bye." Ed felt in full sunlight anticipating Julian's

arrival. To have a straightforward companion seemed precisely the answer. Clear in his mind was the vision of Julian breast-forward to the prow of the boat, wind and sinking sun in the face as Africa rose up over the empty horizon. And he didn't want Claudio tele-phoning to re-immerse him in the murk.

By mid-afternoon the summer sky showed the first stages of relief, an intensity driven from the air by the day's sheer exhaustion, and by dusk it was pleasant to drive to the port through the pretty, ram-shackle streets of Carthage, car windows down and music blar-ing.

The new arrivals were processed individually, tediously, behind a partition. Ed could only loom impatiently round the exit gate, menacing the official there. Thus luckily he saw Julian's fair head bob over the barrier, on the third bounce calling —

"Eddy! Eddy! I forgot to get a visa! They won't let me in."

Ed grabbed at his jacket for diplomatic identification and smeared it in the official's face.

" *Mais monsieur* , oo . . ."

But Ed had pushed through and across the floor Julian fell to him. Instinctively Ed recoiled from the urgency of the boy's appeal, then their past sparked between them and he was sweeping Julian in the crook of his arm to the top official where he began a relentless thrust of bad French, offering the whole United States as security for the boy and at last getting satisfaction.

The evening had begun in earnest outside. People swarmed about in their night clothes, white robes, jasmine and curled slippers, criss-crossing the main road. The sky had revived into iridescent silver. Honk-ing, Ed guided his unwieldy car out into the traffic and overtook a taxi. The boyish driver had a flower behind his ear and Julian was enchanted. The shop signs delighted him too, in Arabic tangle, bleached like the houses on the roadside.

"It's fabulous," said the boy. "I only wish I was up to it. Ed, I feel appalling. The trip was thirty-six hours with only one coffee."

"Is that all they gave you?"

"I had no money. Ed, you've no idea. I got on the wrong train to Genoa. Well, they put me on it — some mother at the station sent me via Marseilles and I had to go all the way back to somewhere or other and change to get on the right line. My God, I had to throw myself at a German woman to beg for her lire to get onto the boat. What would've happened if you hadn't been there to meet the boat. I'd be in the army by now."

They passed an archaelogical site on the left where a row of Punic goddesses observed them, as they were themselves observed by the khaki tents of Englishmen. An evening breeze fluttered in the eucalypts that lined the road, fluffing their leaves this way and that. They reached a slope covered with the lushest vegetation and large white villas dotted in a fairy ring.

"That's my house there," Ed gestured, "the Villa D'Allegrezza."

"Really?"

III

Julian had been in the bathroom as in a bower of bliss and now he emerged, marinaded, hair tossed golden, grinning with a new coquetry at being still and safe. Ed's table was set on the balcony with a line-up of silverware and accessories and candles, which were reduced to a quivering hesitance by the wind off the sea, never so soft. An arabesque arch framed the dining area which gave itself right away over the wrought-iron railing to the disappearing succession of palms and shot-silk blue. The breed of peace was an assault, attempting to smooth the scene into nothingness. Unwilling to give a precise reaction, Julian looked hazily at Ed, who smiled officiously —

"Just sit down, Julian."

"You don't have to ask me."

When Ed left the room, Julian stopped thrilling and relaxed to re-charge himself. He would have to rise to something. Presently Ed arrived with a soufflé that had been pushed to utmost swelling.

"Will you have some now? Come on — while she's still up."

Ed sat awkwardly on a petite white chair. Julian began to let go, although experience had taught him to keep stiff until things were properly defined. He remembered that Ed had had an operation on his shoulder muscle, which left a hole. It was apparent in his way of pouring wine.

"How's your shoulder, Ed? I remember it used to give you trouble."

"All right. It's all right. I'm in good shape here."

They began to eat. The soufflé and later the slab of fillet with bernaise, and then crepes.

"I should've thought that you were just coming from France — "

"No — a fabulous meal. Fabulous."

At least chewing had made talking difficult, a rough

list of cities and names covering the two past years. Ed had explained how a rather too political connexion removed him from Barbados; and now the night was darker than the nearby bougainvillea which sucked and heaved.

"It's lonely here, though," said Ed. "As I said before, I'm glad you've come."

"I had no idea what to expect. So much has been happening. I haven't really known how anything was." Julian chuckled. "I'm tired too."

"You look tired."

"Do I?"

"I was surprised by how much you'd changed when I first saw you. But I guess that's all in the mind. I've forgotten it now. You're still the Australian college kid."

"Do you think so? It's a miracle if I am. If you can do it *and* get away with it."

Ed didn't answer. He stared somewhat bewildered around himself, knowing he was on a brink. Hovering above, in ever thinner light, was the green image he remembered. It worked like an icon, the picture of the pale pudgy boy who had stood on the bathroom mat in Barbados and turned side on with a smile inviting Ed to fraternity. But now the silence was unnaturally edged. Julian's face had gone dull as if an angle of lighting had changed. Ed placed a hand on Julian's shoulders and gave his clasp the fully mustered weight of brotherly affection. But Julian reached for his wine to fizz his lips clean, looked in fervent appeal to the sky and sea and palpitating tree, and when the pitch was wrought highest, spoke. "I'm at your mercy, Ed."

"How come," commented Ed with pleasure at this sign of Julian's engagement.

"I have no money. I have no visa. I'm tired. I'm sick. I need a rest."

"You know you can stay here," he butted in.

"But I can't — be yours. I'm too tired."

"You must be tired. Wait till you've had some sleep. We'll have a great time, going to the beach — "

"Listen, let me tell you about Paris." Julian was determined to shock this athlete of a diplomat. He knew his chances needed pity of the thickest Italian kind, and pathetic tears. In the chair he adopted the slump of a Deposition. "I went there with twenty pounds for a week — to do the galleries — and enough for a return ticket here. It was my first time on the continent. But even before then I was already near the end of the line. In the States I'd been through God knows what. Most of the scenes in San Francisco. But it never got me down. It was incredible, a crazy high. I was flying. You know, Ed, that's the thing even I don't understand. I never lost my innocence. I could always get the buzz, the rapturous feeling of a new high. And I took it here and took it there and gave it with all of me. London was more of a consolidation but I was still flying. Like I'd follow paths further there but never *out* of the scene. I buzzed in Chelsea, and here and there — Birmingham to see the pre-Raphaelites with Barry — Scotland with Roger. But I was always playing off their hang-ups. Those poor frightened fatherly guys I went for in England would never ever dream of making greedy demands. I could always handle it, play it. Then at last Paris, where I always knew I'd be."

Ed stirred to signify that he'd heard enough, that he would forgive and would try to erase the boy's experience. "Don't go on."

"Listen. It was late spring. I'd seen the waterlilies,

the Monets. The light was exquisite — quite unphysical — and I really wanted to be ethereal, you know, all calm and airy. But I couldn't ignore the people. I was in the Cafe des Flores, fabulous bar, having an expensive beer in the late afternoon. And I saw this guy — my God. Denim, leather, thick moustache. Dark eyes, firm, stocky, *so* French. We played eye games but it looked like he was going to leave it. I got up quickly and walked out past him and whispered the name of another bar. Shaking all over."

Ed was caught now by Julian's eyes, duller and inkier than before, in their bruised pouches, and his quiet humble voice revealing oracular knowledge.

"All the afternoon I cruised up and down the shops. I had to pass a lot of time so I'd get to the bar late enough. He kept stalking through my mind. When I got there he wasn't there and I guessed I'd done it all wrong. Then he appeared, literally out of shadow, all in black and eyes like — well, can you imagine black fire? There was loud North African music going. A big song in Paris now called *Été Indienne.* He was called Pierre. I went off with him like a lamb. He had an apartment just beneath Sacre Coeur, neat and old. The bedroom was hung with dark red cloths. We had a lot of whisky together and then got into bed, and on and on it went for eternity, with unbelievable pain. I kept saying, Julian, no, enough. But a woman was singing throughout. *Non, non, je ne regrette rien.* When I screamed he'd say over and over, *Ne bouche pas* . He said he wanted me to stay and be his. I knew I couldn't go further. I was shrieking. He had needles of wire which he forced through my nipples and twisted into rings. I was just muttering, *Je suis votre esclave* . Then afterwards he put my shirt on me and took me out to a party his friends were giving."

Ed said flatly, "Really?"

"When we got to the party I went straight to the loo and pulled out the wires. When I walked back into the room he knew what I'd done. He was appalled to see I'd disobeyed but I had to do it. It made him respect me as a person and we were hooked together after that. I stayed with him for ten days. He gave me everything and was so gentle. He told me stories of his life — he's a graphic designer — and talked about Piaf in that magic accent. When I told him I was leaving for Tunisia he went absolutely crazy. The awful thing was that I didn't care because I'd taken him as far as I could go. He kicked me out into the street and I sat on his doorstep. Actually I went to sleep there. In the morning the street-sweepers brushed right over me. Can you believe it? In the end he saw me off at the station, so tenderly. He begged me to come back. I was crazy for him too, and now I'm a physical wreck. You see, Ed, I've got no money and no desire left. All I ask is that I can stay for a couple of days, till some money comes through from Australia. That's my request. I put it like that because I have no choice."

When the recital broke, Julian's head crashed forward onto the glass table-top. Ed put a long arm across the boy's back.

"You can stay. I'll look after you. None of that matters."

"But I can't give you anything."

"Doesn't matter. You'll be my companion if you're here. I'll be your *esclave* for a change."

Julian picked his head up and smiled weakly. He

told Ed he had to go to sleep and thanked him, squeezing the wounded shoulder.

Ed saw the boy turn and pad down the inside corridor, a slight wiggle in his baby-fleshly hips. Ed poured himself a last long whisky. His head could not be made to spin more than it did already with the shattering of this one vestigial sweetness, and the taunting excitation he felt with it. He stumbled up to his master bedroom, which was his alone. He had no God-almighty to sweep him upwards so he curled up in the bed and lay there, crying silently in self-pity.

IV

The following days brought calm and a certain settling out. The mornings were lucid, the palms limpid and the sheet of sky fitted precisely around things. After a stage of flaccid relaxation Julian also found himself calm. He would sit quietly on the shaded terrace where Fatima the maid brought him coffee. They got on well. Fatima was always failing to subdue her private hysteria and Julian could join her in it. She'd cry "Ooo-la-la" in the kitchen and dance, making her eyes slot madly from side to side. Then she'd restrain herself and gruntingly heave a basket of laundry to the line. *"Ca va, monsieur Shoolyan,"* she'd go, *"ça va"*, with her slatternly Tunisian pronunciation.

Julian spent the mornings flicking through magazines or writing long flowery exonerating letters to his abruptly disengaged acquaintants all over the place. The mail came towards midday and was intercepted by the gardener. From the terrace Julian would hear the young postman and the old gardener gossipping and commiserating outside the hedge. Then the rusted gate would scrape open and the gardener would call obsequiously to Julian. He had no spirit left for work, only a small force of resentful dignity directed against foreigners. Whenever Julian tried to snatch a moment of relief in the garden, the old man would pounce on him, suddenly popping up from behind an orange tree muttering "Hoo hoo hoo". Then he'd go off giggling at his joke.

Today there was an air-letter from Julian's mother. She'd dutifully sent him some money which was on its way by bank transfer. It would take some time, but he could hang on in Ed's villa. They'd come to an agreement. They spent the greater part of Ed's spare time together, in which Julian created ceremonies round Ed as a way of endearing himself without intimacy. In return Ed gave Julian money, to do the shopping and keep the change. Ed wanted to give to Julian abundantly and have him overwhelmed in gratitude. Alternatively he wanted Julian to take greedily and to mock Ed with his callous indifference. But Julian was well schooled in polite, affable discretion. "I'll just treat him as another human being," Ed imagined Julian saying, which meant he would never step out of line and whatever oily fire was flickering inside wouldn't become available to warm Ed.

The man Claudio kept telephoning Ed at the office. He would ring, chat formally, ask if he could visit Ed at home or meet him for a drink at the Cafe Reine Didon; and Ed would resist, giving formal excuses — too much work, a prior engagement — which he took to be finally off-putting. But he felt oddly cornered, when no demands came from Julian, that they should come instead from Claudio. He found himself half-hoping that Claudio would telephone to ask a favour which could be imperiously denied, or even more imperiously granted. Nor were Claudio's motives clear. He'd been immediately alert to something in the man. He felt that Claudio's handsome Italianate quality had been created out of the shifty charm of a man without bearings on the make. Ed was acute about such types. If a man's innermost core was not reinforced by scruples, Ed could usually insert a detecting scalpel and probe with a surgeon's unassailable edge. But he feared to probe and feared the conclusions he was forced to draw. His skill in such matters amounted to a homing instinct for an unscrupulousness he knew to exist in himself. If his victim yielded to penetration, it was tantamount to piercing himself. When Ed suspected the worst of certain natures, he would proceed to calumniate them, as if attributing a similar corruption to himself, with all the zest of self-laceration. It was ultimately an exercise in self-contempt. But that was his job. His method of gauging the lowest to which a man would sink could be glossed as sheer diplomatic professionalism.

One exceedingly hot day Claudio rang to ask if Ed would accompany him to the beach. But Ed regretted — he had to go straight home after work. When he hung up, then, he was stopped by a fearful sense of deprivation. He saw the walls of the office, the desk with its heap of *Middle Eastern Review* s, the telephone, as so much crushing armour, impervious to the merest vibration of martyrdom. For the rest of the afternoon he was in a state of agitation, terrified by the untroubled effortless respiration of his body, rising and falling like the open sea with no rocks to break against, a knight without enemy.

When eventually he left for home he passed three youths in the street, in jeans and Columbia t-shirts with books under the arm. They might have been U.S. college kids and Ed ventured a smile. The middle youth spat at the pavement at Ed's feet and held his head up to bare his teeth in a snarling enunciation of some Arab word. Then, suddenly, as if moved by shame voided of pride, he sunk his head hard into his chest. Ed remembered that the latest aid to Israel had been announced and put the insult down to that.

Julian was waiting for him in the villa. "How's the State Department?" he asked as he went to put on the tea. "Is that guy from the French Embassy still after you, Eddy?"

"No. And he's not after me anyway."

Julian brought the tray with a plate of exquisite French biscuits. Ed sipped his tea slowly and tensely. "I only hope you're behaving yourself, Julian. People notice things in this country. All those big blank eyes are on the look-out for useful pieces of information. People know you're staying here."

Julian pushed his hand through his hair in a gesture of over-ripeness and exclaimed. "What are you throwing away your life for?" Then, "I'm going to get some more hot water. It's fabulous tea."

Ed heard him humming in the kitchen and called out masterfully. "I've asked Marsha and Darlene for tomorrow night. I hope you're going to be here. They're dying to see you."

"They're sweet girls."

"You better put on a good show."

Julian came into the hallway, into the patterned shadow of the shutters.

"You can rely on me, boy."

Ed stood. "No more tea for me. I'm going to the beach."

Ed drove to the beach and slewed his car across the fine sand of the car park. Wearing only shorts and sandals, swinging a towel, he walked through the swellings of sand. People protruded, knobbly and black, from the beach and the water. The workers who came across from downtown Tunis for the afternoon congregated at the end near the car park, where there was an enclosed concrete bar. Ed walked in the opposite direction, where the front was given over to solid beach-houses, found an empty stretch of white and sprawled freely on his towel.

In the distance he saw the efflorescence of a laughing game of football. Already the sunlight was burnished, casting over the sand an oxidized texture. Before long, as Ed expected, a boy came up the beach with beers to sell, a sweet tame animal drawn to Ed by sheer fascination. Ed bought one of his beers and sent him off. Then a pair of brothers arrived and took up a place on the sand near Ed. They began to perform acrobatics with each other, slowly and lazily, half-silhouetted in the deepening light. One did a swinging swallow-dive through the legs of the other. When their performance finished they came up to Ed hoping for something, but he gave them nothing more than a couple of coins. The only beach character who aroused Ed was an anarchist journalist who'd studied in Paris. A dumpy hairy man, he sniffed at the horizon whenever an American passed.

Something about the twin phases of the Tunisian

drama he was involved in struck Ed as futile at the beach, both the pursuit of empire and the stubbornness of freedom, when the end was the migration of all creatures alike to the water's edge. He walked out into the sea with an angry yearning for more than a sluicing frolic. He swam out further than any of the locals, where the clean water accumulated a deeper blue and the bottom couldn't be seen, let alone touched. He dived under and burst out again into the air, and gazed back at the shore hills and houses now made insubstantial. Then he lay back into the water and looked in a streaming way to the sky. He could actually deliver himself up in the sea. No submission, he imagined, could be more real than to the old suntanned One who leans down out of the sky with enormous arms and in a single movement heaves the souls of children to his chest where he licks them and devours them with his extraordinary loving mouth. The old One's chest would have the shape of the cape at the far end of La Marsa beach and the sunlight would be the saliva that smears the innocent soul, finally ingesting it quite. Ed lay back and released his weight in the floating position till he sank underwater. The inertia of his body strove to keep him there until he rolled over, somersaulted and darted back to the surface. Then he swam the fifty yards inwards in one hard dash.

As he stumbled in the low waves, through his saltwatery eyes, he saw a man approaching.

"You have come to the beach."

Claudio walked into the shallows to shake Ed's hand. Ed had not recognized him behind the sunglasses; but Claudio had demonstrated the uncanny directness of the devious person in tracking him down. He supposed that Claudio had seen his car and had covered the beach in a self-indulgent search which ended with the pleasure of meeting his object, fresh and vulnerable from the sea.

"You do not have your country's best interests at heart, Ed. You are always running away from me when I want to talk business."

"I can't imagine whose interests you're serving down here at the beach."

Ed crossed the sand, picked up his towel and shook it. He draped it round his shoulders and stood like some sort of weeping statue, drops falling off him in a shower. Claudio followed.

"I want to talk to you about Memsil-Temim. You know that is my village."

"You told me about it at the party. But what is Memsil-Temim to me?"

"Your government is building its metal-casting factory there."

"My government is not me. You can't talk to my government by talking to a man with a towel round him at the beach."

"I don't want to talk to your government. I want to talk to *you* — about your government."

"For Christ's sake."

"You see, Ed, I know from the French embassy that your government only has permission to operate one factory at Memsil-Temim. But they need a second factory. A separate assembly plant. And the Tunisian government will not allow both factories to belong to the United States. That would be too obvious. So that's why the French government is interested in who will run the other factory."

"You Tunisians are obstructionist imbeciles, you know that?"

"I told you before my sympathies are not entirely with Tunisia."

Ed frowned at so many kinds of sympathy, so many kinds of desire. "I can't talk about it now."

"When can you talk about it?"

The Tunisian was smoothing his hand over his hairless chest.

"Ring me at work."

"I've tried that."

As Ed walked back towards the crowded end of the beach, Claudio walked alongside him. Claudio moved lightly, twisting from side to side in a spiralling movement as if excessively lubricated. To distinguish himself Ed pulled his shoulders back and marched stolidly forward, eyes ahead with resolution.

Claudio had introduced the topic of the nightclub he frequented. "You should come there, Ed. It's wonderful. Come with your friend. The pretty blonde boy. I have seen him there many times."

"Which friend?"

"Monsieur Julian."

Ed turned to look into Claudio's face. The eyes continued to dance and twist, liquidly. "I don't suppose you can leave Julian alone," Ed commented sardonically.

For an instant Claudio's face softened into a terrible openness, which converted for an equally brief instant into a wounded look of offence, then as he at last grasped Ed's bluffing tone he broke into a coarse, stylish laugh. "Monsieur, you are shocking."

V

When they come from every side, waiting limply through the day till they can pounce, from overhanging trees, from creeper smothers, from a woman's phial or the tight bunch behind a man's ear, from the air or the earth itself, even the most sumptuous smells become obscene to the point of nausea. To hold a dinner party in the garden was to sink the guests in a sickly richness they couldn't escape. Ed had therefore taken great pains to ensure they wouldn't want to escape and would be entirely satisfied. Things were laid out splendidly among the vegetation in the light of paraffin flares.

Marsha came first to have a few moments alone with Ed and waltzed automatically into his arms. Ed took her and deflected her.

"Is everything under control? Anything I can do?" she asked.

But he told her that all was attended to.

"You take too much trouble," she commented. "You've been preoccupied lately."

Ed felt her offering comfort and commonsense but he wasn't tempted by her attempt to dispel his mysteries. He told her he was tired out by the heat. She smiled back, strengthened by his refusal to join his power to hers. When Darlene arrived, Marsha was merry.

"Cheers, Darlene. Have an olive."

At last Julian appeared fresh from his bath and provided an object of novelty. He began to entertain the party, saying that Carthage was very heaven, and Ed retired to the kitchen. The meal passed with Julian's glassy brightness never dimming and Ed was able to keep himself thoroughly absent, attending to menial diversions. In the end Julian and Marsha danced, to black soul as thick as the bechamel.

Then the gate clattered and Julian broke off dancing to investigate. Marsha stood with an air of well-founded impatience until Julian returned, pronouncing loudly that he'd got rid of the man. "What a nerve to call at a private house at midnight. He said he was a journalist as if that's any excuse."

Ed yawned and asked if it were really midnight. Marsha had lost the rhythm of the music and wondered why she was waiting for her partner to return. Ed merely said, "Are you going?" and she graciously decided she would, though her face became set to cope with Ed'd frustrating, hurtful abruptness. Darlene pinched a last artichoke heart from the bowl and thanked Ed for a superb evening. Marsha kissed him and the two girls left together.

"Was it Claudio?"

"He's coming back."

"What?"

Julian, pleased with himself, nodded that it was so and wandered off to bed. Ed was annoyed rather than surprised at Claudio's visit. There was as yet no relationship between the two of them on which it could happily rest. Still, much could be put down to Tunisian inscrutability. He folded his arms tightly to fortify himself.

"Julian," he shouted, excessively loudly because he was slightly drunk. "Why don't you stay down and wait with me?"

The night became darker and stiller than it had been. Ed was unable to get a clear line on things which seemed to buzz imperceptibly. He blinked, stretched his cheek muscles, then relaxed again into a buzzing daze. His eyes closed and straining to re-open them he felt the buzz match with the sliding still of a car outside in the gravel street. The carlights were extinguished. This time Claudio managed to open the gate noiselessly and he was over to Ed with just a slight scuffing of feet.

"Eddi, thank you for waiting," he began, the curiously stagey voice the first real presentation of himself. He sat down next to Ed on an upright chair he had to side-saddle. "May I get myself a drink?"

"No — let me."

Claudio's manner was spectacular insolence. He expected a drink as his due. Ed pulled himself up to his full American height. Claudio was dapper by contrast with Ed's shamelessly ill-fitting sports clothes. Yet Claudio's body appeared to disdain his well-cut three-piece suit. The blue shirt open at the collar bespoke raffish calculation, but the fine North African head rose right out of it. Ed stayed apart, in the doorway, columnar. "Where do you work?"

Claudio sort of tucked his head into his shoulder. "I'm in the French embassy."

"French?"

"I'm a local — " he paused before complicating his image " — *contact* for them."

"Do you have a French wife?"

"No," he said weightily, as if revealing enormities and not the fairytale explanation which came. "I married my childhood sweetheart. The daughter of my father's neighbour in Memsil-Temim. We were in love since the first days. We were married a year ago when she was seventeen."

"How nice for you. Do you live in the village still?"

"My wife has gone back to the village. And I have a flat in central Tunis," continued Claudio. "Awful —

because so lonely." He leaned back to contemplate the arabesque grandeur of the Villa D'Allegrezza. His extended swan-like neck sharpened his chin and gave him a cheap look of vulnerability. "I'm really going mad living by myself. That's why I do crazy things like visit you at midnight."

"Why did you?"

"Because you can help me. Because you can help my village."

"I'm an American."

Claudio looked darkly at Ed. His pretty pouting lips had a sinister quality to them. His mouth was fixed in a dead curl. He had his hand on Ed's thigh.

"Listen. You're building a factory at Memsil-Temim. You need an assembly line. I know the French want to run the assembly line. But the Tunisian people could also run it — if you Americans command it. My father-in-law will talk to you. He's a businessman, rich and skilful."

"And it's going to be *his* factory, is it?"

Claudio merely looked sad. "He's a good man. I've hurt him. Poor Nadia my wife. It was so difficult. I had been in Paris too long. She was a sweet Tunisian girl. We couldn't live together." He poured himself another drink. "You understand, don't you, Eddi?"

Ed didn't become even slightly tense nor did he convey any gamey excitement. "Why should I understand?" he asked with dog-like expressionlessness.

Claudio only smiled. The initiation was minute, but now suddenly was checked by a light switched on upstairs. Julian didn't appear, but called domestically from the terrace that Ed should come up soon and get some sleep.

"He's right," said Ed.

Claudio quickly made Ed promise to come to the club and talk with his father-in-law, and the two men departed, each wondering what intimate mesh Julian's deft intrusion had snipped through.

Marsha telephoned several times the next morning, looking for Ed. But she missed him both at home and at work. He was out and about making enquiries. Fatima kept answering the phone and finally in exasperation Marsha asked to speak to Julian, if he was out of bed. She wanted to leave two messages for Ed. She gushed fulsomely over the first, her thanks for the previous evening's dinner, and mentioned the second only casually. She'd discovered that the man Claudio had nothing to do with the French embassy. Nor, she told Julian, was he a journalist. He was involved with one of the groups opposed to the Tunisian president. She wanted the information passed on as soon as possible. She wanted Ed to be careful. Julian assured her he'd tell Ed that afternoon, and smiled when he hung up. Marsha would have found out from Darlene that Claudio had been pestering Ed. She was certainly efficient. But Julian was fed up with the whole business. He couldn't be bothered to leave any message for Ed. He simply picked up Ed's car keys and left the house.

The money from his mother in Australia was due at the British Bank of the Middle East and Julian looked forward at last to dispensing with his unnatural docility. He wanted to stage a coup d'etat and lord it over Ed. He drove the orange Barracuda without respect, using the horn liberally to skedaddle stoned groups of men in robes. The day was crisp, a newly washed blue. He crossed the aqueduct over the stagnant lake in rebellious Assyrian triumph and the flamingo colony flapped their pink-gold underwings to acknowledge him. When he arrived in the central hubbub he overshot a traffic light and circled too fast round the square with its mosque of French trees. In the rear-vision mirror he saw a man in a blue suit, reading a magazine, turn and behold the car with an expression of dumb worship.

But at the bank his money had not arrived. Julian swore at the teller then, to avoid deflation, proceeded to the Cafe Reine Didon, a pick-up place for foreigners where he could flirt at those walking past undecided. Across the mass of tables he saw the back of the man who'd looked up with awe as he shot the light. The man turned at that moment and lighted on Julian with the freshest morning smile. It was Claudio, who hailed him over with his *Time* magazine.

Julian shook his hand and joined him at his table.

"Why do you bother reading that shit?" sneered Julian, indicating the *Time* .

"It tells me things I need to know." Claudio, behaving very properly, offered Julian a cigarette. "You are Ed's friend?"

Julian failed to reply.

"You're driving his car?"

"You could drive it if you wanted to," said the boy meanly. "Is that why you're so interested in Ed?"

Claudio, however, answered with peculiar gravity. "I admire Ed. He's a real Uncle Sam. Big and tough and gold. Like a hero in a movie. His car is immense!" He might have been voicing an unflawed adoration of the old gods and Julian's self-serving scepticism was put out. Claudio smoothed the cover of his magazine and added, "I hate this silly backward country."

"You don't make sense." Julian believed the man was lying.

Claudio clicked his fingers in the air to order mint tea for them both. It was a flamboyant act of fraternal ingratiation and smacked of conspiracy. Besides, Julian was bored — most of all with the webs these people spun round one muddled American. He half-wished that Claudio had a chance to take Ed for what he was really worth. Then he thought.

"Claudio, I won't be at the Villa tonight. I have an appointment elsewhere. I have to leave Ed by himself."

"I see," said the Tunisian, raising his green tea, "yes, I see."

Julian drank his own tea in harmony. Having achieved Ed companionship for the evening he was free once again, his own master to seek something for himself. Claudio's and Julian's eyes shone together in admission of their identical, knowledgable positions. They shook hands firmly on parting. Julian drove back to the glamorous Carthage beaches where he had all day to find himself a genuine appointment for the night. He could seek his diversion wide, spiced by the thought of Ed alone in his villa with not even the car to burn.

VI

Ed raged at Julian's absence. The dusk had already purpled and there was no explanation, only a few half-literate notes from Fatima to say that Marsha had been ringing, and he'd had enough of Marsha. He was betrayed and abandoned and sat perched on the edge of his blood-red rug, drawn into a mooning melancholy.

When the bell rang, however, it was Claudio and Ed immediately covered himself. "I'm expecting Julian for dinner any minute. But have a drink."

"I saw him this morning in your car."

"He shouldn't have taken it. Did he say anything?"

Claudio kept sagely quiet, noticing that the American was scratched and ungroomed.

"Will you talk to my father-in-law?" he eventually proposed.

"Why not?"

Claudio suggested they go straightaway. He'd be waiting in the club.

The father-in-law was of a cut altogether different to Claudio. The old man, Ed knew at once, was honourable, wise and stubborn. Most telling of all was his disdain of Claudio, the agent he was obliged to engage in the interests of a greater end. The man would run a factory to the greatest advantage of himself and his allies; and Ed gauged that the ally closest to his heart was the Tunisian people itself. The whole plan was magnificently feasible and it was quite within Ed's scope to allot the contract to this steely old boy. And that would be, he equally saw, to undermine not merely the French interest but in the long run the Americans' own. In Ed's mind that submission — to the wily domineering plot of an Arab merchant — acquired a certain sweet nobility.

The interview was brief and at a signal from the old man Claudio rose to his feet and ushered Ed respectfully away. When they reached Ed's villa again, rather than losing his interest as Ed might have expected now that business was done, Claudio seemed more than ever intent on coming inside. Ed remembered the empty house and acquiesced, hoping the man would stay for dinner.

During the meal they began to talk about intimate details, that particular dishonest kind of intimacy which presents the tendernesses and the innocence for caressing, while suppressing into jokes the crucial savageries of the past.

"Tell me about your marriage break-up," Ed presumed.

"When I was thirteen years old my father sent me to a school in Spain. To a Catholic school so I would learn my father's religion. We had no money to pay for me in a school in Italy, but there is an order of Spanish monks in Tunis who could send me to their school in Madrid. So I left my village and went there as a small boy. Many tears, you know. But Spain was like — your whisky — to me and I studied the dancing — *flamenco* — I was very good. I was beautiful."

Ed stirred in his armchair and unbuttoned his shirt which was too tight.

"I was sixteen when I was the first young dancer of my company and we went to Paris for a visit. We were the most grand success. A man there offered me much money, his house, a school — a kind man with many connexions — forty years old. A blonde man like you, Eddi. I called him Uncle Pepi. He was in love with me. So I ran away from the *flamenco* and lived with him. For one year, for one year and a half. He was very proud of me — you imagine — made me dance at parties for his friends. One friend of his wanted to take me to America. I loved this friend. I dreamed of America. But I didn't go. Pepi discovered my infidelity and he put me in his cellar — where he keeps his wine — and locked the door. I was a prisoner. Complete darkness! For four days I think he disappeared. I screamed and cried and hit at the door. Then he returned and gave me food and water through the door. I couldn't escape when he did that because he was so strong. And hard! And cruel! For six weeks I lived there in darkness. Lived — *dead* really. I became mad. My head went mad. That was the most horrible moment. I could not understand. I was really really mad, beating my head on the wall. Truly. Then sitting without moving for hours and hours. I was terrified. I knew I would die. At the end there was silence for a long time. I knew he had left me to starve. But I could do nothing. I didn't move. I had surrendered. Until at last again, mad, I beat at the door. And it was *open!* I came out. The house was empty. I was even more terrified then, you understand, so frightened. I found food in the house, some money, my clothes, some things to sell. And I left. I returned as quickly as possible to Tunisia, to my village. I greeted my family. I told my story to no one. I still had such fear. I wanted only to be safe. After some months I married Nadia whom I had always loved. But — impossible — of course — "

The story was so far-fetched that Ed could only take it as some kind of offering. "Mother of God," he said and rose from the table as if he'd just finished an excessive meal.

"Do you desire me, Eddi?" asked Claudio in his thickest accent.

Ed laughed. "Come and see *my* wine-cellar some time. Actually I have a beautiful dessert wine in my cellar which I'll get right now, before you tell any more stories."

Ed padded down the hall, in bare feet, to the door that led downstairs. He fumbled in his pocket for the cellar key without putting the light on, because there was some light from the hall. He found the single key in his back pocket, fallen off the ring, and as he fiddled it in the lock he heard Claudio padding down after him. His hand shook but he got the door open into the dry room lined with dusty racks of bottles.

Claudio exclaimed from behind, "You have a cellar *vraiment*". Then as Ed swivelled Claudio fell to his knees and pushed his head between Ed's legs. "Will you have me, Eddi?"

Ed was thrown utterly. The key fell from his hand and he too dropped to his knees. "Claude, it's impossible."

The Tunisian peeled open Ed's shirt and grabbed at his belt. He looked up at Ed pleading ecstatically. "Please, Uncle Eddi."

But Ed, who couldn't succeed in pushing the fellow away, now succumbed helplessly to his own impulse and thrust his head at Claudio's chest, like a child to the breast, whispering. "*You. You* take me."

In the scuffling Claudio rolled Ed over on top of him so that the massive weight would push him against the dusty floor, and Ed kicked and squirmed not to have to play this role. As he struggled he kicked the door accidentally and it slammed shut, leaving them grappling in total dark, more chaotic than ever, until half undressed they were fighting hopelessly as much against one another as for.

At one point Ed tried to re-collect himself. He reached for the door key and couldn't find it. He guessed at once that the key had fallen outside the doorway. The sure Yale lock had slammed on them and they were stuck.

"There's no way out," said Ed. It was passionate stalemate. They kept fumbling, each striving energetically for the position of passivity, disowning so entirely the desire to master. They were trapped in the dark cellar and finally they wearied themselves out, arriving at unfulfilled exhaustion as a welcome balm. Stark naked, almost yet not quite in each other's arms, they lay side by side on a bed of their discarded clothes, sleeping soundly beyond dawn like celibate brothers.

VII

The morning was bright and soft, full of the perfection that makes July the North African month for good health. The gardener arrived at seven o'clock singing. He started his day's work, first watering certain shrubs, then sweeping the leaves, singing as he pushed the broom with a mild swing down the side of the house. Heaped up around the cellar skylight there were lots of leaves and bits of flyaway garbage. He had to take care clearing them away and he bent down to uncover the slanted barred glass that looked through to below. The window was dirty but he could see, and when he did his face burst into the hugest yellow grin. He dropped his broom and shook, rooted to the spot in unabashed frenzy. The old bloodshot eyes rolled in his head for Allah. When his fit passed he peered again at the two bare forms of his master and his man, laughed again and hurried off with his broom, letting the gathered leaves fly, to celebrate his personal holiday. He squatted on the dirt under the orange tree with one arm slung round his friendly Punic statue and the other scratching his head with sheer contentment as he smiled.

Fatima arrived at eight and saw him grinning in the shade. She took no notice. She knew he was mad and loved him. For his part he greeted her but kept his secret, trusting it would out in its own fine way. When Fatima entered the Villa, with her ordinary grumbling sense of work to be done, she was thrown into despair, all too unfair this sunny morning. Three rooms were in a scattered chaos — like Pompei caught in the act. She shook her head and cursed roundly. Then she too began to sing, only a little less wildly than the gardener.

She didn't realize there was no one upstairs. Though her master would have been at work, Julian should have been sleeping late. She jumped when he walked through the front door at half-past ten.

"Oo, Monsieur Shoolyan," she cried, pointing at the mess. Julian recognized a familiar suitcoat on the back of a chair, with a *Time* magazine folded into one pocket. He giggled and grinned radiantly at Fatima. From the garden they could both hear the gardener chanting to himself like a parrot.

Julian asked Fatima to bring him coffee on the terrace. He was content at last with Tunisia, but tired. He'd had, in one brief excursion into the studded maze of Arabic dark, his thousand and one nights' worth. Now the peace of the day struck him, the hot still air the most comforting blanket, saturated with the dry muted scents of fruit and flowers, the loony gardener beaming as he crouched in the bushes, the facade of Villa D'Allegrezza heavenly white. A rare silence was achieved then, for Julian through his own exertions, for Fatima in her humdrum work, for the gardener in smiling, all other noise far away over the housetops . . . .

When a woman's shriek of revelation, as if the sky had opened —

"Monsieur Shoolyan, Monsieur Shoolyan, oo-lala!" Fatima came crying. She tugged at his arm and floated him inside to the top of the cellar stairs. She pointed down where she'd been to fetch a broom, darting at her discovery. The two naked men had stirred at the intrusion and now blinked in bewilderment from their sleep of impasse.

Julian gasped, "Oh Ed, what on earth!"

"We got ourselves locked in," he said curtly.

Claudio could only make a careless disarrayed mumble.

Then Fatima's embarrassment overcame her and she whirled outside into the waiting arms of the gardener who could now share the joke. Whereupon the two of them danced in a spin with their throats back to the sun in gushing mirth, until the trees revolved with leaves flapping and oranges abob.

Then into the midst came Marsha. She wondered why Ed wasn't at the office and arrived in a hurry, slamming the gate and dashing up the steps, called ahead, "Anyone home?" When she encountered the three men in the hallway, two of them half nude and staggering, she pulled herself up in unimpeachable affront. "I knew I'd be too late."

Ed gave a devastated smirk and began a long extemporization, as freely as Fatima laughed.

For one dead second Marsha looked to the others for confirmation of indictment. Julian's eye caught Claudio's but Claudio remained mute, fearing the insertion of larger issues. Then Julian stepped forward and spoke. "We've seen the divine mockery of the Tunisian night. I defer to that." He went on, weaving Ed's patchy story into a dazzling and impenetrable garment of chainmail.

Marsha grew angry as she saw the truth eluding her. "I tried to warn you, Ed. I was worried for you." Yet she was spun about by the incessant giggling of Fatima and the gardener. "There'll be an investigation. There are things at stake," she affirmed. But her judgment had foundered on the shifty sand of Ed and might miss altogether if she took on these latest, wretchedly fantastic developments. "Speak Ed."

He felt like a petty martyr and yet didn't care if he was consigned to a traitor's Sahara. He agreed. Things were at stake.

Then Fatima flew into the circle of puzzlement. "OO-LA-LA," she cooed finally, joyous as a bird.

The Possession of Amber

for Jan Dalley

I

"Certainly, dear. If you're sure you can cope — "

"I've lived here after all."

"That doesn't stop it being a foreign country," said the lady tour-leader and prodded Jennifer's stomach affirmatively. "But right you are — " Her other charges, staring, were awaiting the sign for dinner.

Jennifer shook out her scarf and draped her shoulders. Now, anyway, she'd told the old nugget. She'd be off for forty-eight hours, free of the whole business, not least the fear that among the others in the party she'd found her rightful place.

In the morning she caught the train to Alexandria, first class with carpet up the walls, and took a room in the Hotel Cecil where she worried the clerk and supposed, from the looks of others, that she was behaving oddly. But it was natural to be in a state until things were properly taken in.

First was the balcony view. The porter opened the shutters and left the curtains hanging, but only when unpacked was she disencumbered enough to slip through the curtains and behold the harbour. She could

182

breathe there before the sea and sky; life's continuance, the crazy dry-skin palms, a monkey man who amused, tenements and mountainous billboard lovers; all making do. How bravely the city tried to remain substantial! She laughed aloud briefly, clutched her scarf, sunglasses, handbag, documents, and went down to the street.

As if foreign to their interiors she idled through some of the antique shops, the dusty glittering merchandise piled up, enshrined. She tried to imagine, as if from outside, the mystery of these clearing-houses, the circle to which had been consigned countless souls' most cherished objects. She fingered jewellery without interest and paused only over an amber brooch in a squirming silver setting, and in one shop an exquisite icon split down the middle to leave half a face and one black eye.

Plenty of time.

Amber was fascinating because no one knew where it came from. She fancied a chain of the dull orange pieces round her neck.

Keeping aimless she wandered and came quite by accident upon a small and appealing gem shop. A government certificate in the window declared it *bonafide* , but nothing was on display. She entered and asked the old man to show her some amber. He moved slowly, as if he had an arthritic condition and all day to spare. Jennifer endeavoured to relax while he fetched his trays of stones — with a caution verging on torpor. Eventually, shaking his wrist gracefully, he lifted a glass lid and revealed to the air little heaped rows of amber.

"Beautiful," she whispered but wouldn't touch them, the little orange eyes dully radiant. The proprietor bobbed gleefully behind the counter, watching Jennifer. Then suddenly with violence she pushed the tray aside and leant back to her full height, addressing him quickly, "Thank you, I only wanted to look. They're lovely, lovely. You're very kind. I'm sorry for putting you to so much trouble, I only wanted to look. Thank you, goodbye. Bye."

She trembled to be out in the light and knew she couldn't continue her disconnected pretence further. She must acknowledge her mission and set off.

The proprietor, who had seen madness in many guises, picked up an orange piece and held it to his eye. Did the light come out of the stone or did you see through it? Even his father had never ventured to tell him.

II

She didn't need a map in this city although it was fully ten years since "that incident in Alexandria", as the family called it. She could still remember leaving England and flying out to Cairo from school much too early for the Christmas break, her secret bouncing within her like a hydrogen balloon, its buoyancy almost tugging her cloudwards. And she still acknowledged now indistinguishable from pain her other innerest memory, never yet shared, the bliss having turned to bitterness, that love by which she the unformed maiden had been fused with the raw other, still unshakeable shadow; changed into a being impossible.

She remembered her mother's fierce take-over. On the balcony, with a sip of gin and a glance across the fingernail minarets, her mother had spoken frankly, "You have sinned, my darling. You must pray for forgiveness. We shall take it upon ourselves to make sure you have a second chance."

From that day she'd been impotent before her mother, and her step-father who mounted guard distastefully for the remaining months. Her second chance began in March, in a limpid enervating Easter season. She'd driven with her mother to Alexandria where they were installed in the Cecil until, according to advance arrangements, she could be committed to the nuns. The baby was born without trouble. She saw its — her — bulging eyes turn to ginger-hazel during the brief feeding she was allowed and she liked to think she had guided its first, quaintly ironic broaching of the world. Then it had been taken away. The nuns escorted her from her bed in the Ospedale to the church, where they prayed for her interminably then led her back mute through the sharp spring sunlight to the Cecil, brazen as ever in its frontage of the balmy port. She had recuperated and returned with her mother to Cairo where she spent the next month as she'd spent the previous five. In the end they were all glad to see her return to school, fit for the summer term, her slate by and large clean.

She had vowed to come back but had never given way. At last, under the guise of a Middle Eastern Swan's Tour, she had allowed her will to surface and encountered all of a sudden a force as strong as her mother driving her across the desert. She would look and see the hospital, that hateful shell, and be free. The street was marked Sharia El Hurreya. She couldn't stop herself walking northwards and upwards and at the top she turned to see the place. She stared bravely without bothering to cross, watchful for transformations in the building or herself. She saw that the face was dead, yellow powdery skin flaking off its flat poise. The high iron fence, a Byzantine neckband, needed paint and the tree, like an off-centre neck supporting the place, was thin and grey. The untended shrubbery had been given over to a terrible lush rustiness. A meek gardener was pushing an old mower at the bare lawn. In the upper storey two windows, like eye sockets, had their shutters open. Jennifer saw a pyjamaed figure in the dark of one, unfortunate under cure, and smoke came from the chimney above. Evidently the place still functioned. A new wax-like statue of the Madonna smiled from her niche and Jennifer felt denied. She was able to look back with blank calm, sensing no exorcism. Her superstition had come to nothing.

She walked back to the main square and took a coffee in that decent cafe she hadn't forgotten. Drinking the gritty syrup she puzzled over her lack of reaction, partly believed that nothing had happened. An abrupt hubbub broke out in the square and she was happy to be meditative and separate from it behind the cafe's grimy glass. As she drank, an indifference to inside as to outside spread through her body like a narcotic tingle and she decided to welcome her fresh fearlessness by venturing a second coffee and an exquisite cake from the Nubian waiter. Nor did he remember her.

In the hour before dark she bought, from the square, roses of that sick Venetian yellow the church uses for its optimistic festivals and continued her tour of duty. Her memory pulled her along its jagged route to St Catherine's, honeycomb without and within gloomily cubicular. Jennifer shuffled to a front pew and squeezed in between two hunched devotees. In her heart she called her stolen child Hope, because that along with Happiness had been taken from her. She bent forward to lay her roses, vaseless, on the altar steps. It was harder this time. Her eyes, unnaturally bright, teetered between tears and desiccation. Across the circle of ten years the source of her grievance was almost within her grasp and she could hardly not anticipate a perfect purifying annulment ahead. A devotee gathered up Jennifer's roses and submitted them to arrangement. Jennifer closed her eyes strenuously over the flaming encrusted cross; then rose to leave. She lit a candle, frivolously, and once outside was swept along again, by the skirts of evening Arabs kicking up their mindless wisdom at her, her ghosts for the time laid.

III

She lay on the bed peacefully and rested. She had faced the church and the hospital with remarkable ease and now that her unhappiness was to become simply a familiar accessory, like her scarf and sunglasses, now that she was divorced from the struggle with missing life, how much easier things would get. No more odd-ness, no more awkwardness. She brought to mind her marriage, as if to ditch that overboard while she was about it. It would never have happened if only — After "that incident in Alexandria" she'd been a dutiful daughter. At school and university she'd managed well enough to become a professional translator and, to her step-father's relief, had married a young man in the foreign service. The marriage had worked, the first posting an excitement, Jennifer "hauntedly beautiful"

always in demand. But throughout she couldn't relin-
quish hold over her loss and this had confused her. Her
sadness became muddled, incomprehensible, embarrassing sometimes. Then she learnt to appear composed as
if in a dark silver light. She and Richard never had any
children of course and after five years, because of irri-
tation, imperfection, loneliness, their connection
ended. Half-dozing, she found nothing of the marriage
to remain.

She wanted to sleep now but couldn't. Nor could she
sit or read. She wondered whether she should buy herself an amber necklace as a reward. Some sort of obligation nagged at her, an unvoiced arrangement. The
sheer foreignness of the city was calling her out. Her
ritual seemed not *yet* over. One bead did remain unsaid
from the string of her life, but it seemed unfair, irrele-
vant to insist on that. Still if release was at stake, im-
palpable like the lights on the water outside —

She would be obliged to contemplate her brother. To
avoid this last she got up and went out, down to the
Corniche where the sea swarming against the concrete
wall in the semi-darkness laid to rest the idea that a life
might, hidden elsewhere, continue. In truth he was her
step-brother but had been her Brother, her twin despite
a difference in years and colouring, she dark, he the es-
sence of fair. The horrible matching of their single
parents brought them together and they'd been grafted
onto each other through an impossible series of obsta-
cles and interventions: the family's lurching moves
around the Middle East, the educational stream, the
efflorescence of prospects left, right and centre. Now
he too was gone. A year had accumulated since the
postcard from Kampala. No one ever got round to
following it up. After all he'd been out of touch for

other long periods — the eight months in Chad. He'd written a year ago that things were getting sticky and he hoped soon to be out. But the land was lordly, he said, and he couldn't imagine a greater pleasure than covering the place properly; if he stayed on he could push his activities to the far north where all sorts of types were after coffee-growing patches. He sent his love to his Sister, not knowing whether to add condolences or congratulations for the divorce. But he was certainly gone now.

Over her shoulder she heard a gentle splashing, and turned to discover two men hauling up net from a tipping boat. They were disentangling odd wriggly creatures. She shivered, shook her scarf vigorously to free all the dust, and returned for want of other to the Cecil.

Later she sat in the bar. A desultory festival outside in the square spoilt the peace and she watched as the bands of people indulged their silly games.

A fat mercantile man had nodded graciously to Jennifer from the bar counter and now he came across to ask, politely, if he might join her. He turned out to be a Libyan, exiled in Alexandria, and she accepted a drink.

"Why have you come to Alexandria?" he asked.

She hesitated over a tough-shelled pistachio.

"I've come for no reason really. I suppose I'd like to find some good amber. That's what I've been looking for today."

The man nodded. "You are alone, no?"

"My friends are in Cairo," she hedged.

"If you allow me I could take you tomorrow to a very good man for amber. An honest man. He will treat you kindly. And his amber is absolutely the best. Many years, many many years I know him."

"That's kind of you," said Jennifer. "I'd love to."

"But if you are here for pleasure," said the Libyan, "why do you not look more — happy?"

"I'm not the happy type," she claimed hastily, and explained that at the particular moment she found the pointless festivity in the square rather depressing. "Their lives are so difficult, so weary, so stupid in a way. And the causes of misery are so many. I can't bear to think of all the disappointments and all the gratuitous suffering — even going on right now outside."

"Ah, my dear lady," began the merchant benignly, "you take a too small view of things. Think again. Perhaps in that crowd in one man, in one woman, somewhere, there can be the little miracle. Do you understand? The little moment that will fill the life of the one man or the one woman. And if it only happens one time and all the rest is miserable, that does not matter. The little miracle makes the life. You understand?"

Jennifer smiled with respectful disbelief.

"Perhaps in England not so much," said the Libyan and laughed heartily, at which Jennifer's smile became even more blandly sphinx-like.

IV

Nothing remained. It was near midnight when she handed in her key and the clerk nodded, *"Non, non, madame"*. She ignored his warning and walked out into the dark. The emptiness of the square was balm to her and as she continued along the western arc of the Corniche she encountered only a few harmless homeward-striding men. On her way to the furthermost fort the curve of the harbour was so marked that looking back the hotel became unrecognizably distant. She stopped finally to revel in her broad-front divorcement from things and briefly she dared a last luxury. Before the waters she saw herself as an empty boat blown to sea. Then to her dismay she felt a disturbance in the stillness of the night and from nowhere all her familiar winds came brushing her.

"Jen . . ." she heard a voice call behind and turned sharply. "Jen . . ." again, and discerned up against the building across the road a low crouched heap. "Jen . . .", the uncanny first word became part of a long anxious Arabic chant. Her name was just a sound in his wail. Jennifer had stared so intensely that the man, legless on his little cart, thought it worthwhile pushing out towards her. He bumped down over the gutter and wheeled across the road. No cars came. By the opposite gutter he stopped and looked at her, chanting again "Jen . . ." as he made a new start.

When she saw his greasy, distended face Jennifer's fear broke, swelling and swamping her. A vast distance was between her and this nearby mutilated form; she was entirely safe; but her discomfort could not be avoided. From every direction, out of interminable cold distances, she was struck. She took her purse out of her bag and gave the man one — two — pounds and then, in case he trundled after her, fearing her self-control, she walked rapidly in a sweat back towards the centre. A taxi honked at her. She clenched her fist, as if around a stone, and was reminded strangely of tomorrow's appointment for the purchase of amber. Originally the Libyan's suggestion had annoyed her but now, blown with unexpected apprehensions, she was glad of the friendly arrangement.

V

She passed the first morning of her new freedom in the Graeco-Roman museum, bright and bleached. From the truncated bodies there she derived a haphazard companionship, and when she came upon the sunny cluttered courtyard she sat quietly, not too distant from a group of women gossiping under the lemon tree.

Half-reluctantly then she kept her appointment with the Libyan, who by daylight looked less philosophical and less interested in the prospect than the night before. Jennifer let herself be led through the angular thoroughfares of the city, through the markets where racks of chickens and rabbits waited to be sold and eaten. Her guide was talking about the cuisine in Tripoli and Jennifer began to feel nauseous. The blackened fish, the plastic footwear, the hanging tripe, nauseating, the whole business. Only the force of indifference kept her going.

She recognized the shop immediately, the same dirty *bonafide* today as yesterday. The Libyan ushered her inside but the arthritic proprietor was missing. They heard his voice from within, behind a muffling curtained doorway, high-pitched gabbling in business French. Jennifer couldn't resist fingering a yellow chain of stones while her companion took out another foul cigarette. When the proprietor, presently, came out he embraced the Libyan arduously and apologetically, and when he passed his hand to Jennifer he murmured curiously that he recognized her from the day before. She grinned with embarrassment and began to explain why she'd come back. Assuming in any case that she'd returned for the amber the old man moved across to the locked case and after a time produced the first wooden tray. He signalled that she should examine the stones. Behind her back the other unseen man, the business interlocutor from the inner room, was pushing through the curtain.

" *Pardon* — " she heard him begin patiently, now that he too had been left waiting. Tall, lean, he had to bend in the doorway; a fair untended moustache drooping round his mouth to match the fair matted hair hanging down his neck. In the iris of one eye he had a crescent fleck.

"Bill — " she scarcely mouthed.

"Jen."

For a moment both stood tentatively, to consider if a trick had been played. Jennifer looked to the Libyan, Bill to the shopkeeper. Then Bill went on decisively. "Jen, fancy seeing you here. Are you here buying amber? I'm here for the amber too. I never expected — M. Sarhan runs the best shop in Alex — but I never expected — "

He stammered while the old man bowed to acknowledge the compliment.

Gesturing at the fair Englishman in an attempt, as much for herself as for the Libyan, to establish the propriety of things, Jennifer started, "An — old — friend. From England."

Bill cut in, "We're old friends, M. Sarhan."

"Beautiful!" The shopkeeper knew an occasion. "Let me show my most beautiful stones."

"Bill," she pleaded, not quite able to smile, half whimpering.

"I know." Bill's dim slowness had switched to a breathless taking things in hand. "M. Sarhan, we'll come back later to see the stones. Now we must talk — you understand. An — old — friend — from England.

Goodbye. We'll be back. Come on Jennifer. You *are* coming, Jen? Come on," he urged.

She tried to nod politely, gratefully at the Libyan. But he only insisted on leering, as if he'd uncovered the lack of respectability he'd suspected in her all along. "Please — ", he flicked his wrist, casting her off onto the chance encountered Englishman with worldly disregard. Jen was immobilized by the awkwardness.

"You've been very kind," she blurted, but Bill had seized her arm and she was with him alone.

"What on earth are you doing here, Jen?"

" *Me* ? I thought you were *dead* !"

He took her hand tightly and as they walked along bent his head, kissing, into her ear. "Sister mine." And grinned at her slily, pleased with himself.

"Brother Bill," she replied.

They found a large empty bar where they could sit opposite each other, reflected many times in the mirrors round the walls. She ran a scratching finger over his hand and felt her face burn in the longing that he be there, really. Now she stopped herself. Had she gone mad? The man opposite her, straw man, winking eye, ungainly stretched out arms, was no more her brother than the mirror's image. Was she away from her mind? She'd let herself be picked up by a smooth French gemmerchant. Could it be? As the man gazed intently at her drawn face and her long black hair she felt herself pulled back. As if his look ran a thread through a hundred of her faces, lost inside, he was drawing her together and towards him. She could not resist his scrutiny and found herself in the grip of the severest faith, compelled to believe.

"Are you really there? *Here* , I mean. Bill?" As he answered she reached out to touch his mouth and broken teeth. "You have to let me lip-read. I don't trust my eyesight." When they spoke she became sceptical again. She told him she was in Alexandria playing truant from a package tour, and he explained that he was trying to organize coffee contracts for Tanzanian farmers.

"To get round the almighty profiteering concerns."

Was any of it to be believed?

He laid a string of amber on the table. He meant to sell it. The little sections had a strange opaque glow, like irradiated bone, and she smoothed them timidly.

They shifted in their chairs and chatted about the cafe. No effort could bring out suitable conversation. Bill felt himself awkward and without words.

"Will you come back to my hotel?" he asked.

"I don't mind. Yes."

It was a dingy serviceable place lacking the effrontery to overlook the sea. There was nothing to look at in the room. They stood divided by the bed watching each other, purposefully making the uneasiness so great that it had to be broken. Bill considered the thin, dark, staring woman. He struggled to wrench himself free of all he remembered, so he could circle round to face her in the present. Her eyes became wide as he approached and put his arms round her head.

"Jen — "

The eye-to-eye manner simply terrified her as she slackened and was enclosed in ten years' worth of yearning.

Her consent was complete in the first kiss and they undressed and lay on the single bed, coupled like key and casket.

Bill was heavy and slow, stubbornly violent. She couldn't remember her last man and she feared for herself, gripping the pale ropes of flesh round his waist as he pushed himself down and her against the bed. She'd forgotten the weight, almost suffocating, and let it come. His straining face and his bursting eyes wet and heated hers. His face burnt her as if she had been hurled, breathless, into the first fire. She clung to his arms and sides, her brother's. He was shoving her from inside, she was thrusting herself, her spine almost to snapping. And then suddenly she knew herself flung against the hard root of the substantial world. She was calling out, no longer lost. With her mouth she gripped his shoulder, hard clenched his wrist, slumped against him and her body was growing from his. The fierceness of the return — of severed flesh re-healed by searing — left her near puking, crying, bucketting against his weight. But it was through and she was stroked by him, watched by him in peace.

He splashed cold water onto her face. She shuddered and they laughed. He opened up the shutters onto the clanging, emptying street and then he flopped on the bed beside her, unable now to be strong. She saw untense the known angle of his eyes, the sad thin moustache, the familiar curve of his half-open chafed lips. Expressions that had been momentary when he was younger had been marked on his face with lines. And again she felt herself in the fullness of recognized, believed love, start to whimper. He heard her and touched her, to make sure of her, and she finally to make sure toppled gently across him. "I don't want to sleep," she half-said, frightened by the time ahead.

And sleep took them both.

VI

The woman in the bed surprised Bill when he woke at dawn. Warm light sloped across him like a beam and he stirred sleepily and content. With his hand, idly, he rubbed the woman's shoulder, hidden by the sheet. The vague pleasure of morning lust came to him until, ashamed, he understood the familiar posture of his step-sister beside him. He got up stealthily and dressed as quietly as he could, bending down like a child to tie his shoelaces. He closed the shutters so Jennifer would not wake, and wondered about her. He imagined her drenched in all the obverse brilliance of the pain that had dogged her. There she had been in that long marine summer; there her young self like Eve among the trees feeling a way towards bliss; there with him her better-than-brother, reckless and strung and fine. She breathed composed; he pulled back his shoulders and went out.

No one was yet about in the street, which relieved Bill, solitude his accustomed state. He needed to think. The light was wondrous — cool heavenly yellow — and the milky sea. On top of the morning he felt a physical brimming within his own body. But what was the meaning of the sign? As he dawdled near the harbour wall he found himself playing with the amber beads in his pocket. Could it all be taken up again, after so long? He had a choice, didn't he? The empty space of the sea reminded him of the comfortless spaces he'd known all his life, in which he'd grown, toughened and thrived. The fat Libyan with his rank smoke had brought her, in conspiracy with the bent old Arab shopkeeper. They'd be grinning brazenly after passing two more lives through their hands — secondhand

Alexandrian merchandise — the middleman's favourite joke — bequeathing the complications. Things were better left.

The first men were setting off for work in the continuing day. A large new cinema advertisement was going up. A child ran out to Bill and for three piastres, smirking, sold him a copy of the *Egyptian Gazette* . This was the world's news.

That Bill had *no* choice was as straightforward suddenly as the simple breakwater protecting the harbour and he turned his back on the blue space. When he returned to the hotel room he found Jennifer compact on the bed brushing her hair.

"You here," she said quizzically.

He didn't bother to explain. "Do you really have no ties?"

She nodded and her hair fell down, slightly off-centre.

"Did you go and look at that hospital?"

"Yes. I felt hollow. There was nothing — there or anywhere."

"What would you have done? If I hadn't been — "

He wanted a sign and walked to the window to look at the sun.

"Bought the beads. Gone home."

"Home?"

"You know what I mean."

He caught himself in the mirror and sought confirmation there. None came. All he could do was speak. Jennifer had moved away from him nervously and sat on the bed. He wanted her back.

"The kid's here." He had said it. "In Alexandria. She's well. She's in the Catholic convent. Ten. They called her Anne."

He looked for her reaction but at this final unveiling she could give none. Before she could take in what her step-brother had said, she had seen before her in unflawed re-creation her forbidden memory.

"The baby was meant for a Jewish couple without any children. That's what your mother and my father arranged and that was enough for them. But in all the war-mongering of that year the couple decided to go to the States. So the baby stayed here. You could've found out easily, though our parents didn't bother. Leave well enough alone they would have said.• I knew she was here years ago. I've seen her a few times. That's why I kept apart from you, because I knew too much. It was too much of a responsibility. You were fifteen when you had her. You had a right to be free of her. It was up to me to keep it a secret — she's been all right here, and I've given the sisters money — "

She interrupted his flat rapid account. "But I haven't been all right."

"I didn't know that. I wondered if I should see you when the divorce came through, but that could just as well have messed things up."

She frowned keenly, fixing her attention on this new situation, and he likewise as they disembarked together onto their weird *terra incognita* .

"But you deserve to know."

"What will happen?"

Jennifer was pained, stopped. She needed to reflect but the current rushing swift and white gave her no chance. She smoothed her hair, as actually and domestically as she could.

"Shall we get married, Bill? There are no laws against it. No one can stop us."

"Do you want to? Can we manage the whole thing?

"In the face of it, is there a choice?"

Outside the taxi horns sounded like the blaring of lusty elephants. Bill was at the window again, searching the early streets for orientation. There were no irrefutable signs. But everything out there delighted him only because he knew that Jennifer was behind him in the room. She was still confused, shivering slightly at the great doubling back of her — their — destiny.

He turned back into the room and moved forward to take her hands. They looked, most endearingly, like performing animals.

"I love you."

She responded in kind.

"Now come with me to see her. This was meant for her." He dangled the amber beads.

In a lazy inconspicuous fashion, hand in hand, they walked along the street. The many faces of the morning city were open to them. The clash of smell and colour, those faintest that once were sharpest; the youths kicking and slapping and hugging; women with jauntily ship-shape dignity; the dying old. No city had seen so much intricacy come to nothing and beneath its sky the puzzles of human outcomes most readily reduced to dust. But Jennifer and Bill felt easy in the midst. Once it had taken a golden barge driven by cupids to make that sky gleam. Yet today the sky seemed to salute the couple veering along an edge of truth. Otherwise their walk passed unnoticed among the diverse transactions of the street.

Dear R.

Michael knew he needed help but hadn't bothered to do anything about it. He had the house and the rambling garden and his work seven days a week. Then one Saturday morning he noticed an ad in the local shop, someone called R. Hill looking for odd jobs. It was worth a try. He took down the details and drove out to the address given, a farm further along the valley, in the rain shadow of the Adelaide Hills. But no one was at home there. He kept knocking and scouting around and at last, slightly cross that his impulse had been frustrated, he decided to leave a note. "Dear R.," he wrote and invited whoever it was to make contact as soon as possible. The person came that very afternoon. He was a schoolboy with a slight build and glasses and didn't strike Michael as much of a handyman. He claimed rather nervously that since he was from a farm he knew how to do most things. Then Michael smiled, the boy took off his jumper, and they set to work together.

The first job was the trellis which had to be stripped for repainting. They cut back the old creeper and scraped at the wood with palette knives, paint flakes flying everywhere like sparks. They worked more or less in silence. Michael was wondering whether the boy would ask him questions and eventually one was put. What did he do? He answered that he was a lawyer working on the commission into the law of privacy. The boy was impressed. He wanted to do law too, next year when school finished. "I don't want to work with my hands for the rest of my life," he said, brushing paint chips off his forearm. "If there's anything I can do to help," offered Michael.

The work progressed and Michael came to feel that somehow he should explain himself to R. Hill. But the boy asked no other questions of fact and seemed to have no interest in personal details. So Michael had no pegs to hang himself on. Halfway through the afternoon they broke for tea and went into the kitchen. The wiring had been faulty there for ages and unless you fiddled delicately with the wall switch the electric jug wouldn't work at all. When the boy saw this he insisted with great enthusiasm, with glee, that it should be fixed immediately. He really was a handyman and in a few minutes the job was done. He didn't even look pleased with himself except perhaps for a slight touch of pride, unconscious and natural. "Let's have tea now," said Michael sitting at the kitchen table. "You deserve it, R."

After that R. came every Saturday and Michael looked forward to it. He liked to be out in the air getting things done, and home-making was most proper in autumn. The boy was sharp, eager to talk about deep things, but Michael didn't mind because they were the things everyday friends would never broach. R. asked whether the law was a force for social equality or for difference. And he asked another time if you could believe in anything if you didn't believe in one thing absolutely. "Some people manage," Michael answered fliply. His own situation was stranger than strange but R. accepted it apparently without realizing that there were puzzles to be explained. The boy's mind was so much on the world at large. He knew the botanical classification of all the plants in the garden and one day when dusk came early by surprise he could name every visible star. The things that made Michael ache were so different. Driving home from work on weekdays, for example, he compiled catalogues of spare facts about himself. The lists were designed to give an accurate account of himself to any would-be disinterested observer; but his facts didn't really add up. With mutual consent and approval he was separated from his wife. She had taken the children and moved into town to make a new start. He stayed on with the house which they had bought as part of a general plan when they decided to have the children. Tumbledown, roomy, deep in the hills, it was perfect for making a life. They had renovated thoroughly, intending perpetual residence, and added a modern wing with a sun-trap studio for his wife. They had a scheme for the two-acre garden too — a blend of landscapes — but got distracted. After two children and much else the grand plan exhausted itself. Nowadays Michael's work as a professional took up most of his time and energy. It was curious the way getting older, improving himself, filling gaps, remedying lacks, in the end remaking himself, he'd become the opposite of what he used to be. He'd been very much a people person once but the person who first set out had vanished. Now here he was alone with the new picture of himself, wanting badly to show it and tell it all to R.

The boy was tired when he came next time. He'd

been doing homework all morning and his eyes had a dull protective lustre about them. He kept looking at the ground. One of the paths was overhung by a deodar pine which had got out of control. Its low branches blocked the way and it was sending runners up through the path in great numbers. The whole lot had to be cut back. They worked slowly, cutting the fan-shaped foliage with secateurs and chopping the new growth back to the base. The leaves were bright green, oily to touch and almost acrid to the nose. R. said the fronds showed the same growth pattern as a kind of seaweed. Soon there was quite a mound of cuttings, some dry but most green. Michael fetched a swag of old newspapers out of the shed and they began screwing them up into balls. If they stuffed paper under the leaves then the pile might burn. They worked fast now to keep warm in the cold and when it was ready Michael took his cigarette lighter, reached to the innermost centre of the heap and put the flame to the crumpled paper's edge. The fire was unwilling to burn at first. It couldn't pass through the green pine branches and died instead into thick dark smoke which sat round the leaves in a sluggish aura. "It'll burn in the end," said R., "if we get the inside up to a good heat. It'll ignite then. If we cover it and keep it burning underneath. Stick more paper in." Michael kneeled down and blew into the black smoky centre. A glow came and went along the fringe of the newspaper. He kept blowing and at last a free-burning flame got going, but R. threw on another armful of green leaves which smothered the fire. "It's the only way," he said. "Starve it of oxygen and you push the combustion temperature up." His eyes were watering. Michael suggested throwing on petrol — but it wasn't necessary. The heart suddenly became bright and orange, radiating outwards, flickering, devouring whatever they threw on. Michael and the boy stood on either side of the fire, tending it. Their faces were hot and their backs were cold in the shadow of the huge liquid ambers that bordered the clearing. The fire burned well, smoking a little, until the heap caved in completely. R. raked up any odd bits lying around and threw them on, making a last small pile with those branches which hadn't yet burned away. And in the end the fire was a spread of ash. Michael stirred it with a stick, thinking of himself. He was inspired to make a comparison, a leading comment — but stopped.

"See it did burn," said R. cheerily.

"It did."

They stood in the sphere of smoke. Then R. said it was time to be going and Michael was left unexplained for another week.

Next Saturday he had to be away. He left R. a note, wedged in the backdoor between the wire and the wood. "Dear R. Sorry I can't be here today. There's nothing much to be done anyway so go home early. See you next week. M." But he was annoyed to miss R. It was more than ever imperative that he should make some sort of breakthrough with the boy and really talk. He had come to believe that R. understood him but he needed confirmation. He was late home that night and saw that his note had been taken. In the morning when he wandered out, a misty pious Sunday, the radio playing old hymns, he found that R. had done some digging. The red-black soil had been turned over. It was lying open to the air now and in a few days could be planted with potatoes and carrots. Michael pressed his slipper down on a clod until it crumbled. The bed could be planted next Saturday. But R. telephoned on the Friday evening to say that he was sick and wouldn't be coming. Michael felt disappointed, extraordinarily, as though he had suddenly found out that there were ten more miles of lugging his knapsack before he could rest.

In the end R. announced that he wouldn't be able to come anymore. Although he appreciated the money he couldn't afford to take Saturday afternoons off from his schoolwork. When he came and said this Michael just blinked then grinned quickly and falsely. "Yes, you mustn't waste this year. It's an important one." Michael felt he should blurt out an apology for some mysterious failing but with relief managed not to do so. R. was looking at him placidly with his sunny alert face. It was as if he were staring through Michael, seeing nothing of what had been kept hidden, seeing nothing at all. Actually the boy was noticing that the oaktree kept its full cover of leaves even though the leaves were well and truly dead. There was some pruning to be done and they set about it without talking. Normally Michael found it easy to chatter. In the office he chattered to everybody continually. But on this occasion he couldn't even rehearse in his mind what he wanted to say. In a way he wanted to confess, but what he wanted to confess was himself. He wanted to say that purely in fantasy R. had taken his measure and plumbed his depths. He opened his mouth to speak. "R. — " The boy, sawing at a bough, turned his head and looked blankly over his shoulder. "What?" And Michael in a flush of cowardly charity suddenly felt no reason for interrupting the boy's content task. "Watch your thumbs." "Yeh." They shook hands at the last, R. giving a fine impression of a bloke's eye-piercing gaze. "If you want any help," they each said, and "Good luck." When the boy was gone Michael went to his study, switched on the standard lamp, opened his desk drawer and took out a sheet of paper. He sat and wrote: "Dear R." For two hours he kept on writing beautifully, explaining everything. He included not merely facts but an extended and subtle interpretation. It was on paper, all laid out, to the splendid peroration in which he wrote down all that he had ever felt: of love and transports, of touching hand to hand, of feeding mouth to mouth, of knowing and being known face to face. When he had finished he folded the paper and slipped it into an envelope. On the front he wrote "R." with no other address. Then he ran his tongue along the flap, sealed the envelope and firmed it with his index finger. In a purposeful, almost sprightly manner he went on foot down the hill to the shops. The night was freezing and brilliant and through the overgrown barricades of trees at the ends of drives he could see into the houses. It was Saturday night and people were meeting or going about. At the bottom of the road cars were swinging one after another into the pub carpark. Naturally the post office was shut at that hour but the slit was there beside the numbered private boxes. He slipped the unaddressed letter through and it landed softly with a slight scrape of paper against paper. There it was, unrecoverable.

Outstretched Wings and Orient Light

Oil-green firebrands of poplars lined the Memorial Mile as a ute travelled jauntily between them. Brendan Lynch at the wheel allowed his head to bob from side to side, as the road curved upwards, in sceptical wonder at what the town might be. His ute was pink and battered and although the passenger door was orange, being a replacement, he travelled without a passenger. Just himself, Sheba his dog, and his sausage bag. He reckoned the town would be soft. The valley it overlooked was pastel and you approached across a willowed river, up an easy slope. Brendan drove into the main street as far as the intersection at the heart of the town. Two pubs and two churches were ranged on opposing corners in worn enmity, solid goldrush buildings. When Brendan did a U-turn and proceeded back past the shops, people started to notice. People stopped to look at his car and Brendan whistled as his head rocked. His vehicle was quite a character and made blokes follow with their eyes, sneering. When he braked hard the carpet rolls in the back jumped up in a cloud of dust — and people were looking. When he had backed into an angle park Brendan wound his window down and peered over his shoulder at the town, at his observers. He grinned tightly with approving hatred. "They just dunno what the price is, do they? Eh?" A junk-dealer mate had taken Brendan on and sent him to Worrong looking for rugs and carpets, though he was proud to say he had no previous experience of such work. His car was his own, and his mate had given him money to cover the rounds of the district. Barely enough money, however, and he'd spent most of it. He ran his fingers down the wedge of his face to the tip of his beard. The solidity of the town was before him and he wondered how he'd tackle it. "You stay here," he said as he shooed the dog off the blue wool jacket he wore at the commencement of a visit. He pulled his sleeves down and patted his wispy hair and chest. Only in parenthesis, between farewelling himself in the rear-vision mirror and locking the car door from the outside, was he aware of painfully wanting this town to take his measure.

It was glamorous to walk along the street intending to make inquiries. People noticed him, knowing he was a stranger, and he looked back brightly into their eyes. His shirt was pinned against his belly by his baggy, holey jeans; his jacket was shaped chiefly by his bones; but his clothes were not the thing they should see and his eyes reduced to glinting slits to tell them so.

He asked in the newsagent's if he could put up a notice. He told the proprietor he was willing to collect any carpets or other junk people wanted to get rid of.

"You won't get much response. In my experience people don't like giving things away."

"I'm taking it off their hands. I don't mind driving out to their place. But it would help if they knew I was around."

"Go ahead, son."

Brendan printed a message and then the newsagent pruned the sheet of paper and stuck it in a spare corner of his window. While his back was turned Brendan picked up a magazine.

"Thanks mate."

He wandered in the street gauging the town's prosperity. It was extraordinarily quiet. There were people moving quietly from door to door always under cover of the overhanging verandahs that kept the life of the town secluded and discreet. Friday was food-shopping and as Brendan walked, hands leaned forward into shop windows selecting steaks or loaves or buns or fruit, to be wrapped in newspaper and stuffed into baskets, piled into the trolleys some ladies used, or settled into cartons for quick transference to the backseat of the car. Brendan rolled up his magazine and tapped his thigh. He passed an overstocked frock salon, a real estate agent, and, outside the post office, notices behind glass about functions in the hall or at the school.

The town's most imposing building was the Orient, a red-brick painted two-storey facade hotel. If the blackboard on its steps spoke true, lunch wasn't yet over and it was time to forget his reconnoitre and his rugs for a plate of roast beef. Brendan had been made ravenous by Worrong and the wide streets that withheld themselves. In the foyer a sign pointed down the floral track of corridor and he visited there first. He relieved himself carelessly and playfully, spraying a yellow steaming jet all across the tiles, then soaped his hands, splashed, and fixed himself up neatly. When he entered the public bar it was as a clean newcomer who nodded to the barman with whimsical benevolence.

"What's yours?" the man asked, drooping his protruberant nose.

Brendan ordered food and drink and smokes, settled himself square on to the counter and drained the first beer in one. When he came near again, Brendan lifted his eyebrows and asked the barman quizzically if he'd been in Worrong long.

"Is forty years long enough for you?"

"You must like it then?"

"It's a comfortable place."

The barman, when he wasn't fiddling with his tea-towel, stroked the length of his nose. He saw that the stranger was trying for a conversation and stood back suspiciously.

"It's my first time here," said Brendan, "on business. I'll have another one."

"Your sort of business must be all right," remarked the barman as he pumped the beer fountain.

"Bill! Bill, would you be so kind?" a woman's voice called all of a sudden, ripely projecting and catching Brendan off-guard. He slopped his beer. As the barman came forward to mop up he gave a shrewd glance to the stranger who'd swivelled round, in turn, to look at the woman. The bar was empty but for her, a pale old woman sitting in a low lounge chair, in a shadowy corner, behind Brendan's back.

"Good afternoon," said Phoebe Deslines graciously, holding up her empty liqueur glass. Bill the barman, constrained by the visitor's presence, came out from the bar and poured her a muscat.

"There you are, Phoeb. This once."

Then Bill made a point of taking his form guide to the far end of the counter where he curled over it intently. The others drank quietly and the afternoon light through the pearly windows became progressively browner. Until Brendan, needing another, shoved his glass along the counter in the barman's direction.

"Eh? Bill, boy?"

The beer frothed temperamentally and Bill had to swill half of it away. "That'll be forty cents," he said sharply, holding out one hand while he pulled his nose with the other.

"Listen, mate," replied Brendan. He could ride the barman's hostility. "I wonder if you'd help me. I'm in Worrong looking for old junk, old carpets mainly. If people will give them to me, I'll take them. It's a bugger of a job. Jesus!" Brendan pushed a jet of air through his teeth and took a gulp of drink. "Got any clues?"

Bill was more interested now. A fellow workman was at least engaging and faced with such a hopeless bearded fellow Bill felt worldly: "You might try driving round some of the rural properties. That would be your best shot."

Brendan nodded earnestly until, all of a sudden, he lost his concentration and his eyes became wide and remote. Then he snapped back, "Yeah. Thanks. I'll have another beer on the strength of that."

The barman shuffled towards the trays of glasses to oblige, but disapprovingly.

At half past three when school finished Joe Dunn turned up. His small son had been instructed to wait outside on the bench while dad had a couple of drinks and a yarn, and Joe pushed the door open purposefully, a stocky good-looking man, strongly in command.

"G'day, Bill. Middy, thanks."

"Well, are you back now?" grinned the barman, giving an accustomed greeting.

"I'm back for a bit. Lorrie sent me down to fetch the kid from school."

Joe was sitting with both hands round the bottom of his glass. He took matters seriously. His hair was cropped and his manner was trimmed by reserve.

"You should have been up at the site, Bill. It was tremendous. Yesterday we blasted the end of the big hole through the hill. Christ, you can't imagine. I've never seen anything so huge."

His bullish neck flexed as he talked and his eyes glowed dreamily.

Brendan interrupted. "Where's this you're talking about?"

Joe Dunn pulled himself up at the stranger's interference. "Up in the Snowies. Over towards Kiandra. The new dam."

"You blokes blowing up the hillsides, are ya? Reckon that's pretty good?"

"Eh?"

Bill fidgetted anxiously from one man to the other as he sensibly cleared off the heavy ashtrays.

A pink beery flush filled Brendan's face and he couldn't stop himself insisting at this Joe.

"Do you reckon it's impressive to blow up a bit of a hill? I've seen whole towns blown up. I've seen whole people exploded into nothing. You don't need to look at me as though I'm nuts. I'm talking about the war, mate, when I was in Vietnam. I was there a few years ago when it was all on and I seen things *you* couldn't dream about, let alone handle in real life. You're looking at a bloke who's killed twenty human beings with his own gun. About as far away from me as you are, some of them were. True. And from the air I seen what explosives can do for mile after mile after mile. It isn't all that tremendous at all, I can tell you. It's enough to make you chuck." His hand was gripping the bar rail.

"Give me a beer, will ya, to shut me up?"

Brendan shook now and Joe Dunn frowned hard to make sense of the weird ginger bloke.

"You've been unlucky, mate. I'm sorry for you."

"Come on, easy does it," said Bill. He put a hand feelingly on Brendan's shoulder and jollied him gently. "Haven't you had enough? You've been here for hours."

"You're all children," muttered Brendan as his head slipped forward against the counter, which was wet with drink. He hauled himself up again and spoke, this time to the whole bar. "You sit round here in this fucking town, taking things quiet." He leaned over at Joe. "Getting your thrills."

Bill chuckled. "You make it sound pretty attractive."

"Do you ever think of the price some people have to pay?" Brendan panted and would have continued, fiercer than ever, but that suddenly all the air was taken out of him. The immensity of what he wanted to say twisted his tongue and he could only fall against the bar, thin and quivering, cowering round his glass. "Forget it," he mumbled. "Forget it. Never mind."

No one spoke until, when it was clear that Brendan had indeed winded himself, Joe Dunn reasserted his position. "You want to watch out."

A young woman had come in from the street and entered the silence between the three men. She was smiling. "Hallo, Bill, I'd love something long and cool, a gin and lemon. It's been a hard day." She brushed her plain thick hair out of the way and looked a little exhausted, though still lively. When her drink was ready she took it over to Phoebe Deslines's corner and kissed the old woman cheerily, with a squeeze. Then to her annoyance she discovered a patch of chalk under her elbow and brushed it away briskly. "Damn," she said, smiling again broadly, and sank down into the chair contentedly. She was a big girl who looked hampered in her gay cotton shift, yet, beginning to talk to Phoebe, simmered with enthusiasm.

When she saw Joe Dunn she waved and he winked back. He was her parents' next-door neighbour and she liked seeing him. She liked his swarthiness, his fine hair and his sure front.

"Better not let the schoolkids catch you in here, Harrie," he called, "not in the middle of the afternoon."

"Well, you've got your own son waiting out there for *you* ."

"Yeah, I should be off." He noted the amount left in his glass and finished it.

But Phoebe Deslines, eager to confide, took Harriet Varney's wrist and bubbled. "That chappie there has been in Vietnam. It sounds quite ghastly."

Harrie took in the back of the quaintly dressed red-haired man shrunk over the bar. Pathetic and exotic. Brendan cocked his head since he was being discussed and looked sidelong at the girl, a fat angel whose face was white and keen and had been inflicted with nothing. She was like a milky Chinese whore he'd known, who took anything and never stopped being happy. Only at the end had he been able to make her confess her pain.

He gave Harrie a smile and, without allowing her the option, started to explain — about his brother, a sweet bloke who'd been in the army too.

"So you see, lady, I'm not the one to feel sorry for."

But Harrie could never bear to hear such things and

215

Joe Dunn, having had enough, stood up and belched softly.

"Before you go," Brendan addressed him, "could I touch you for a drink. I'm broke."

But Joe didn't see that he should be drawn further. "Nup. That's the price you pay. You've had plenty, mate."

"Joe, won't you stay," Harrie jumped up and almost put her arm round Joe's sullen body. "Let me buy all of us a drink." She looked challengingly at him and he was bowled back. What on earth was Harriet Varney meddling for?

"I couldn't let you do that," he said.

A gold panel of light had spread across the bar as the door from the street opened and little Ben Dunn was standing there. He wasn't able to mouth anything. His round black eyes skimmed about the room and sank gladly upon his father.

"Benjy, all right boy, I'm coming. I'm coming right away."

Joe Dunn edged round Harrie and the tables and reached the doorway where he pulled his son to him. Hypnotized for a second, the boy beheld the funny man on the stool, who beamed from a bush of carrot hair, hunched funny. Then Ben had gone and Brendan turned away. The child had made him tremble and he clenched his fists. He bent close round the bar and the cords in his neck, the muscles round his heart, tightened into straps. Bill watched Brendan's fit, rubbing his nose with careful curiosity. And before Harrie could fully take stock, Brendan had recovered and swung round to the girl gesturing rakishly.

"Forgive me. Could I keep you to that drink?"

She felt for her purse hastily. "Of course."

216

Phoebe perked up now and called across to the man. "Still, it's always wonderful to travel, isn't it. The East must be marvellous."

"Phoebe!"

Harriet Varney moved up to the bar where she sat on a stool next to Brendan Lynch and chatted about Worrong for a number of drinks. Finally when she decided to leave she and Bill escorted Brendan, teetering, outside to the public bench. In the evening air they laid him out. His eyes flickered like bobbing half-moons in pink seas and when Bill returned to the bar Harrie lingered. Although he accepted his position on the bench it was obvious that the man wouldn't sleep. It was early evening, yet he was in a trance that removed him from her and his surroundings. She took five dollars out of her purse and pushed it into his pocket, deliberately nudging him. Startled, he shook as if finding himself and jerking violently pulled himself up onto his knees, kneeling before Harrie on the bench, thrusting his leering face at her.

"I don't know what you're after, lady, but I can tell you this much, I'm not the one to get it from."

He'd fallen down again before she could be upset, face on to the bench, and lay there heavily. Harrie was properly reproached. "You'll be all right," she said and turned away in the direction of her parents' house. The uphill walk would calm her down. She was always glad to get home on Fridays. And as she walked upwards she was staggered by the gentility of their community under the spring dusk. The hoses' sizzle, ducks at feed, the gargle of currawongs, chatter from the porches or the television all blended and was audible.

◆ ◆ ◆

Harrie had come back to Worrong after doing an arts course and a diploma in Sydney. If other young teachers had gone way out to Balranald or Bourke in search of experience, she had returned to her home town to work subtler manipulations. She wanted of course, ever so modestly, to raise the consciousness of the place and, if it seemed at times unlikely, she at least had youth.

Most of the kids in Worrong were transplants with little sense of their surroundings so Harrie specialized in local history. For her part the town's seed was the Orient Hotel with its goldrush foundation stone. Named after the bright light that dawned with the gold discoveries, and nothing to do with the Chinese who came from afar to camp and pan there, the Orient had marked Worrong's shift from crossroads to settlement. It had been in the Varney family for three generations. It was only for their old age that her parents had sold it and moved up the street. For their daughter, who loved old ways, it was still the best of Worrong.

Harrie had her life. In the evening she'd sit on the verandah and dream. In the morning she'd sip the tea her mother had got up early to make and sieve the dregs through her teeth so the leaves would slide back in disarray to the bottom of the cup.

This particular morning when she peered down they formed no pattern, unless a thick arched eyebrow. She smiled as she tried to conjure up some innocent foreboding. When she shifted in her seat and looked again she saw a crow's outstretched wing. It was enough. Something would happen. Though the dull heat held the morning in unproductive stillness, she anticipated an event and stirred herself for school.

"It's going to be hot," said her mother and the two

women gazed out together over the papery mass of hydrangeas tumbled against the kitchen window. Harrie drew in a sharp thrilling breath, the taste of tea still in her mouth. She was sure in her heart that a blaze would irradiate them all and quickly before leaving she brushed herself with powder and combed her long thick hair once or twice from the crown.

Her headmaster was a tired efficient man. She'd won him over by taking charge of those things he couldn't manage and he'd agreed, all too gratefully, that she could produce the school play. Directly after assembly then, when the sunlight fell on the blackboard, she took her place before her class and was illuminated.

"Will you call the roll, Dennis?"

Dennis Casson sang-song down the names. There was Adams, Andreotti . . . Kincaid, Lindfors, engineers' kids . . . Wilma McCloud, the little Aboriginal girl. She was the oldest in the class. O'Donoghue the clerk's son, Yvette Pidou, Sinclair, who was difficult, Tavistock, who was from a property. The cleverest.

She liked Martin Tavistock. He sat at the front and looked at her, slightly gangly but his face, pointed and alert, unified the diverse stages of development his parts were at. He suffered less than some under the cruel kneading of puberty. She couldn't write *that* on his report, however, nor how reassuringly blue his eyes were.

"The headmaster has asked me to be in charge of this year's school play. It's going to be *The Wind in the Willows* by Kenneth Grahame." In memory of her fine girlhood days in cubbies under trees by the Worrong River. "Have any of you read the book? It's about animals that live by a river."

Elaine Berkdon put her hand up in pique. "Isn't it a children's book? I mean for little kids?"

This caused murmuring.

"It's for children *and* adults. Grown-ups can appreciate it greatly. That's why it has been chosen. We can make it fit in with us here in Worrong. We can perform it down by the river and introduce local animals and things. Put your hand up if you'd like to help with it."

The whole crowd went up in a vote of confidence and Harrie, to outline the story, wrote the characters' names on the board. Although she loathed chalk, because it was merciless, and on a bad day would hold it loosely between her fingers flinching at any that came near her, today she would cover the board with madly inspired connections and wouldn't mind being in whiteness even up to her neck. She swam among the motes in the light.

"After recess we'll go down to the river and read the play through. And don't forget to be thinking about your magazine contributions either." Then she smiled to indicate she had no further claim on them. They were very young and strange sitting staring in rows. Only occasionally did she feel their roving senses stop to absorb something from her. Wilma McCloud was digging a heart in the desk. "Don't," said Harrie, pointing. Outside, the groundsman was dragging the sprinkler into place. A far bell clanged. A few seconds later the electric bell in their own ceiling returned the din.

Having approval for the play, Harrie could move through the staffroom in triumph. She spoke to Janet Frawley the language mistress. Janet had returned to Worrong at the same time as Harrie, but after a much longer absence. They had been new at the school together. Janet — mousey, but she'd been around.

"Coffee, Janet?"

"Yes thanks, dear. Make mine strong. Two spoons. I'm dropping on my feet."

She put two heaped into Janet's mug and one level into her own. "Oh?"

"I had a hell of a night. A mate of my good husband's decided to look me up. To offer condolences. They're all the same."

An older woman floated in their direction. "Lovely day."

"Isn't it heavenly," Harrie said. "I'm taking my class down by the river."

"Really."

"Let's sit outside, Harrie, get some sun," prompted Janet.

"Now you girls aren't fair." The third teacher was mopping hay-feverish sniffles from her nostrils. "You know what happens to me outside."

But Harrie had strolled out after Janet.

"He was a nice chap, I suppose. His family are stuck in Wagga. We drowned our sorrows as usual, till all hours."

"They come round you like contenders, Janet."

"Wish they did. He's put on weight — all across his back."

Harrie was embarrassed, preferring it when Janet spread her eyebrows and laughed at her desertion.

In the middle period, in the Gardens, Harrie introduced her children to the play. The monstrously bright annuals were at their bravest. Harrie reclined elegantly on the grass, regretting her dark dress in the heat and feeling slightly beached among the children and flowers. Still, she conducted the reading keenly. Some of their voices were uncontrollable, others shrank into an inaudible shyness, but surprisingly Wilma Mc-Cloud read well, and Martin Tavistock. She would cast Tavistock as Toad certainly, although she shouldn't have favourites. But for little Mole? A very special child was needed for Mole.

In the lunch-hour she met Janet Frawley again, who was looking satisfied.

"I've just taken an aspirin. Migraine."

"Wouldn't you like to go swimming, Janet?"

"I'm feeling a bit weary."

"Come on. It'll be lovely. It'll fix you all up."

So the two of them drove together to the best place, a deep clear pool with a grassy bank for stepping off. Janet crouched up against a willow to change.

"It's only because he loves me that he's doing things so cruelly," she was saying. "He can't admit he loves me. That's what Barry said last night. He said Jim doesn't want to be a softie."

Having pulled her dress over her head and struggled into the full black costume that best coped with her body, Harriet dipped one foot into the water, only distantly attending to Janet. She groped downward through slime and reached out with her other foot, down and down without finding the bottom, until in the end she plunged forward and swam. The middle of the stream was muddy and flowed with unexpected rapidity, leaves and twigs burbling past, and Harrie breast-stroked peacefully. Yet she was hurrying. Looking to Janet on the bank she realized the downstream tug. "It's lovely," she called. "So cooling."

Janet dived neatly in and, surfacing, was turned and carried towards Harrie, her hair slicked against her head in tails. "The current's so *strong* ! You have to swim flat out just to keep *still* !"

"Let yourself float away."

Janet bumped against Harrie, their feet and legs slithering together as they passed.

"It's too exhausting."

Janet made an almighty effort and Harrie steadily brought herself along behind. At last both of them reached the bank and clambering out lay panting, drying off, side by side on the grass.

"Joe Dunn's back," said Harrie.

"That's rare. Have you seen him?" asked Janet, who could have imagined anything.

"Only in the pub."

Harrie recalled the barricading set of the man's face.

"Harrie, I've got to be getting back. I'm on after lunch."

"Feeling better?"

"I'm all right."

Janet dressed in a businesslike way, as if she had things to do. When Harrie heard her car engine she was relieved and rolled onto her back to look at the sky. It was pulsating forward, like a billowing sheet, but splendidly intangible. Harrie closed her eyes on it and felt hot. Sometimes she was irritated by Janet's mantalk and her clinging so much to her Jim. In any case Jim had left because no one knew who the father of their daughter was. Harrie's closed eyes enveloped a great world of chocolate against which colours swarmed in unfixed shapes. She let her eyes trick her. When she remembered her play, in which the kids would sigh and strike their breasts, joyful thoughts surged in.

She rolled onto her front till it was time to swim

again and then once more she glided into the river. Before reaching the current she could control her movement and floated sleepily, propelling herself with odd wriggles of her tiny flippery feet. But she was attracted by the faster stream. She liked to be carried along, happily not contacting anything, simply enjoying the movement that seemed to come from nowhere. It pulled her as irresistably as the gumleaves, rocking her, and she was tireder now. Her arms were washed back against her sides and couldn't reach forward to make a stroke. It would be easiest to go. When she tumbled under, the sky through the water was thick orange and tasted dirty in the mouth, and underwater she delayed and delayed . . . .

Some holidaymakers shouted to her when she was taken round within sight of the caravan park. She couldn't bear to be yelled at and she couldn't have borne being rescued. So that's what made her, sighing primly, commence at last her upstream swim, but the water wouldn't stop forcing her down and it was hard swimming back against the current. Concentrating on her breathing she reached the bank, and climbed up amphibiously onto a sunned patch of earth. She admitted that she might almost have had it and chuckled in quiet amazement to herself. As her hair dried she raked it with her fingers. Her eyes smarted a bit though nothing had happened. All right, said Harriet Varney, she needed an anchor. But she didn't want a slab of concrete dragging her all the way down.

There was no need for her to choose a man.

When her dress was on she smoothed out its crumples, slipped her gritty feet into her sandals and set off for town.

◆◆◆

The front bar of the hotel got the light, orient and occident, tinted the colour of a bath by the opaque window glass. This suited Miss Phoebe Deslines, who had a permanent room upstairs and would descend at eleven for her morning piece of restraint, a muscat nipped like a rose between finger and thumb. Her programme of juvenescence needed sunshine but not too much. Her skin, renowned for its blanche, was easily sabotaged. In the front bar her chair was placed to receive just the right degree of murky light and to allow a shadow to fall not too sharply across her chin, which wasn't up to scratch. She sat with her best angle to the door, in case, but no one would speak to her before noon.

By late in the day she was bickering at Bill who scrutinized his form guide and quietly forgot to refill her glass.

"It's not my fault if I was brought up to fine living. I can't *help* appreciating luxury. The little things. You think I'm a silly old woman, Bill, I know that, but I've seen more of this world than you have. It's the smallest things that make life . . . *gorgeous* . Oh, how would you know!"

Only when she became cantankerous enough would he sleepily wield his bottle.

"It's a question of vision," she added, sipping. "Thank you, dear."

Harrie had seen Phoebe from the street and hopeful of a welcome went in to the old woman, falling to her and kissing the cool cheeks, almost pickled in eau de cologne.

"I'll have to fix myself up," she said and slipped out to the ladies' while Phoebe flapped. She had been heated on her way home after the swim; her hair had stuck together.

225

"Yes, darling. You are a bit of a wreck. Bill," Phoebe summoned, "hasn't she got her father in her?"

"That's no pity." When it came to history the barman wouldn't have his authority questioned.

Phoebe Deslines pitched her eyes on a point in middle distance, a jewel of a memory, and hummed. "He had something that man. He was a real man. So good-looking. Before he went away, I mean. He married Hazel after the war, wasn't it, in Sydney? I remember meeting her. We used to go drinking after the show, a Victory show we were doing. There she was in her little boosie hat talking about New Guinea or something."

"Hazel's a capable woman. If she hadn't come back to take this place in hand we wouldn't be here now. This pub was really on the downhill run when the first Varneys had it."

"Bill, Bill! Stanley and Hazel came back to Worrong to save this hotel. That's no excuse. He shouldn't have come back. The hotel's been a millstone round his neck all his life. He couldn't get rid of it. That's why he married old Hazel."

"You talk a lot of balls sometimes, Phoeb, if you'll pardon the expression."

He had dried his tray of glasses and continued proudly. "Hazel completely re-did this front bar. And she got the hydro-electric people coming in here — like Joe Dunn and his mob. They were only lads when they first came to Worrong. No, Hazel's a capable woman."

"Well, she didn't stretch herself when she decorated my room. It's the same wallpaper as was in the reception parlour of the Calvary Hospital, Wagga. She doesn't think I'm long for this world. Still, I have my things to make it nice."

Phoebe was excited. She pursed her lips in annoyance, shaping them incidentally into a cupid's heart; but Bill was fed up. He poured Harrie a gin squash and left it on the counter, smoothed his nose vertically and his moustache laterally, took the paper and retired to the backroom. Phoebe rasped. Her glass had been left empty and it was a house rule that she couldn't help herself. Fortunately, though, Harriet emerged.

"You look pretty now, dear. You've got lovely skin, you know that." Phoebe ran a finger over the cheek of the girl who could pour her a muscat.

"How are you, Phoebe?"

"I have my fun but it's difficult. Worrong's so small. Sweet place, but it *is* small. You young are so lucky being able to travel."

Harrie wanted to ask Phoebe's advice about the play. Miss Phoebe Deslines had toured with Tait Bros. and Harrie had a vision of Phoebe in green tulle, drenched in moonlight, appearing as a guest in *Wind in the Willows.*

"I'm happy in Worrong, Phoebe. There's something about it. Is it the air?" Harrie felt herself on oddly equal terms with the old girl. "I'm doing a fabulous play at the school. Outside by the river."

But Phoebe had to offer her wisdom. "Harrie, listen to me. You'll go on to gorgeous things only you can't stay here. Everyone gets out."

Yet as Harrie loudly reminded her Phoebe had ended up in the town.

"I suppose so. But it isn't right. This *place* , ho!" She swayed and put out a hand for support. "Harriet —

what I mean really is — oh, I don't like to say it but between friends — I've known your parents, oh, heavens — years! They're sweet. Your father's a glorious man. Harrie darling." She took the girl's hand between her palms and fell silent.

"Would you like to do something for the play, Phoebe?" ventured Harrie once more. "Would you come and talk to the children? You could show them a few tricks."

The woman raised her head, swelling her bosom to a rapturous crest, then subsided pitifully to ask Harrie to get her next drink. When the girl returned Phoebe grabbed her wrist tightly. "Just show me your palm, dear. I always know a palm." Harrie flopped her hand into Phoebe's and waited. "You've got a long life. I don't know if I envy you that. It's a long strong life, a fabulous life. There it all is."

Ashamed that she could give credence, Harrie drew her hand back to her lap. She shouldn't need prophecies, so sure were her hopes. Phoebe smiled prankishly and began again. "What makes it hard is the people here in the hotel. They're nice people but they don't understand. They don't know. When I think of the exquisite theatres I've played in. There's a devilish noise in the night here, comes right in through the cracks, awful, makes me quite frightened. And they've replaced the soft toilet tissue with shiny stuff. Oh! It's not that I'm fussy, but well I'm not as strong as I used to be."

Harrie followed the aria of complaints generously and had a handkerchief ready for Phoebe to squeeze.

"They do know you're special."

"Harrie darling!"

"By the way, has that man been back? From yester-day. From Vietnam."

"Not if he can help it, I shouldn't think," pro-nounced Phoebe as if it proved her case. "He was a different sort of chap. He'd travelled, of course."

They drank so Harrie was flushed when she rose. As if compulsively Phoebe seized the girl's wrist yet again and pulled herself up. Her pink creased face was half in love, half lost, as it groped to see itself across the years in the clear and serene flesh of Harriet Varney, and Harrie disengaged her wrist with a slight yank, protec-tively, not unkindly.

"Do please take good care. You're very precious, Harrie. Come and see me soon."

And leaving the girl unsteady Phoebe Deslines had made an exit.

Harrie was mildly awash and, preferring to avoid her parents, took a deck-chair onto the verandah where in the dusk she could seek her clarity.

The neighbours were out on the lawn, the man and his son. Joe Dunn's well-tempered frame leaned on the slope of his property surveying Ben as he might have sur-veyed terrain at work. His light shirt rippled, having come untucked in the game they played. Ben in return eyed his father tremulously. His shoulders and knees shook in their readiness to respond. When Joe Dunn flicked the ball low to the ground the boy would fly blindly to catch at it. Joe played to excite the boy, egg him on, so he could perceive and admire his child's development. Now the boy was standing on a spot while his father circled, clapping his hands from different positions, suddenly behind Ben's back posing him a harder test. Then he would halt, cock his head and scratch as his hard-working eyes assessed the boy. It was like a sheep-dog trial and across the fence Harrie Varney joined in, absorbed in Joe Dunn, expectant of the least twitch of a sign.

"Come on," yelled the man. The ball had rolled through the fence into the vacant paddock at the bottom of the Varneys'. They ran to the fence where Joe picked the kid up and plumped him down on the other side. "Now watch me, Benj," he said as he showed the correct method of crossing barbed wire. They prowled for the ball in the thick phalaris and daisies and when they found it tossed it casually to and fro. The father did all sorts of fancy throws, from between his legs or backwards. He did a cricket bowl that looked like a contorted windmill and Ben tried to bowl back over-arm. He ran spiralling his limbs but let go too late and the ball dribbled only a few feet in front of him in the weeds. Father and son ran to retrieve when suddenly Ben found himself picked up and flung about in the air. Joe Dunn had grabbed a wrist and an ankle and whirled his son now squealing and giggling round in circles above the spinning grass. It was marvellous that the man could keep his balance on the hillside, supported by his widely planted legs, rocking from one to the other as his body rotated. He swung Ben high and low. His wrists and hands strained as he clung to his son, their linked arms taut as a spoke.

The boy began a strange high hum. He had relaxed and was a swooping jet. The dizzy blurred world was loosened about him and he soared, secured by centri-petal force to the axis of his father, and it was ages before the motion slowed. Joe Dunn was lowering his son now. "Okay," he called and dropped the weight onto the ground, making Ben fall and bump in grass that hid him.

For a second Harrie was worried about snakes but didn't dare intrude. Joe left Ben lying and headed up, giving a nod to Harriet Varney on her verandah as he crossed the fence to his own patchy lawn.

"G'day," he laughed. "Having a bit of fun."

"Yes, it's beautiful out." Ben had fetched the ball and came running behind his father. "I bet that felt terrific," she called to him. But the boy was content to be silent about it and hurried after the man so they could enter the lit house together.

Harrie was wanted inside too. The lamb was ready.

"He's home for a change — next door," said Hazel her mother in the kitchen, flopping her wrist towards the sunset as she searched for the knife. Her husband Stanley would carve.

Harrie's mind was still giddy after the meal and she closed herself in the bedroom early. She hadn't stopped staring at Joe Dunn. She had been whirled too by the operation of his body, intricate, mysterious and easy. And while she took in the father she studied the son. Little Ben was six and had never been so lively nor so beautifully, nervously confident as in front of his dad. She wanted his shining face. She wanted her play to have the simplicity of the child. She wanted father and son to know her worthiness.

Sleep came, welcome. Its stillness was opportune and Harrie revelled beneath its surface. In unaccountable phantasmagoria she laid her palm before Joe Dunn and seeing his face said, "I give you my hand."

♦ ♦ ♦

In the morning she put her face closer to the mirror than usual, widening her eyes and baring the teeth she had brushed and brushed. She bit her teeth with determination. Her vision of the thing, freshened now, would sustain her, green and full of her own special life, oceanically abundant. She could be businesslike and she could be womanly. She would have the children she wanted and draw from them the peculiar sap of their selves.

Before leaving for work she went next door to ask Lorrie Dunn about Benjamin. She hoped, although he was so young, that the boy would be Mole. But his mother stood suspiciously at the front door, preventing Harriet Varney. She didn't know. Ben was funny with strangers. He was too shy and gullible.

"I'm sure it would help bring him out," urged Harrie, as if that was what Lorrie wanted. Ben held his mother's skirt and looked at the lady with open eyes. But when Harrie bent to ask if he liked plays he became near tearful and ducked his head. "I wonder — is Mr Dunn in?" asked Harrie, implying that the man might respond more sensibly.

The wife stiffened at this, adopting the expression she saved for the bank. "No, I'm sorry. He's still in bed, love," she chortled, hooking Ben's neck in a grip. "You know — he's not at home all the time."

So Harrie couldn't pursue things for the moment and merely allowed herself to touch Ben's silken head.

Rehearsals commenced by the river and the children ran all along the bank in the tall rushes with the brushy pokers sticking out, in the uncut grass thick with weed flowers.

"Hey Martin! Martin! Come here Martin!" called Wilma McCloud to Martin Tavistock. She was standing in the willows in a white rose-patterned dress and he tore across to her. "Guess what I've found." She scampered off, hopping sideways, and Martin vanished after her behind a curtain of trees.

When it came to the rehearsal, Tavistock was a professional. He had his lines learnt and kept his eyes on the move for someone to pin down with his performance, usually Miss Varney who had an inkling now of what her play might be.

At the end of the morning she distributed ice creams from the back of her car. As she leaned into the cooler someone tugged at her bottom.

"Miss Varney?"

Ben was there. He was holding a milk bottle full of river water and wildflowers and he thrust it forward at Harrie.

"Ben! Thank you! You do want to be in the play, don't you? You're a big boy, aren't you? Do you know the names of these lovely flowers? There's dandelion and everlasting daisy and that's salvation jane. You dear boy. Do you want to be Mole in the play?"

Harrie drove Ben home to Lorrie Dunn who was cross because she hadn't noticed his absence.

"If he really wants to do it, he can," she said now. "But promise me you'll look after him. He's a sensitive child. He's got a nice nature. He's not as tough as the other kids." Mrs Dunn let her own toughened frame slacken as she talked. It was Saturday afternoon again when all the chores were done and Joe was off at the pub.

"He'll have a fabulous time — Lorrie. Won't you, Ben?" Harrie insisted as she passed the boy across the doorway. The parents were always the worst. "Bye now. And thanks. Bye bye Ben."

The milk bottle vase of river flowers would stand proudly on her dressing-table.

In the next days dust appeared in the distance and rehearsals took place under a browning sky. Her time was taken up. She spent loving hours with Ben probing his natural quality and although he didn't speak up at first, being shy, and would just stand there staring vaguely about him, unwilling to tell what he thought, she was patient. Being the youngest he didn't fit in and he preferred to wander off by himself up the bank where he could watch the river creatures leaping and throw in leaves or paper boats that sidled away.

Her evenings were busy too, with costumiers, technicians and parents, and she would have to walk home late up the vacant main street. Summer was coming and at half past ten on a warm Sunday night she passed the Orient. On the day the bar closed Phoebe usually had one of her times and Harrie considered going to her. The old trooper would be on the bed immobile, moist cotton-wool pads on her eyes, immersing herself in the fortitude required to endure a night without sleep. Harrie could have done with a lift but suspected that on Sundays Phoebe liked to remain inconsolable.

A film had just finished in the cinema hall and a mass of people was bustling out, overly gay in the night. Harrie saw that Wilma McCloud was there. She was a shapely girl.

Then Harrie flared and panicked briefly. At once she crossed the road to put herself at a distance and under cover. Wilma McCloud was making a couple with Martin Tavistock and a teacher should never see such things. Besides, Harrie was nervous at the fullness of the fragrant dark and the blossoming of younger youth. She had to be thoroughly intent on her own green vision, and pressed on home. And Martin Tavistock fretted that Miss Varney saw him with Wilma, meshing her fingers with his, directing him away downhill. But he was happy to be led, for the first time holding a girl's hand like this. By the river a few reassuring cars were parked, under trees whose roots snaked in the shadows. It was so dry that sounds sparked underfoot, against the river which made no noise and was invisible. Wilma and Martin found the path. It should have been awful to be so close. But it was glorious, worth the boring film and mouthful of lies, as Martin said afterwards when their hour was up.

Brendan Lynch had given up on Worrong after his behaviour in the pub. He'd moved on from the bench in the middle of the night and without waiting for dawn had burned his ute recklessly along one of the dirt roads that led higher into the mountains. When he found some thick scrub to stop behind he curled up on the seat with his terrier Sheba nestled in his crotch and slept till light.

When he sat up in the morning he swore and testily arched his creaking neck. "Shit!" If he'd only played it lower, damper, in Worrong. But once the match was thrown onto the straw of his mind — booze and memories — he burst into a hell of fire which danced through him. He had a drum of water in the back and heaved it over the side of the ute so he could douse his face and fill his mouth. He was hungry too, as well as broke now, and kicked the passenger door ferociously. But he wouldn't go back to the town. The track he was on climbed higher into the Snowies.

When Brendan Lynch returned to Worrong he had been out in the bush for a week, shifting about, bludging a bit, taking scant meals in exchange for junk removal. His body was all bone and knocked about on the seat as he followed the last winding hurtle down. The dog looked sick, in sympathy perhaps or just sorry for itself. But Brendan whistled merrily and allowed his head to bob as he felt good, seeing Worrong again spread vulnerably in front of him, halfway up from the rich river trough. Brendan would get satisfaction, thrillingly, beneath that ramshackle complacency of roofs.

He began his rounds straightaway, starting at the top of the street at a fawn brick house. The bell chimed at his fingertip and, inside, the shadowy figure of a woman prepared herself to open the door.

"Excuse me. I wondered if you had any old floor covering you wanted to get rid of."

Lorrie Dunn kept herself on the inner side of the threshold, unsure what was being offered.

"We've only just moved in," she said. She imagined the man wanted more than he was asking for. He seemed mockingly to know all her needs and to be ready to meet whichever of them. When he moved his shaking hand, she jumped as if he were about to grab hold.

"Mum," called a child's voice. Ben saw the funny bloke in the doorway and timidly came to smile. The carrot bloke from the pub. With a twitch of a blink Brendan concealed the recognition from the boy's mother. Only the boy's blank innocence was lit up by the stranger; and Brendan felt a gash in his own heart exposed.

"Sorry I can't help you," the woman was saying.

"Here, take this," crumpling a dollar into his hand as she closed and snibbed the door.

When Brendan tried at the next house, the Varneys', no one was home.

Harrie Varney was in the classroom keeping a lookout despite herself for signs of romance between Wilma McCloud and Martin Tavistock. She got the girl to call the roll. When Martin wouldn't look at her in Miss Varney's presence Wilma read his name extra loud to summon him to her. Although Harrie freely admitted jealousy, she was niggled by a wish to find something blameworthy.

Monday was dreadful. She was overworked all day and there was an intrigue about photocopier abuse. On Tuesday during break she had Janet Frawley weeping in a corner. She had to take her home and arrange a substitute: the husband's friend had left. Wednesday was cheery and the magazine contributions were due. She flicked through the heap guardedly for Tavistock's and found a poem in free form. Snickering she pulled herself up in her seat. It described a bank beneath willows —

> My eyes have gone out.
> Our bodies find each other,
> like lips that touch and sing —
> a dark song of pleasure and pain.
> It drums us to dissolving
> in a flow of love.

Harrie's cheeks reddened. Tavistock was bent over his book like a lamb. His pastoral hair was a fleece of hay. If it hadn't been quite so specific she might have enjoyed his adolescent rhapsody; but she couldn't discuss it with him ever.

Wilma's contribution was on a scrap of paper, a three-frame comic strip. A stick girl with black curls and a large gun was talking to a stick boy. "Hey look!" she says. "What is it?" he says. "A gun, stupid," she says. "Does it work?" he says. Third picture: "BANG BANG YOU'RE DEAD," she cries and the stick boy is flat on his back. Without smiling at the sinister joke Harrie put her face into her hands. It was disturbing. The girl wasn't gunning for Martin Tavistock alone. Wilma sat poking a pencil up her nose, her white eyes mooning into space, the redness of her lips answering the shade of Harriet Varney's blood. Thank God the period was ending.

The air was still thick on Friday for the next session in the Gardens. Harrie was labouring to bring it all together now and odd bystanders gathered. She was pleased to see the chap from the pub there. He'd parked his pink ute at a vantage point and leaned against the side of the car with his dog, half-dozing as he watched, his nutty face lost in a ginger fuzz. She gave him an ample wave across the grass and Brendan swished a daisy in return, acknowledging the girl with a friendly leer from his strip of a mouth.

Harrie had timetabled Wilma and Martin for late in the day because she didn't want to be put off by any charge of love their scenes together might betray. But when the time came, they were missing.

"Bugger," she said and marched off from the others. She had a good idea where they might be. The boy's poem ran like a map in her mind and took her straight to the riverbank, pushing through the trees. She chewed her cud feverishly and when she heard giggling from inside a willow shoved the fronds aside as if they'd been plastic strips in a butcher's.

The two kids, noiseless and helpless, shuffled together on the earth, their ankles manacled by their clothing. Miss Varney was annoyed. "That's enough, you two. We're trying to hold a bloody rehearsal. Your attendance would be appreciated. Come on now." They were clumsily assembling themselves, wondering what they'd have to face. "Just you behave yourselves in the future and there'll be no more said about this."

When she left them she forced her way through to the river to splash herself. The water steamed off her cheeks. It was trying but she wouldn't cry. Not for her frustrated anger, nor her hope, the play, the kids, Martin Tavistock with the sky eyes. There were other receptacles for her faith. When she returned to the group she was imperiously in control. "We've wasted enough time already. Now let's put some effort into it."

Little Ben had seen Miss Varney coming red and hot, and hopped aside. When he wasn't needed he drifted off, straying wide out of her range so she couldn't call him back. The grass was yellow-green from too much bore-watering.

"Hey, sonny," someone called.

Ben grinned eagerly. He hadn't noticed the red-bearded fellow and now ran over, making the terrier yap crazily.

"You're acting in the play there, are you? Must be fun. Can you come here a tick? You can help me."

"What are you doing here?"

"Me? I'm just watching."

Ben hesitated. He saw how far he was from the others and wondered if Miss Varney knew he was gone. She happened to turn then and catching him in the distance smiled hazily, pleased that the boy wasn't shy of their odd spectator. So Ben came forward.

"I've lost one of me cards," Brendan said. "The Queen of Spades. She's usually somewhere here in my bag of tricks, but I can't seem to find her. Well, come here, sit yourself down and watch close. I take this pack of cards, see, and shuffle."

Ben peered at them as they sprayed between Brendan's skinny fingers. They were mixed, divided, put into piles and re-united. Then the man closed his eyes, groped for Ben's hand and pulled the boy against him.

"Walla!"

He clicked his fingers, blinked and plucked the Queen of Spades out from behind Ben's ear.

"Wow!"

"Have you ever heard of China?" Brendan fished. "Well, that's where these cards come from. See the pictures on the back." The colours changed like butterfly's wings.

"I don't believe you. Dad's got some like that."

So Brendan did another trick to establish his power and made Sheba trot on her hind legs. He was sweating and drops ran off his stubby carrot nose.

"Why do you sweat so much?" asked Ben cheekily.

"Because I'm wearing a thick woollen coat, all right? It belonged to my brother, who's dead. He got it in Vietnam. That's a sorry story I don't like to go into, mate." Brendan laughed in his soft wheezy way and made his body tremble so much that he had to whistle to calm his throat. He showed Ben how to whistle with his hands cupped over his mouth, and kept on with endless fragmentary stories of his travels. Brendan had never been listened to so intently and he wanted to tell the boy everything. Ben believed Brendan and would

understand even the most fabulous, even the most horrible of what the man had to tell. In piercing through to
the child's capacity for enthrallment, Brendan's power
was felt as if it always deserved to be.

He pulled a piece of fool's gold from his sausage bag
and gave it to Ben. It was from Saigon.

"Why are you giving it to me?"

"Because you're my mate. You understand about
these things. Will you come back tomorrow and see
me. And don't tell anyone. Cross your heart and hope
to die."

Harrie was searching for Ben now. "Ben," she called,
advancing. Why weren't all the children as responsive
as Ben?

"Shake on it," whispered Brendan to Ben, "and will
you bring me some food tomorrow? Fair change for the
gold, see?"

"Okay." Ben put his hand into the man's rough
freckled one. The dog Sheba was gouging fleas from her
belly and yelped at Harrie.

"Hallo. Have you been watching?"

"Yep."

She leaned over them. "We've got to be going, Ben."

The boy secretly slipped the stone into his pocket
and let Miss Varney take his hand.

"See ya later, sonny. What's ya name? Ben. See ya."
Brendan gave the fat girl a dry sort of smirk as she
swept back her hair.

"How are things going?" she asked him sincerely
and he shrugged. In spite of her tiredness Harrie's
round face beamed at the prospect of charity.

"I get by."

"Of course."

Brendan heard her say as she walked to her car with

Ben, "Have you been talking to that funny man? Was he nice?" He spat into the dirt after that bag of an angel.

Ben clutched the gold in his pocket. "Don't ever stop believing," murmured Harrie, her thoughts miraculously running with the child's. Ben's quality was never more precious to her. In him she found the intensity of wild open-eyed-ness she needed. If all the children had greenness as shining as his, then the play would be blessed and the Gardens, the river, the town itself, might break through to radiance.

Harrie delivered Ben and ignored Lorrie Dunn's surliness. Joe was overdue again. But Harrie had earned her night off in the Orient.

It was windy and the dust had been whipped up again, infiltrating nose and mouth. All of Worrong hoped the storm would reach its peak and pass. Harrie met Phoebe that evening in the hotel foyer, wearing a hat brimmed with frayed chiffon.

"What a foul wind, Phoebe!" she said.

"I have wind, dear, and I'm not staying in this place another minute. Darling, where can I go? I can't go to another hotel in this wretched town."

The new manager's wife swung through from the side bar, coughing. "Evening, Harriet. I'm glad you're here. I've *had* this performance. Talk to her, will you? She owes us four months' full board — not counting the bar bill."

"I would be completely within my rights not paying you a penny. I could be paid to hold my tongue about this place. But I will settle as soon as is feasible. It's not your fault, dear. You just don't understand."

Harrie took the woman aside and smoothed things over. If she left her luggage as surety, Phoebe could go up to the Varneys'. Harrie lugged Phoebe's cases back upstairs and then took her to Hazel and Stanley who received her placidly in the lounge, taking out the brandy and embarking on a batch of their familiar gossip.

"They say an odd looking bloke's been hanging round the Gardens," said Hazel, "where Harrie does her play. Have you seen him, Harrie? He's got a painted up ute apparently."

"Yes, I've seen him."

"He's nothing to do with you, is he, dear? They say he's not all there."

"He seems all right."

"They say he's funny."

Phoebe squawked. "You and your funny people, Hazel. You haven't changed." Phoebe had been pacified but now started to kick again. "It's in God's hands, I suppose. If I could do anything about it I would. I'd get out of this bally place." Hazel and Stanley on the couch found it hard to sympathize. Phoebe sucked at her glass. "Although I don't go to church," she went on, "I do still believe. Believing is the most terrible thing. You know that, Harrie, what faith and hope can do."

Presently Phoebe became drowsy and nodded off. Harrie feared she'd passed on altogether but Stanley, slow and gentle, could rouse her. He escorted her gallantly back to her room in the Orient and saw from the street that she'd extinguished her light.

After that day, as she laid her head on her pillow, Harrie felt like a pin-cushion.

♦ ♦ ♦

By Sunday morning it had cleared. Down the back of Varneys' a flock of cockatoos baubled the gumtrees and magpies made their bell sounds. While his parents rested after lunch Ben walked out, down to the willows near the caravan park as he'd promised. Brendan was lolling on the front seat of the ute, Sheba beside him. Ben surprised him when he peered through the grimy window.

"Hallo mate," said Brendan, bouncing up, "good to see you." He had a doll in a hula skirt dangling from the mirror and quickly straightened out his hair and beard. Ben handed over an apple and a block of chocolate and Brendan started to eat at once. He was talking already, about the possibilities of things, if you were prepared, and what it cost. He told the story of a man who wanted to fly. He found a teacher who put him through all sorts of tests which he passed by trusting. In the end the teacher took him up to a high crag — in the Himalaya mountains where it was freezing cold — and told him to fly. The man jumped off, right into the clouds. "They say that he flew, because no one can ever say that he didn't. You see?"

Ben giggled and nodded as sagely as he knew how. Brendan's fingers now were going like knitting-needles at a piece of newspaper. He folded it into a package and told Ben to pull two corners. He did so warily and the paper blossomed into a sort of prehistoric bird that flapped when you twiddled its tail. Brendan's eyes were glinting. He gave Ben a warm hug. He hadn't dreamed he had so much up his sleeve. But he had to keep on talking in case the spell broke.

"You know, there's a kind of knowledge only very few people ever have. It's something you see, eye to eye." Ben was settled next to him on the car seat and

Brendan put his hand on the boy's arm. "Your arm is warm, blood temperature, right? It's brown and smooth and covered with little golden hairs. But what makes it an arm is the bone in the middle, even though you can't see it. And that bone is nothing more than a dry old stick. But if you could see that bone then there'd be nothing else to see."

Brendan spoke almost desperately. For the first time he had someone to receive his secrets and Ben didn't dare move away.

"That's what knowledge is. It's looking into the sun. Seeing the flowers of light. I told you about my brother. He saw them."

"He's dead."

"That's something different. I've seen the magic flowers too though no one will believe me. Do you want to?"

The perspiration ran down into Brendan's beard in runnels. He couldn't stop now.

"I can show you something that teacher of yours can never show you, mate, and that father of yours can never show you."

He took from his bag a paper tube with a purple twist.

"That's a cracker," stated Ben.

"You do what I say."

He put the tube firmly into Ben's upright fist and made the boy swear to obey. Brendan was grinning now and rubbed the boy's shoulder.

"You're joining the club, mate."

He set Ben out of the car and switched on the ignition, then while the car idled he lit up a cigarette. Finally he bent to kiss the boy, filthy and slobbering, on the forehead. Ben stood dumbly and Brendan's eyes sparked. He held the butt of the cigarette to the wick and quickly once it was smouldering slammed the door and was off. The car rocked and clanked over the track through the trees out of the caravan park. Ben heard it along the road. He held the tube carefully because he was shivering. He nearly threw it away because the smoke smelt awful, but remembering his promise he stayed studying the wick with his giant eyes. Holding tightly to the fizzling tube, staring, his legs rooted to the ground, his heart beat in loyal hope for the flowers of light.

When the explosion came he didn't move. He continued standing and staring until he began to scream, holding his bloody hand in front of him as the pain of a degree never before conceived pushed into his brain. Then he howled, running.

He ran across the grass, tears eating his face. His hands were knotted together high in the air before him, the one squeezing the other throbbing burnt one. Yelling still he ran into the circle of caravans and people came. They took him to the hospital in the next town and someone rang his parents.

Lorrie Dunn was hysterical when she arrived. Ben's eyes were completely covered with a thick wadge of bandage. His eyebrows had been singed and worse damage was suspected. His hand was a great white mit. Lorrie Dunn shouted in fury at the matron. Who had done this to her boy? Who had taken him away from home in the first place?

"Accidents happen, Mrs Dunn."

Lorrie took the boy's good hand in hers and demanded, "Ben, sweetie, what were you up to?"

But the boy wouldn't speak except to say, "Mum,"

and with the white gauze across his face you couldn't tell anything.

Harrie's mother had already received the news on the phone when Joe Dunn came next door to talk about it. She wanted to go to the hospital at once but Joe let her know that the boy's mother was there.

"The top of his first finger's nearly blown off. And the webbing's split. His whole hand is a mess of burns. The poor kid." The father spoke in a calm dead voice. He'd been gardening in the morning and was wearing only his shorts. Harrie was faint in the doorway.

"Dear God, the poor poor kid. What about his eye?"

"They dunno."

She couldn't endure the child's pain, nor Joe's judgment of her.

"Someone did it to him. It's the only explanation. They reckon that weird bloke's been hanging round again. A real bloody animal. The cops are after him. They've got his number. You haven't had anything to do with him, have you?"

She felt vainly for strength and squeezed the doorknob urgently. The man was naked to the waist. She could have clutched at his chest and he seemed to flinch in palpable disgust, knowing what she proposed. When the girl didn't answer but bowed her head and blubbered, Joe Dunn bit at her. "What do you know about it?"

He confronted her in the doorway and she spoke what she could not deny. "That chap was down by the river yesterday. Ben was talking to him. They liked each other."

"They'll get him," said Joe. "Jesus, woman. What did you let that bloke near the kid for. Couldn't you see he was a nut-case? Ben wasn't to know. He's such a trusting one. He'd trust a stray dog."

Joe was dirty and brown from the garden. His thin mouth and his tufty eyebrows were unable to match his bitter righteousness. He was fed up with not understanding.

Harrie took his words until he refused to give any more, flattened into a more terrible silence.

"They'll put him away," Joe concluded and rubbed his chest. He had a great pelf of hair across his chest in the shape of outstretched eagle's wings. Harrie for a moment felt herself dislodged, as if she'd dug her fingers into the wings, mounting to soar. She blacked out; but before she could slump to the ground Joe Dunn reached out an arm to support her.

When she came to, Janet Frawley had arrived and was ministering tea. The news was round that someone to do with Harrie Varney had let off a banger in a kid's face. On every side of her was shame. Then Phoebe was on the phone with a more exalted version of the story. It was impossible. She was stranded. The only being near her was Janet whose stained features were at home with fate. The tide had drawn back, right back, and deprived her even of the brine to sluice her aching eyes.

In Chinese

They came from the various sectors of the city, the
diverse walks of life, travelling intently by car, bus or
bicycle, or on foot from the residences. They con-
verged with purpose on the bare hilltop of the College
of Advanced Education, gripping their coats and books
closely and hurrying through the cold and dark to the
Union or the instruction block. They had an air of
eager concern and commitment to the evening classes
which took them away from their homes and families
at the dinner hour. They were very active. A few con-
versed briefly in small groups. But most, single and
alone, were engaged in brisk, rigorous internal dialogue.
Yet it was all semblance and John, heading for his class,
had a theory. He theorized that the appearance of action was only a foil to the passivity within. Not that he
disapproved. He was the same. Passivity was the only
approach possible to the modern sort of education.
Front up and be worked on. Get knowledge by submission to programmes, courses and the aggregation of
percentile bits. Entering the classroom he chose a place
not too far forward, not too far back, and tipping,
shoving, scraping, he adjusted his chair to accommo-
date his body in a position of maximally receptive iner-

tia. He waited. The others as they arrived did with their chairs as John had done, and fell to cursory, woeful chat about the ordeal of study. Then they flicked in their folders for a clean page and doodled, stilling their thoughts. John drew a spiral round the punchhole in his page. They were not to be condemned. He had a theory that, whatever their life elsewhere they wiped themselves blank when they entered the teaching environment. Automatic primal therapy. They were ready for knowledge, in a dry fashion, yawning, shuffling, awaiting the lecturer who was late. John was passive too, on principle because he was dedicated to openness and, anyway, he didn't stop at passivity. Beneath that layer he seethed with inventiveness, energy and decision. Did the others realize? He wondered if it was the case with them too. They eyed each other indifferently, no one much talking. They looked content and compact. Except for the old Christian Italian lady who gave watery smiles to the air. They were dried fruit hoping to be dunked and reconstituted in the syruppy sweetness of truth.

The lecturer was a solid chap whose commitment to the subject had led him to acquire a Chinese sense of humour. He joked as he unpacked his bag and the class stirred familiarly to reassure him. *How to tell the time in Chinese.* Like everything else in the language it was sagely and wonderfully at odds with the way things were done in English. The lecturer was giving the first example when the girl walked in. He stopped in his tracks to usher her to a seat. She was a new girl. John had never seen her before. She certainly hadn't been there in the first semester. She sat on her chair, book and paper in her lap, and smiled. She leaned forward at the lecturer, smiling keenly. With her hand under her

250

chin, smiling, she seemed to reach out for the foreign
sounds and the information. Her eyes were bright blue
coals.

Behind her back the others in the class turned and
made querying faces. Some frowned and were
affronted. She couldn't just walk in like that after half a
year and upset the group dynamic. Others pulled
themselves up, or slouched back coolly, to intrigue and
allure her — but she didn't notice the rest of the class.
Indeed, John saw, her look of attentiveness kept giving
way to a tired glaze, though without·losing its dazzle.
She didn't sit back until the end of the lecture when she
said to her neighbour —

"Isn't it *fabulous* ! I'd forgotten how *fabulous* it was!"
She laughed, bubbling. "But it's insanely *difficult*. I'm
never going to catch up." She flicked her fine, dust-col-
oured hair out of her eyes. Turning to the people on her
other side she looked, for a moment, terribly worried.
"What am I going to *do* ? You're all so *good* ." Then she
gave her bubbling rising tickle of a laugh again.

Her neighbour was Kevin Spike. He was the
hawkeye of the class, always on the ball, never missing
a trick. He stood up, buttoning his maroon blazer and
waiting by the girl's seat, encouraging her to rise and
leave under his escort. "How come you're just picking
it up now?" he asked confidentially.

She gathered up her things, still smiling, and with
half a turn of goodbye to the others walked quickly
ahead of Kevin out of the class. "Well, you see, it was
hopeless . I first — "

She was gone round the corner of the door and John
couldn't catch her story. There was only the string of
images trailing behind her down the corridor, flashing
through John's head, twenty-four per second.

The evidence was considerable. On a normal day John spent his time working methodically in his room. Now he was passing unaccustomed hours drinking coffee in the Union, looking up from the cup whenever a fair-haired girl of medium height appeared, whenever a brisk lively moment occurred on the edges of his vision. Where had she come from? Perhaps she had a connection with the lecturer and was given special treatment. In his mind John saw her park her hair behind her ears where it should have stayed. Except it fell forward and made her look mysterious and late-night. John couldn't wait for the next lecture. Having theories for everything he speculated that this might be love.

He took the seat next to the one she had occupied. He peeled off his parka and laid it across *her* seat. It was an opportunity not to be missed. If his behaviour was obsessive, well, then, the others in the class were his rivals and were equally devious. Then running all the way up the stairs a clicking of heels announced her, rushing ahead of herself. John retrieved his parka only a fraction before she appeared in the doorway. She beamed, took the hint and collapsed in the empty chair. "Hi!"

John responded as softly, as significantly, as he dared.

"What's the *time* ?" she said. "I thought I was ages *late* . God I'm disorganized. It was bumper to bumper all along Belconnen Way and I just couldn't *move*. My watch must be wrong. Anyway thank goodness I got here. It's absolutely pouring outside. You couldn't see a *thing* ."

When she shook her hair one of the raindrops fell on John's hand. As she settled herself he drew the hand back. Ceremoniously, with the tip of his tongue, he licked up the drop. She unwrapped her scarf and took her coat off, and her chequered vyella smock underneath looked so warm John wanted to touch it. She gave a determined heave to slow her breathing. When her breasts rose they sent out a soft wave, as if she was throwing something off, stripping herself back to a kid ready to learn. But since nothing was happening in the classroom her vitality swelled up again and she bent over to John, whispering that she'd *love* a cigarette. In his dream, as she came near, he could do nothing but point, silently, at the No Smoking sign.

After a decent pause Kevin Spike leaned forward, offering a gold packet. "Cigarette, Ginny?"

"Oh no, I don't think I will now, thanks."

So that was her name.

When the lecture started she turned to John again, mouthing: "I've forgotten my *book?*" He looked at her humorously and pushed his own book so far in her direction that it tipped off the little table attached to the armrest. It spreadeagled on the floor and he had to crouch inelegantly to pick it up. At the end of the lecture John said, so flatly it was neither question nor statement, so warily it showed total disinterest: "Off home now."

"Well — " she grinned, shrugging, "via the bar."

Kevin Spike pushed forward and asked if she was still coming.

"Are we *coming* ?" she asked generally. "We," with John at her side. But she was walking towards the door in front of Kevin.

"I wouldn't mind a drink," declared John.

He *would* mind it; he would hate it; but he would hear more of her magical chitchat.

He discovered that she was doing Chinese as part of a Dip. Ed. and had deferred the whole thing after six months to go travelling in Asia with a *really wonderful friend* . Now she was back to finish off the second part of the *year.* When she spoke she gave the last syllable of every sentence a rising accent, filling her speech with ecstatic unanswered possibility. After the first drink a tall goodlooking man in his middle twenties came and took her away. He was got up like a battered schoolboy in the punk style. Was he the *friend* ? As quickly as possible after she'd gone, because there was nothing to be said or done to Kevin Spike, John took himself off. He saw them then, in the distance, Ginny and the man, gliding behind the sheetglass wall of Life Sciences, short-cutting to the carpark.

They learned many essential things in Chinese. They learned that in the opinion of some linguists there was no passive voice in Chinese. There was only greater and lesser activeness. There was no chance of withdrawing irresponsibly into a state of being worked on. On the other hand there was the compensation that *our* habitual passive could be strangely transmuted through Chinese eyes into an active living force. For example the character 愛, pronounced "ai" or "eye", meaning "to love". Typically it combined with other basic words to make binary compounds: you could take 人 , pronounced "*rén*", meaning "person", and put it with "*ài*" to make 人 愛 : *àirén.* Literally it means "love person". In English it must be translated as either "lover" or "beloved". There is nothing in between. In the People's Republic it must be translated as "nonsexist spouse", in Singapore as "mistress". But "love person", the actively loving or the passively loved, in Chinese John reckoned there could be no distinction. Simply by loving you would necessarily have to be loved back.

The day they learned about love persons John was sitting behind Ginny. He looked at the back of her head and willed love over her in waves. It was an experiment and if the theory were correct she would become aware of him, start to fidget and, finally, turn for a quick smiling glance at him. But she didn't and on the way out he couldn't look her in the face.

The class dispersed in various directions. John went by himself down the several flights of ill-lit stairs leading to the back concourse. As he approached the glass doors to the outside his eyes, at a certain angle, were dazzled by the low sunset. It was fiercely orange away off behind the black mountains, throwing light to the ends of the sky in stupendous spears. He was bewitched and pressed on, lost in it, until crossing the concourse he all but collided with Ginny.

"Hi," she said and stopped for a conversation. She was wearing sunglasses.

"Is it the same colour to you," asked John, "through those things?"

She smiled but didn't take them off. "It's better." They looked across ten miles of suburban development at the orange fusion. Four students with squash racquets came out of one door, walked along the building, entered another door. "There aren't many people *round* ," said Ginny.

"There never are," said John, "not real people. It's illusion. That's my theory." His legs were apart and he had the weight on both feet, confronting her.

"That's what *they* say about *you*," was her reply.

"They?"

She laughed and made her eyes bulge. "A thousand million Chinese! Can you believe they actually communicate in that language? Anyway, see you." And she pursued her geometric path towards an exit from the concourse rectangle.

John lived in a room in a hall-of-residence. By his bed, in a pot, there was a comfrey plant, an ancient medicinal herb which died in winter and came again in spring. But John, although he watered it carefully, had little faith that anything would grow out of the remains of last year. He looked at the old leaves, shrunk and crinkled like grey potato chips, and wondered if the comfrey were technically alive or dead. A book called *The Secret Life of Plants* had talked of the incredible sensitivity of all organic forms — to emotions, to events, to desires, needs, hopes, stimuli of every kind. So John stood in front of the pot and repeated his experiment from Chinese, emitting waves of love. When nothing happened he was consoled. If a minimal plant didn't respond, why should he ever have thought a human would? Such ideas were superstitious snow!

That night in the remotest passage of his sleep he felt something tugging him up from the solitary deep. He kept his eyes shut, tightly resisting consciousness, wanting to stick with his unknown dreams whatever they were. But slowly, sluggishly, he was rolled over. He was edged across to hug the body in the space beside him, reaching out his arms to encompass the warm loved shape. But the sheets were cold in that part of the bed. There was nothing there. He woke properly then and opened his eyes on the claustrophobic pitch of his room. A sorrow as strong as fear filled him. He found his body balancing along the very rim of his single bed, making a place for the one he had imagined — and loved — in the night. But no one was there.

After the next Chinese class John intercepted Ginny in the corridor. "Do you feel like getting together to practise for the oral?"

"Yes," she said immediately. "Yes, *great* ," nodding, "come round to my place?"

"When?"

"Tonight."

He nodded cautiously. "Okay."

Ginny lived in a group house. The group consisted of two females and two males. The girl Marilyn suffered from *anorexia nervosa* and worked a computer in the Department of Veterans' Affairs. The blokes Ted and Todd studied Natural Resources. The house was a townhouse in the far new suburb of Holt. When John arrived the group was eating vegetable casserole and rice around the television, Marilyn and Ted in their running shorts, Todd in battle trousers and a t-shirt.

"Will you have a drink," challenged Todd, "a beer?"

"Ah — no, thanks." John stood there.

Ginny began to talk rapidly. "Did you get here alright? It's incredibly difficult the first *time* . You've probably been driving round in circles for *ages*. Have you?"

"I rode my bike."

Ted looked up with interest. "Great," he judged.

Ginny quickly scooped a heaped forkful into her mouth and, chewing, rushed with the plate to the kitchen. "That was delightful," she said, swallowing. "Now John." While she was in the kitchen she continued calling to him although he stayed awkwardly in the living room, looking at the others who were looking at the TV. When she returned she was in command, smiling and carrying a teapot and two small Chinese cups on a tray. "We can practise better in my room," she said for the benefit of the others. "It's quieter there."

Though it was not yet spring her window was wide open and the room was fresh. There was a line of books in the room, a line of plants, a line of non-commercial lotions and a mushroom ring of jars, vases and boxes on a little chest. On the wall was a green Asian cloth, otherwise the room was white. Ginny closed the curtains and lit two candles. They sat on the floor with the teapot between them and talked for hours about many things, with many long silences. Ginny talked in excited bursts, then fell soulfully silent for a stretch. John spoke in single, laconic, equally spaced sentences. Whenever they ventured into Chinese they giggled, although the Chinese tea was good. They were still on the floor at two o'clock in the morning. John was propped against the bed and Ginny had smoked endless cigarettes.

"I better be going," he said at last.

"You don't have to," she said.

He put his hand on hers and she welcomed it with her fingers.

After a respectful silence he shuffled near and kissed her. When they were in bed, when he was lying against her skinny, beautiful, fragrant form, when with her hands she seemed to treasure him, when she whispered "John", he couldn't stop wondering why he had been chosen. On the ride home, seven miles, tingling, he sang his tremendous luck. His luck which he knew was his love.

But was it love? He could afford to step back now. He noticed that the comfrey plant by his bed had put out two tiny spiky shoots. He regarded them with approval but was too exhausted after his ride to wash energy over them. In the morning when he woke he was refreshed and the shoots had doubled in size. There were four of them now, and the sun was shining. From his high position in the residence he could look out and see mountains. In the morning light they were violet and airy, as if they belonged somewhere else, and they made John feel different. That day he began to feel differently about many things. He saw a maintenance man sitting on a stone under a willow by the artificial pond in the college courtyard. For a moment the man was an elder in a scroll painting. On the approach to the residence block there were black plum and cherry trees studded with pale buds. They became Zen foreground. They had their mode of being as John had his, yet something linked them to him. Even the other students shambling about in the Union could be seen as fellows on the path, on the way. But was this love?

He came early to the Chinese lecture and sat on the chair beside the one Ginny had taken previously. He opened his folder and scribbled as the others in the classroom were doing. But the idleness and inconsequence had vanished and the occasion had acquired

259

fantastic meaningfulness. Just before time Ginny dashed in breathlessly and whispered that she wanted to speak to John outside.

"How are you?" she said, pressing her back against the wall of the corridor.

He looked at her blankly.

"Listen, I can't stay for this lecture. I've got to see a *friend* ."

He continued to gaze blankly. His tongue was a tangle of inexpressibles. He might as well have tried to speak in Chinese.

She was saying: "What happened — last night — it was just something I wanted to happen."

He gave nothing away. "I wanted it too."

"I know. That's all."

"That's okay," he confirmed.

"Anyway, look, we must see each other *soon* ," she said, smiling at him, turning from him, spattering down the stairs.

John spent most of the twenty-four hours until the next Chinese class in the Union drinking coffee. His favourite theory of all was that the individual should exert no pressure on the world. The being should be as if non-being. The world should do all the determining, all the moulding, all the pushing and shoving. He sat at one of the plastic tables overlooking his cup, moving only when the wiping-down lady came. He waited until he was actually late for the lecture so he could make an entrance. But Ginny wasn't there. During the hour Kevin Spike tapped his shoulder and passed him a message on a piece of Defence Department notepaper.

Kevin had written *I saw Ginny on the way here. She wanted me to tell you she's feeling crook and will catch up with you later.*

John's room in the hall-of-residence was very small but that night it was so enormous and empty he couldn't stand it. And there was the whole weekend to go. On Saturday at midday, after he had busied himself all morning, he rode his bike out to Holt. It was the first sunny day of the season. Marilyn and one of the Natural Resourcers were playing frisbee on the nature strip. "Hi!" they called stridently, bouncing, offering nothing more. John went up to the front door and knocked, and Todd the other Natural Resourcer answered. He was in his dressing-gown. He allowed John to walk into the living room where the curtains were still closed and in the gloom, above the music, John heard Todd say that the group hadn't seen Ginny for a few days.

"She could be at her parents."

John had not imagined she would have parents.

"Wait if you want to," said Todd.

But John wanted to return to the hall-of-residence. On the ride back an insect got in his eye and he cried. Why wasn't it working?

That Monday he was walking up the steps to the top concourse of the College of Advanced Education. It was early dusk and the view towards the sun was a fairytale. John couldn't help being enchanted. It was so clear and gentle. The mountains were blue-violet wash. The sun was silver. On the horizon a single green cloud rose in a zigzag like a cartoonist's squiggle. All the way

261

down the valley the planned development looked like nothing more than scattered futurist cubes and carefree twinkling lights. John ascended the stairs as if advancing towards an unveiled dream city. The concourse was a high concrete plateau. It might have been an open-air stage for the mountains, or a slab from which the suburbs could witness sacrifices. At that moment it was depopulated, save for one couple. They were alone among the select native shrubbery. John saw the man put his arm around the woman. The woman stood up on tiptoes to kiss him quickly on the cheek, leaning into him, then she lowered herself, pulled her sunglasses down, and was gone. The man walked on as if he were going somewhere. The woman was Ginny. John looked at the revealed city. It was a death metropolis fuelled on human dreams.

He and Ginny sat next to each other in the lecture. She was demure and greeted him rather solemnly. He felt the sharpness. They had a further lesson on binary compounds and the lecturer, beaming at the mysteries he imparted, introduced the word 博 愛 — *bó ài* — and its derivation. "You know the word *bó* meaning 'broad' or 'wide', as in broadcast, sowing the seed wide. You know *ài* meaning 'love'. Put them together and you have 'wide-love'. What is this concept?"

"Promiscuity," snorted Kevin Spike in a stage whisper. Beside John Ginny giggled.

"For the Chinese," the lecturer continued, oblivious, "*bó ài* means 'universal brotherhood'." He paused in order that the class should contemplate the celestial simplicity of this truth.

Wide-love, thought John. He could almost accept the concept, quietly and soothingly, almost. He turned to Ginny whose eyes met his with an expression of indecipherable wonderment. He had a theory. All right, he understood. It was wide-love that she practised. It was her version of universal brotherhood and was only proper. He had no special claim.

Afterwards John and Ginny went to the Union together, to speak in Chinese over their coffee as training for the oral. Suddenly he remembered so intimately the sensation of being with her. It came back naggingly, trying to assert itself. She held the coffee cup daintily in her hand, not quite keeping it level. It was surely that hand he had touched. But the more her sharp eyes shone at him the less he knew whether it had happened or not. It was imperative not to be deceived by the illusion of an action. Everything reduced to passivity in the end. Everything reduced to receptivity. Everything reduced to dream. His own love was only one drop in the universal sea.

Ginny suggested they should arrange a time for further oral practice.

"It can wait," said John gallantly. He didn't want to push her into something that wasn't real. "Are you free on the weekend?"

And she at once gave a great long uncontrolled speech about *all* the *things* she had to *do* , her *assignments* , her *parents* , her *house* , her *hydroponics* , her *really wonderful friend* , concluding that Saturday was fine.

John nodded. She brushed back her hair and laughed wildly.

"Great," she said. "See you."

His theory was that it had never really happened. That seemed the right approach. That evening he put himself in front of his books. The comfrey plant had exerted itself and now four large green leaves sprouted out of the pot. They were ridiculous. He laughed, to distract himself. He would see her next Saturday and they would talk in Chinese. He had behaved well. He had done nothing possessive towards her. He had done nothing at all. He shifted restlessly and turned the first of many pages.

Hours later there was a knock. The midnight intrusion startled him. He had been deep in study. Anxiously he went to the door. It was Ginny, face rosy, puffing. She'd been in the bar.

"Sorry," she said clumsily. "I'm sorry. Are you asleep?" Something had changed her since the afternoon.

She walked in and sat down heavily on the bed, bowing her head guiltily. John was at a loss.

"At least I got the right room," she said. "Sorry to bother you. I couldn't wait — "

John stood away from her, wanting to go to her but not doing it. "Is anything wrong?"

She kept her eyes to the floor, shaking and altering position in great uncomfortable heaves. Nervously he couldn't stop thinking about what was happening, watching for signs, wondering. The comfrey leaves had pricked up: the charge in the air would do them good. He prayed that she would speak, to explain and release.

"What?" he said, thinking she'd made a sound.

The room was monstrously vacant. Sunken on the bedspread, crouching round her knees, Ginny looked like an unwrapped parcel. John was hot and heard thumping in the cave of his chest.

Suddenly he went to her and put his hand on her head. At the same instant she spoke. "What are you *doing?* Why don't you say *anything ever?* Why don't you do anything? What's going *on?* She had been talking to the ground but now faced him. "I'm sorry. I can't help it. I haven't done anything wrong. I don't want to hassle *you* but - oh God! -" She put her head down against his knee.

She had done it. He gasped, laughing, half-yelping exultantly, half-mumbling in embarrassment. "But *I* love *you* !"

In a convulsive motion, strong as shock he jerked towards her.

"John," she said.

Quite involuntarily two tears flooded his eyes.

Then he was there with her. She was soft and it was real. Squeezing each other they understood that they filled the curiously matter-of-fact hall-of-residence room.

In the morning they opened the window. It was the world. They faced the furthest mountain, visible tipped with snow, and the nearer ones, glowing purple. Nearer still the suburbs were busy, packed with green. It was spring proper and the cherries and plums made pink and white spray. All was proportioned, as they looked, background, middle and fore. John yawned sleepily, gulping the air. Then she touched him. Following her example he touched her too and, though each traced a separate path over the other's body, their hands met and compounded.

They called the scene outside On a Road to the Yunnan Mountains, or, Approaching the Capital of the Southern Province. Overnight, overstimulated, the comfrey plant had produced two bellflowers which now tinkled in the morning breeze. There was no theory to cover it. Love person, love person, blew John in Ginny's ear. Together they looked out at the sprawling houses, all similar, containing rooms containing people, as blank and deceptive as Chinese boxes. Wide love could know them all.

The Mares

Rick was in the drive standing not quite straight and got the dust from the car when Karen drove up. He came and kissed her through the window; stood back and grinned appraisingly as she got out; hugged her. All the way from town her mind had rattled on and she had slowed down only for the last strap of road, when she saw the squat house in its honied circle of garden and outhouses. But now she was happy to let Rick put his arm round her and take her out the back to the hot close weatherboard place, his bedroom.

"I have to show you everything," he said. She had already picked up two snail-shells from the bedside table and recognized them as the ones from the Ada River in New Zealand. "Correct," he said. He had told her about it all but it was disturbing to discover that his talismans really did exist, apart. His eyes glinted at her like stones embedded in their earth. He nudged her. "Come and meet Mum."

"Wait."

She tucked in his new blue striped shirt, smoothed it and held his wrist. Then they went.

His mother was in the kitchen and she dried her hands on a tea-towel when they came in. She had fine glamorous white hair and blue eyes, unlike Rick's but as open as his. "You're probably ready for a drink, dear?"

They sat down round the table and Rick talked about the reluctant stallion at the stables. One service was worth thousands but they couldn't make the old boy do it.

Mrs Turner had two foals to feed in the home paddock and she got up to go. When she'd gone Rick slid his hand across the table to reach Karen's.

"Can I go and see your mother's foals?" she asked.

"Sure. Mum'd love you to."

Outside it was almost dark and full of dusk noises. Karen could see Mrs Turner's white hair shining out. The two horses were sidling against the railing, anxious for attention, but when Karen came down they paced nervously backwards.

"I get them when the mums die. Usually one or two a year," Mrs Turner said. Karen helped her break up the bundle of hay. They threw it in handfuls over the fence, then walked back to the house together. They could see Rick moving about in the open lighted window. "Rick never draws the curtains," his mother said.

His father was there now too, a small dark man watching the cricket round-up with Rick. He squeezed Karen, not just with his hand but with his eyes and words too. By the time they sat down to dinner things were crackling with laughter between them all.

Rick's parents had an awkward unnatural faith in the new and were eager that life should work. Their other son was off travelling somewhere and their daughter was married in Adelaide. Rick had been off too, at university and working, but he always came back to the stud for the three months of Christmas. Rick talked all the way through the meal. Only for odd seconds would he fall silent and search round the room for something missing. Then when he landed on Karen's face he would start up again, generously.

Afterwards Rick and Karen were left alone to have their coffee on the verandah, in deep armchairs. Her coffee tasted black and strange, like oil, and his fingers pressed down on her neck, a strong dry pressure coaxing her to him. His head rolled onto her shoulder and he gave a huge slack grin. He so much wanted her to be happy.

"Look at the hills," he said. "Like great big cushions, aren't they?"

It was true that their contours suggested an opulent mound of protection, and the white fence-rails chalked out the paddocks in a blanket pattern.

"I can't imagine a kinder place," he said. "When you're here."

Their faces were glossy, with a hot sheen, as he rubbed her neck and tickled. "It's too much," she said, giggling.

"Let's go to bed."

In the kitchen, as they passed through, his mother was laying the table for breakfast.

"I'll be there in a minute," said Karen.

She was suddenly inclined to follow the road down. In the home paddock the foals were whinnying in brief unanswered snatches and the moon was clear. She ran her hand along the fence-rail and the wood pushed abrasively against her skin. So she turned back, going with the grain.

Rick was sprawled across his bed in the fashion of one who sleeps alone and she moved him over. His body had measured her a space and when his flesh touched her she roasted. A flash of startled laughter burst between them. The dungy smell, the scraping touch of him, his earth weight — was all over her.

The sheet was twisted round her shoulder like a rope when she woke. Rick had gone off to work hours before and, feeling immodest lying there, she found her dressing gown and sat on the desk chair, robed like a matron. The room had lost its wonder without Rick. The crumpled clothes, the dust surface, the arcanely ordered books didn't yield up their meaning any more.

Karen's breakfast setting had been left in the kitchen. Mrs Turner was hoping to break off from the chores for a cup of tea with the girl. The radio's quarrelsome jollity made the morning seem all the more silent and still.

"What on earth's in that jar?" asked Karen as Mrs Turner stooped to the low cupboard where the jams were kept. Gleaming in the gloom on the bottom shelf was a jar full of green and white worms.

"Bean shoots. Rick's. He keeps them down there in the dark till they sprout. Then you eat them with salad." She brought the jar over to the table for Karen to see. The tender white shoots were twisting about each other, feeling round the glass sides for a way to the light. "They take no time at all. You put in a handful of beans and in a few days they're pushing the lid off."

"They're incredibly pale."

"A bit watery but crisp. Look, we'll have some for lunch." The kettle shrilled and Mrs Turner marched round the kitchen making the tea. "I love growing things. That's one of the nicest things about the stud. You're surrounded with it." Her own smile was almost wearily fertile, endlessly benignly encouraging, like the ideal mixture of sunshine and rain on well-ploughed vernal soil. She took the pot to the kettle, dashed some warming water in, swilled it round and out into the sink. Three heaped spoons and back to the stove for the boiling water, splashing down onto the black leaves.

"What time does Rick get back?" Karen asked.

"About twelve. Off again at two. It's hard work but he loves it. I don't know why he doesn't stay on. If only he'd make the stud his home and settle here. He loves that room out the back. Won't let anyone touch it when he's away. And he's not a boy anymore." Her thoughts had passed through her mind so often that she hardly knew this time whether she'd pronounced them aloud or not.

Karen saw the beanshoots move in the jar. Mrs Turner renewed the pot and, assuming, poured out two more strong cups. Suddenly Karen spoke seriously. "I can actually feel myself becoming more relaxed here."

The older woman smiled knowingly, her face moist and almost tearful from the steam off the tea. She savoured the obscure configuration of Rick's future and Karen's well-being; then automatically started clearing away. Karen offered to help.

"No no dear. It's all right. I know where they go."

It was cool inside the solid green-painted walls of the kitchen.

"Are you feeding the foals this morning, Mrs Turner?"

She laughed and turned, smiling again. "I've already done one feed — at the crack of dawn."

The pans clattered as they found their places on the shelf.

"How long till they can look after themselves?"

"It takes a couple of months. They're slower to get going without their real mothers."

270

"What about normally? Do the mares give them up easily?"

"Poor mares. They don't have much say in it. The men go out to the paddock and the mares always come over. They're drawn to the men. Then the men separate the foals off — with lassos." Her tone had altered. "It's all over in no time. The mares are upset for a while usually but the foals don't mind. It's marvellous to watch them spark up when they're all put in together." When the dishes were done she stood with her hand on her hip, with her unqualified smile. "Now Karen, I've got to go out shopping. Why don't you take a chair outside? It's not too hot yet and it's lovely round the side with the view of the hills."

Rick and his father came in for lunch and afterwards, while Mr Turner was reading the paper, Rick and Karen went to the bedroom. He smelled pungent and, lying on the bed, she nestled her head in the soft sweaty hair of his armpit.

"I talked to your mother," she said.

"You seem to get on. She wanted to like you." He yawned, snuggling against her.

"Rick?"

His hair sprayed out against the pillow in haywire clumps. Pretending to sleep he allowed himself to be undressed. He would hold her against the lumpy mattress and take her into further drowsiness and they would sleep until Mr Turner called tactfully from outside that it was time.

She wanted to keep on sleeping after Rick had gone but finally got up and dawdled into the alien dry afternoon where the trees and shrubs and the components of house and outhouses were clearly defined, in isolation, by the sunlight. It was a landscape without attachments. She followed the drive as far down as the stables and passed without being seen, skulking, along the avenue of pines. Nothing obtruded on her dull contentment. The gums plumed themselves airily. The clouds plumped up and dissolved. Dust billowed from a car in the drive and the odd balloon of wind bobbed across the grass, flocks of birds fanned out in speckles, the blue ocean itself advanced and receded.

The creek had muddy patches of clover on its banks. She crossed on a log and continued in slack mindless movement, following the horses' exercise tracks to the top paddock, ankle-deep in stubble, and down the other side into one of the land's shallow, unimagined dips. In the centre of a flat windless arena of grass the mares stood idly cropping: thirty or so mares, some hugely pregnant and some with skinny foals. A couple whinnied and started to circle about or foot the ground uneasily as she walked down towards them. She had never seen such animals, sensing the meaning of her being there with their high heads and their loose then taut lips. They gave the air a peculiar charge. She expected them to turn and run but they were held there by curiosity. And she was held by the feeling that circled from the mares round their foals and reached to her as she stood puzzled in the dry grass on the slope. When she started to move, crossing to the gate in the opposite corner of the paddock, the foals stayed close to their mothers and she heard a mild breeze breathing behind her.

When she turned she saw that the whole number of the mares were following, at a safe distance, slowly, dutifully, moving in one body with a beautiful steadiness. Animals were usually shy of Karen but here they were, drawing after her. When she reached the gate they kept coming, staring and quivering their lips. Then Karen knew that her body was not her own that afternoon. The smell of Rick was on her, his work and his pressure, and the mares were pulled to it. They were disturbed that she wasn't him but they were drawn anyway, poor loving creatures, as they had always come and would come again this year when the men arrived. To give up their foals to that sweet smell. She climbed the gate quickly and half ran between the fences of the exercise track. The mob pressed against the gate, neighing after her, and some followed down the fence line. She heard them calling, their cry cutting out everything in a sharp line.

Rick was already back and asked her if she'd like a drink on the verandah. He wanted to relax. He'd had a long day and not much sleep the night before. She had to tell him. Though the weekend at the stud wasn't over she couldn't stay. It wasn't his fault. She couldn't be with him there and when he ran his hand over her neck she pulled away. She told his mother she was leaving but didn't explain. Mrs Turner didn't protest. It was terminated. Rick came to see her in Adelaide later. He was pleasant and unhurtful, and though she had jagged herself on a nail climbing that last gate she was under her own star now, pearly and free.

Within the Hedge

If he wasn't active again soon he would go mad. He attacked the air with his stick. "I've got to get going again. I've got to get back into the swing of things." Insects were leaping in sympathy with his restlessness, the gravel on the road crunched underfoot and against drabber gums a youthful pine flamed. He disliked the rural atmosphere. He'd borrowed a friend's house for his convalescence, in a pretty place only an hour's drive from Adelaide. But it struck him now as excessively secluded. The hills were steep and thickly covered, the valley was hedged in, the houses and gardens were lost in growth as if misanthropes wished to rot there undisturbed. English greenery abounded and the whole place had a gently deathly aspect. It was perfect for metaphysics which irritated him further. He had a term off lecturing and had hoped to get down to the research demanded of him. Under a shadow of morbid scepticism, induced by his illness, he had planned to write a couple of philosophical papers. But hadn't managed to do so yet. He'd merely speculated idly on the pleasure principle. What did it all matter anyway? That was the finest consolation of philosophy as he discoursed guiltily with the spring air. His only attachment was to the golden morning.

He itched himself under his woollen trousers, feeling the old Narcissus return. The wattles hurling pollen at him made him want to possess a crumb of this sunny world. He stroked his beard like a bristling physical thing and continued walking. When the road stopped, passing between wooden posts to become a foot track, he kept on, stepping with dignity over blackberries and observing the red and white toadstools, dwellings of fairies, up the hill until finally the track was in parallel with a high cypress hedge.

During his illness he had led an ascetic's life. It amused him that with his fleshless arms and face he might pass for an ascetic, when his dark eyes, his dancing crow's-feet and the dimples in his beard were proof that he had used and been used. He was a libertine, so he styled himself in accordance with his profession and his needs, and now the sun had him scratching in his beard.

The path followed the hedge which was huge, half lit by the sun and half in shadow. It smelled strongly of medicinal resin and when he poked at it with his stick dust rose in clouds off the branches. But he was bored with walking and the hedge annoyed him. It annoyed him that he had got tired so quickly and he guessed that the hedge had been planted by a purposeful neurotic. It was too high and too impenetrable to be natural. He couldn't see behind and its greasy scent repelled him. At the bottom it grew close to the ground and at the top it had been left deliberately uneven, so the branches rose high and low in sequence, like battlements. It gave him a headache and he was about to turn back when a sudden strange change of light made it for a moment possible to see something behind. He was picking his way across a patch of soggy clay at the time, when a flash of movement caught his eye and made him jerk his head round. There was a bright white dart of motion inside the hedge. Then nothing. A quick balletic leap, it seemed, that made him feel wretchedly unhealthy on his unsteady legs. He found his mind fired and when he was home later, sitting in the armchair, his desire focussed narrowly on that spring of white.

The shock of it made the glimpse fascinating. The whiteness must have been a dress — pearliness or simple cambric? a white sea-bird or a cloud above a bay? a woman in a green fort? Next day he would find out the property's entrance.

The gate was at the very top of the hill. It was an old picket thing, leaning but padlocked. He peered through and saw the garden which was peacefully spectacular, a thicket of rhododendrons unfolding their tissue flowers, camelias with tight buds, azaleas beneath with small pink trumpets, and spindles of erica. Further down the garden was wilder, with a scatter of daffodils and irises, and up the slope was an orchard of old misshapen trees. Some had tiny rosy balls which might have been unseasonal apples, crisp as ice. He couldn't help feeling excited. In the middle was a sunken garden to which five slate paths led across a luminous lawn. It was well-kept and looked like a quaint green and pink amphitheatre. One frozen plaster Greek set the scene, and a stone bench at an angle. But there was no human centre piece. He shoved at the gate crossly as though he'd been looking into a viewing-machine and his one coin's worth of time had just run out.

Not many people knew Lucy. She had little desire to

go out and, since her mother's friends seldom invited the daughter too, she wasn't often organized out. She was quiet, serene, seventeen — dutiful and diligent: qualities which came to her easily in the hedged house. She and her mother were well enough off for duty and diligence to mean not a great deal. But the innocence visible in her made Lucy remarkable. Not a quick open smile nor an eye that twinkled, but rather a kind of innocence located in her absolute calm. She walked in the garden calmly and took everything as unquestionably beautiful. She listened to her mother with genuine concern, with round polished wisdom. Such were the impressions others had of her too, when leaving at the front door they would say to her mother, "Lucy must be a great comfort. Such a sweet nature." But they would pause then, being unsure what was nature really. And the men, whenever she left the room, would talk as if released and sing her praises without mentioning her good behaviour at all. She was the most beautiful young girl most people had ever seen; or at least she could make them think so.

She did nothing during the day except wander round the place. She sat in the sunken garden and drew sketches of roses. She twirled the chosen flower and stared at it in order to comprehend, but it wasn't easy. She would press her lips so tight that she broke her pose on the bench. It was impossibly wonderful that the rose existed at all.

One morning she couldn't concentrate because the weather was so bouncy and she walked down through the rhododendrons to the least kempt part of the garden, where the season could be enjoyed best. She lay there in the dank wet grass and the bright arriviste flowers, and when her dress was damp she felt part of things. A butterfly reminded her how years ago she had been taught to imitate a butterfly's wings with her hands. She did it again now and was pleased. Though she didn't recall it often, her childhood training in classical dance was utterly part of her, the strictures of perfect grace. And today she would be Primavera. It was a long way off. She remembered when they had lived in Northern Italy and she had lessons in the house beside the lake, the splendid lake that dissolved in Alps. She could picture the teacher clearly and began to stretch and wave her forearms, stepping into the longer grass. Then an ordinary starling halfway up an oak tree, terribly agitated, suddenly threw itself off its branch. She could only gape. In the crook of its wing there was something she knew, and all at once she was fluttering. After a second she realized how ungainly she was and stopped. But on the other side of the hedge a man had seen the flick of her white skirt in that funny moment of leaping.

He walked past on successive days until he found her there. She didn't see him at first and he was able to observe her clearly for some time. Then, impatient finally, he made the gate creak and she noticed.

"Sorry," he said. "I was admiring the garden. Hope you don't mind." He spoke with uncharacteristic politeness. "It's lovely."

She was neither surprised nor suspicious.

"Is this your place?"

She came over.

"Do you live here?" he tried again.

"We've lived here for eight years."

"Are *you* the gardener?" he asked. "The azaleas are in great shape."

"No," she smiled, " — my mother. My mother's interested in landscape gardening. She likes Japanese gardens. But it's impossible here, really, with the summers. Except for bonsai," she added.

He explained that he was convalescing and found the warm weather a terrific boost. She talked briefly about the house. It belonged to her father but he never came there; he worked overseas but anyway her parents were separated now. She didn't explain how it had all happened, while they were living in Como, outside Milan; how her parents' fighting had disturbed and finally wiped out her childish vivacity, leaving her formless; how she'd retreated with her mother to this hills house where she could be licked into the shape of a child from no marriage at all.

Suddenly she said, "Do you want to have a look around?"

"I'd love to."

She made him follow her along a path, leading first to the orchard.

"What do you do? If you don't mind my asking?"

"I'm a philosopher. I mean, I teach philosophy."

She bobbed ahead of him irresistably, one arm's length away. He couldn't tell if she was flirting with him or not. But it was his duty, at the least, to entertain this lovely little girl, the poor tender sea-bird longing to be free. He reached out his hand, touching her back to steady her as she went ahead down the slope.

"What do *you* do?" he called to her, hoping she would turn brightly. When she did turn, the calm of her face shocked him.

"I do things. I read books. I talk to my mother."

They were in the sunken star-shaped garden.

"This is mine," she said.

He didn't hide his sneer. "You spend most of your time here?"

She was about to speak but stopped abruptly, annoyingly.

He pointed at the Greek statue. "She's pretty brutal!"

"I like her," she smiled.

The girl was a coquet, he decided, and he had better do something about it. She was sitting on the bench, leaving half of it free, and he dropped down beside her, held her and pushed forward to kiss her.

Without any suddenness of movement she rose and avoided his body, stepped forward and said quickly, "Excuse me," before turning her attention to a rose bush, quite oblivious, apparently, of his presence or his action.

He wanted to shout at her but restrained himself. "What's your name?" he inquired instead, demurely.

"Lucy."

"Mine's Mark."

He stared at her in an attempt to reconcile his desire and her flourishing separateness. Here she was positively throbbing — in a refined way — with spring energy. Then he announced that he should be going. But she still didn't take her eyes off the rose bush. She had turned from her companion to crimson roses and vague airy vistas, deliberately and provocatively. Yet if spring could explain her absurd bounce, it might explain other things too.

A few days later she invited him to a picnic lunch and after the eating and drinking she showed him her sketch-book. It was ridiculous. Mark was accustomed to country bacchanalia and he felt she was practising on him, driving him to reveal his basic ardour. She stretched out on the rug. Timidly remembering her earlier wordless reproach, he reached out to touch her near the knee. But instead of any murmuring drowsiness, or any of the other responses he could recognize, she simply asked: "What's *your* philosophy, Mark?"

He was checked. He had no philiosophy with which to entrance the girl. "I don't believe in the inner life," he said. "We define ourselves only in action. Not to act is not to be. And by extension to act half-heartedly is to be half-alive. We make ourselves by moving out into the world and making it. Not by staying rooted like a rose."

Pricked, she sat upright and blushed. "That way you never see anything but your own reflection. If you're always making things change."

Her face hardened and set.

"There's enough inside for me," she said.

He was talking to the statue now. "But you don't know what else there is. Can't you get excited by freedom? Or at least the images of freedom? Take the sea — "

She registered nothing and, not wanting to offend her, he stopped. She was more impossible than the sea herself. He excused himself quickly and left.

But she felt abandoned. His final image had hit. Why hadn't he noticed? How her face must have shown the loss of that childhood lake. And she'd never actually been to the seaside, she confessed to herself. That really didn't seem right.

◆ ◆ ◆

Mark's health improved and his attitude towards Lucy changed as required. The season had settled into its proper business of bearing forward to the hot fruitful summer and the sense of evanescence had gone. He went to visit her twice a day and they talked widely about books and ideas. He felt bound to chastize her narrowness, priding himself on his own expansive sympathies, and she declined to argue, setting her face at the slight tilt that betokened graceful disagreement. The days passed. The tension he had contributed to their relationship eased. Neither wanted to behave any differently with the other. When he pushed the gate open he would have been disappointed had she not greeted him in her particular manner and continued, in the very brushstrokes of their friendship, to maintain the same chaste joy.

They were in love in a way, but the way they had specially evolved. He had a passive way of dancing his reactions to her, and she had a new response to him. There was a change in the way she viewed his habitual beard-scratching, though she would never admit it. But he was leaving soon.

To mark the last evening he invited her to dinner. It was their first meeting outside the hedge but had no symbolic meaning on that account. It was a chance for him to play her some of the records he had talked about.

Yet he fretted and couldn't catch the right note of simple decorum. When he fetched her he watched her nervously at first. When she threw her fluffy shawl down he wanted to hug her — but things had to take their course.

"What perfume are you wearing?"

"Do you like it? It's made from daphne. We've got it growing in the garden."

He bowed to the couch. "Sit down." He was too busy adjusting the curtains to notice how precious the two of them were. "What a moon!" But she showed no enthusiasm and they drifted on to a halting half-hour's talk about novels. The meal followed. She had brought flowers which in the centre of the table met Mark's need for finishing touches tonight. He pulled out her chair and when she sat he pushed it in for her. In place of grace he offered apologies for his cooking. If his gentle intentions hadn't been quite so obvious she might have felt herself satirized.

"It's strange that we met at all, really," he said. "It's because I felt so adventurous that day."

"Spring affects people like that. They want to do something to say 'Yes, spring! It does exist after all.'"

They often talked about the weather.

"Like country folk," she added, laughing. Her hair had fallen forward. For a split second he knew he would lean across the flowers and kiss her — but held himself back.

"It was a delicious meal, Mark. What a clever man!"

He was easier now. Each time he overcame the temptation to touch her, the particular light on her face became more wistfully exquisite. Vaguely drunk he had become an aesthetician. He brought in a tray of coffee and bell-shaped liqueurs, and they settled on the couch for the special symphony. He clowned, rearranging the lighting before he put the record on. The thin fine unravelling of the music was just right, and she half smiled at it oddly.

But Mark wanted a cigar. Time was passing and for all his efforts he was no closer to Lucy. He opened up the curtains and the windows. She looked at his back, as she sank half-amused into the couch. Then he remembered her properly and turned to face her. But the record had finished and she was standing again. She didn't know what to do and turned away towards the window, so Mark saw her from behind. She had become as he imagined her, formally composed, blanched by the moon. In the foreground the domestic objects had lost their beloved quality and returned to the strange still-life state they were in before he ever laid his hands on them. The nightscape background had become equally foreign. Mark judged from the set of Lucy's elbows that her hands would be loosely clasped in front, with peculiar precision. In his wish to compose he wasn't able to observe the firmness with which her lips were shut, until a sly draught stirred the bottom of her dress and pulled him back to the living. She turned and blurted at this puppet-man:

"It's been an unusual experience knowing you, Mark."

"Likewise."

"You've disturbed me. You've made me changeable."

"Have I? That's my job."

Her words were hints he didn't take up.

He rounded things off. "It's been perfect."

They had approached each other tangentially once again. Towards midnight she reached for her shawl. He drove her home because walking would be too cold to be romantic. Their attitudes to each other had swung round without much effect. But Lucy couldn't bear the deception of letting themselves part with memories that had already mortifyingly received their finishing touches. The car had reached the beginning of the foot track through the hedge. There was confusion. Could she act now, against the finality that had fallen so terribly easily? There were strong cypress smells and weird gum forms all round and barely visible blackberry tangles. All this strangeness gave her courage to speak, not commenting or stating harshly, mouthing a distant wish.

"Will you do something for me one day, Mark? Will you take me on an outing to the beach? I've never been to the beach. Isn't that incredible?"

It was extraordinary that she was holding his wrist. Only at the last, when the unbearable irony of a neatly managed parting came so close, did this particular slip of desire utter itself. She had asked for the sea.

Miraculously he understood. He spoke calmly, with the calmness he had learned from her.

"That's a good idea. Lucy, we must do it. Go down to the beach." He smiled. "Sun and surf. We should make a day."

"We should," she said.

At this last minute the girl looked at the man. They leaned forward and kissed with equanimity. Both had compromised themselves but something was released. She thanked him and walked briskly up the path until she became an indistinct white patch which suddenly darted through the gate. She had led him a merry dance but he hadn't compromised himself too much. They had come out of the maze and met. For this happy well-lit moment of meeting at the gate he would remember the acquaintanceship, though they wouldn't meet again, at the sea or next spring, and she would stay one of the ungraspable white things.

More New Fiction

FROM AUSTRALIA'S LEADING CREATIVE PUBLISHING HOUSE, UQP

War Crimes, a long-awaited new collection by master story-teller Peter Carey (author of *The Fat Man in History*)
"*War Crimes* establishes Carey as one of the finest short story writers in the world today." Geoffrey Dutton, *Bulletin*

1915, by Roger McDonald — a brilliant and authentically based narrative which shows Gallipoli as it has never been seen before. Winner of the *Age* Book of the Year Award. "A first novel of astonishing maturity." Maurice Dunlevy, *Canberra Times*

The Haphazard Amorist — pornography or new classicism? A funny new novel by Graham Jackson

Pieces for a Glass Piano, stories by Gerard Lee
"A most enjoyable book . . . bawdy, shocking, philosophical, understanding . . . the author never loses his Rabelasian humour." John Orrell, *Cairns Post*

The Peach Groves, a new novel by Barbara Hanrahan
"One of Australia's most stylish, original and sensitive writers." John Miles, Adelaide *Advertiser*

Something in the Blood, by Trevor Shearston. Stories of Australians in Papua New Guinea before Independence. Gritty, often amusing, always readable.